# BEHIND THE WATERLINE

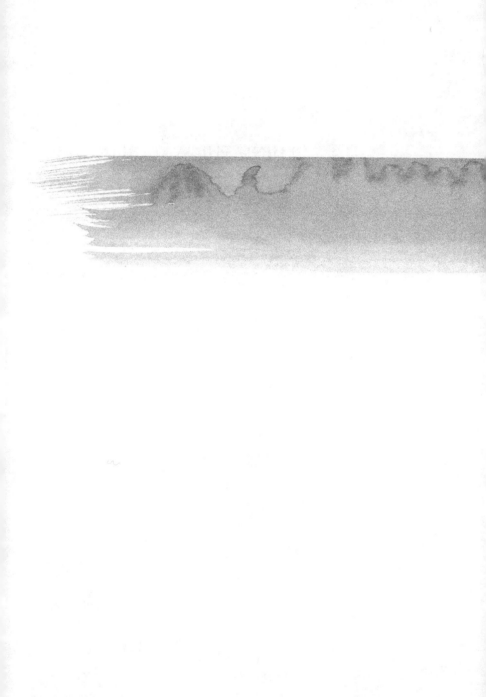

# BEHIND THE
# WATERLINE

*Kionna Walker LeMalle*

BLAIR

Printed in the United States of America
Cover design by Geronna Lewis-Lyte
Interior design by April Leidig

 Blair is an imprint of Carolina Wren Press.

*The mission of Blair/Carolina Wren Press is to seek out, nurture,
and promote literary work by new and underrepresented writers.*

We gratefully acknowledge the ongoing support of general operations by the
Durham Arts Council's United Arts Fund and the North Carolina Arts Council.

This novel is a work of fiction. As in all fiction, the literary perceptions
and insights are based on experience; however, all names, characters, places,
and incidents are either products of the author's imagination or are used
fictitiously. No reference to any real person is intended or should be inferred.

Library of Congress Cataloging-in-Publication Data
Names: LeMalle, Kionna Walker, 1975– author.
Title: Behind the waterline / Kionna Walker LeMalle.
Description: Durham : Blair, 2025.
Identifiers: LCCN 2024047022 (print) | LCCN 2024047023 (ebook) |
    ISBN 9781958888216 (hardcover) | ISBN 9781958888469 (ebook)
Subjects: LCGFT: Magic realist fiction. | Novels.
Classification: LCC PS3612.E4454 B44 2025 (print) | LCC PS3612.E4454 (ebook) |
    DDC 813/.6—dc23/eng/20241104
LC record available at https://lccn.loc.gov/2024047022
LC ebook record available at https://lccn.loc.gov/2024047023

# PART 1

# WEATHERING
# THE STORM

# CHAPTER 1

My mother's dead, and the rumor is that after she died my father ran off because of my crazy grandma. I don't know if that's true, but it could be. The thing is, nobody can tell me what happened, or nobody will tell me. I get bits and pieces. Like, one time, this girl at church said her mama told her my daddy was white and my grandmother hates white people, so she ran him off and told him never come back. I don't believe that's what happened though. Because I've seen pictures of my mama, and she looked like a white woman—which raises all sorts of questions. But whether my daddy is white is not one of them. Judging by my skin color, my daddy is a deep brown. That's the only way I could see being as dark as I am with a mama as white as she was. My hair's curly too. So, that settles it.

The other thing might be true though. I heard Sister Harriet Jo say Grandma used to have friends when she was young. She said they used to be friends too, good friends, but Grandma came back from college different. Mad. Mad like in angry, and mad like in crazy. Double mad. Paranoid they call it.

I asked Pastor Charles once. He's her only friend as far as I can tell, and he said, "Your grandma's not crazy. Just hurt. She got a whole lotta hurt." He didn't tell me more than that though, said I have to wait until I get old enough to understand. When's that supposed to be? Adults always think you need more time, but twenty-four hours a day takes a long time to go by. Especially when you're bored, and I'm bored a lot. I don't have nobody to hang out with. Grandma runs everybody off, and sometimes it makes me wonder if that rumor about running off my daddy might be somewhat true.

And Grandma, she won't talk about nothing that happened yesterday. "Don't dig up old corpses, Eric." That's what she says. "Be grateful for the here and now." But ain't nothing here now. Not much anyway. I don't even have cousins. Grandma was an only child, only had one child, and apparently dumped her friends after college. So I don't have cousins, aunts, uncles, or nobody to tell me the truth.

That's the worst thing about not having my daddy around. Having to imagine him with nothing to go on. And the worst thing about my mama being dead is having puzzle pieces that don't fit together quite right. Like someone put the puzzle almost all the way together then just stopped right before adding the pieces that make the person, and the person is the point of the whole puzzle—but all you have is houses and trees and shadows, stuff like that, but nothing that really matters.

"Hey, I'm running late today, or you're early."

Shelia comes up from behind me, and my heart drops. I'm used to walking to the bus stop alone. I plan it that way on purpose because nothing good ever comes out of it when I get on the bus with everybody else, especially if Neil's there. So, I just stay to myself. But here Shelia is, our feet moving in unison like we're together or something, but we're not. I wish she would speed up or slow down because seeing her feet next to my feet just reminds me that I'm two sizes smaller than a girl. Well, to be fair, Shelia is the biggest girl in school.

I can hear her panting, short breaths between steps like it's a real struggle, and she's only walked from her house, past Ms. Carolyn's and

Old Man Jake's. She caught up with me right between the barbecue man's house on my left and the cat siblings on her right. We're walking in the middle of the street because with the way the roots of the oak trees raise the sidewalk, it's easy to stumble, even easier to get shin splints. Besides, something about walking in the middle of the street just makes you feel like a part of everything. Even if you're walking alone, which I usually am.

Behind us we hear, "Hey," and the sound of a brass band rises in the air.

"He's at it again." Shelia turns around to look back at Old Man Jake.

I take a few more steps, and for some reason I feel guilty about leaving her, so I stop and turn around too. The old man has his boom box on the top step of the porch, an orange cord running through his front door.

"I guess he burned out the battery," I say.

Shelia does a slight laugh like she's not sure she thinks I'm funny. But I don't hear her panting no more, and I think that means my joke at least made her smile.

Old Man Jake is in the middle of the street second lining to that music like he's in a crowd, dancing with the Mardi Gras Indians. Today, he has a beer in his right hand, a tambourine in his left, and he's hitting that tambourine against the beer can in the perfect beat.

"Come on," Shelia says. "We're gonna be late for school."

"Already late," I say.

"You're always late, but I'm not. Come on!"

She grabs my hand and starts running because the bus is within view. I don't want to get on the bus with her, but I can't wait for the next one to come. I'm usually late, but only like a few minutes, not enough to get in trouble. So, we run, side by side, our feet slapping against the pavement, dodging the potholes. My backpack slips off my shoulder and Shelia stumbles a bit, landing her foot right in the pink gardenias Ms. Nguyen planted in the pothole at the end of the block. Shelia gasps, but she don't stop. I don't stop either because now the bus is at the corner, and I know Mr. Lionel is waiting for me.

When we get to the bus stop, he has the doors wide open. He nods at Shelia and smiles at me. "You're not by yourself today," he says. He winks and leans his head right in the direction of Shelia who's walking down the aisle, heading to the back of the bus.

"Guess you're not sitting in the front today." He smiles and turns his head back to the road. "That's good. Real good."

My stomach tightens. I always sit in the front, but when I look down the aisle, I see Shelia at the back with her backpack in her lap, her hand tapping the seat next to her, her eyes telling me to come. I walk down the aisle. The bus ain't so crowded yet, just the usual— two nurses dressed in white, a man with a long, dirty beard and thick glasses who talks to himself, a guy in a gray suit with a briefcase, and a pregnant lady with four little kids who all look the same age. When we make the transfer on Canal Street though, the Esplanade will be crowded with people standing up in the aisles, holding on to the silver bars. Some guy with an armpit Afro will have his arm up, white specks of deodorant trapped in the hair, and someone else in a dashiki will be selling bean pies or pralines I can't afford to buy.

"Ms. Nguyen's going to be mad about those flowers," Shelia says when I take my seat.

"No, she won't. They're moving."

Shelia looks at me a few seconds, then shrugs. "I was surprised she planted them in the first place," she said. "Seems like some crazy thing your grandma might do, but not Ms. Nguyen." Shelia laughs. "You know what I'm saying."

I look out of the window and take her words quietly like a punk.

"I'm just playing," she says. "You know that, right?"

I pull my backpack close to my chest and stare out of the window.

"Don't be so serious," Shelia says. "I thought we were finally making a connection."

The rest of the bus ride is equal torture. I just keep looking outside, acting like I'm not bothered. Every now and then Shelia taps my leg. "Did you hear me, Eric?" She laughs real sweet and soft like you'd expect a real short, thin girl to laugh.

"Yeah," I say, but I'm lying. I stopped listening after she decided to tell me a funny story Neil told her about my grandma. According to Neil, who's a big fat liar, my crazy grandma refused to open the door for his mama. "She was just trying to bring the mail that got put in our box by mistake," he had said. Then, he did an impersonation of what he imagined Grandma doing on the other side of the door. "Oh Lord, Eric, get my bat! There's a person outside. A person! Oh, never mind. I have a bat right here." Shelia reenacted this whole thing, laughing her too-soft laugh the entire time. She pretended to pull a bat out of her shirt as if Grandma was fat enough to hide something like that. One of the little kids with the pregnant lady laughed and repeated the motion.

I wanted to tell her that's not what happened at all. Grandma just turned out the lights, peeked through the blinds, and whispered for me to hush so they wouldn't know we were home. But I just chuckled a little because what else could I do? No matter what I say, Grandma'd still be the crazy lady who hides from neighbors. Randomly at that, because every now and then she seems normal. It's easier to just stare out of the window and ignore Shelia. She's got a weird way of being nice.

I'm still staring out of the window when Shelia hops off the bus and calls back, "Eric, you gonna miss the Esplanade. Come on!"

By the time I get up, a flood of people are getting on. I have to squeeze my way through the crowd and out of the back doors. When

I get off the bus, Shelia is out of sight, already seated on the Esplanade. There're people packing the sidewalk, standing against the side wall of Maison Blanche—young people, old people, dressed-up people, and stinky drunk-in-rags people. A bunch of girls in blue-and-yellow plaid skirts and white button-up blouses are sharing a cigarette on the corner of Canal and Basin. I make it to the next bus stop just as the Esplanade is pulling off. Through the window, I see Shelia shrug her shoulders. She looks genuinely sorry. Maybe. Maybe not. I don't know, and I decide that I don't care because she probably can't be trusted.

When I finally make it to class, Ms. Hornwell is standing front and center, pointing to the words *Traditional Literature* on the whiteboard.

"Glad you decided to grace us with your presence, Eric."

I hand her my pass, and she gestures toward my seat. I'm walking to sit down when I hear her say, "Unexcused again?"

"He should get detention," Raheem says.

Neil daps him up, and Shelia shakes her head.

"As I was saying before Mr. Calhoun arrived, today we begin our unit on traditional literature. At the end of the unit, everyone will turn in an original legend based on a real family member. So, who are the legends in your family?"

I sink into my seat near the back of the room. Ms. Hornwell has her room arranged in rows but not in a rectangle or square. It's something closer to a U, and I sit in the first row of what makes up the bottom of that U. I can see almost everyone in the room except the people who sit in the one row behind me, and everyone can see me. I hate my assigned seat.

Ms. Hornwell walks slowly from one end of the whiteboard to the other. "We all have family legends, so, as we begin our unit on traditional literature, I want you to begin to research. Ask questions. Talk to your parents. Discover."

"What's a legend, Ms. Hornwell? Is that like a hero or something?" This comes from Shelia.

"Maybe," Ms. Hornwell says. "It could be someone who did great things for others, like a hero, or it could be someone who overcame some big challenge, had a masterful skill, or even someone who was notorious."

"Notorious B.I.G," Raheem says. His laugh comes out muffled like the crumpling of an empty bag of chips then ends with a sudden snort when Ms. Hornwell takes her first step away from the board.

She walks over to Raheem and gets real close to his desk. Then she kneels as if preparing to whisper in his ear. Only her words come out in full volume, "Are you related to Biggie Smalls, Raheem? Because if you're not, leave him out of my class. Do you understand?"

Ms. Hornwell stands up, straight and tall. Raheem slumps down in his chair. Everyone starts laughing, but it's quiet laughing because he's one of the cool kids. Shoulders rise and fall, heads bob up and down. But don't no one ever laugh at kids like Raheem out loud. My stomach tightens—the laughter trying to find some place to explode. Ms. Hornwell makes her way back to the center of the room.

"This person doesn't have to be famous. Who do people in the family talk about? Whose stories come up over and over again? Who do you think of most often, and why?"

There's a period of silence, like a moment of organized prayer. I look around the room. Shadows of various hairstyles and head shapes are frozen on the pale yellow walls. Everyone's head is down like they're reading their desktop for hidden stories or something. Ms. Hornwell's heels click as she moves back to the whiteboard.

"What if there are none?" My throat feels dry. "No legends, I mean. No one to write about." The words come out all raspy.

"There is always someone," Ms. Hornwell says. "You may have to dig, but you'll find them." In the sunlight her Afro glistens like a halo. "Let's start by brainstorming."

Several students shuffle for paper and pen.

"No, out loud," she says. "Today, we are going to talk and listen."

I keep my paper out. I want to write down my answer ahead of time, but I end up drawing circles around the holes punched on the page. Ms. Hornwell waits. She is known to wait. The clock on the wall ticks sixty times above our nervous breaths, and I count every second.

Then, Neil Rose of all people gets started. "Well, I have an uncle who fought in Vietnam."

Ms. Hornwell nods.

"My cousin beat colon cancer last year," Raheem says. "Does that count?"

Ms. Hornwell nods again.

"My daddy works three jobs and takes care of five of us as a single dad. I think he's a legend," Alejandro says. "For real, you know. That's real legit. Not everybody got a daddy like that."

"My grandma was the first Queen of Zulu," Marielle says.

"Wow, for real?" Shelia asks. "That's dope."

Everyone chimes in with stories about aunts, uncles, cousins, parents, and grandparents. I am quiet. I don't have nothing to share, so I sit there drawing stupid circles.

Shelia starts talking about her aunt, a bodybuilder and female bouncer who worked for some big dance club and was known for throwing out drunk soldiers when they came home from the war in Iraq. That would be the case with Shelia's family. Not only is she one of the biggest girls in class—bigger than all the boys—she ain't afraid to lay hands on the boys if they do one of her girls wrong.

"You have an aunt who fights men?" Marielle says.

"If she has to."

That gets me thinking about how I can't fight at all. I mean, I'm real bad at it. I imagine my daddy was a fighter. Maybe he stopped a carjacking or bank robbery, punched the burglar right in the gut, got several good licks in, almost knocked him out, but then something went wrong, and he got killed. But he didn't just walk away from me like they say. I bet he was handsome with brown skin and lips like Dr. Martin Luther King Jr., or maybe he was reddish brown like Malcolm X. Probably had a real nice speaking voice too. If he was alive, he'd be teaching me how to be a man and what to do about jerks like Raheem and Neil, and how to stop my body from doing random stuff, so I can stop putting my hand in my pocket every time a pretty girl walks past. He'd be teaching me how to do some fancy footwork like Muhammad Ali too. We'd be dancing around each other in the backyard, throwing and dodging and blocking punches. "Come on kid, show me what you got." He'd be ducking and diving and laughing, then I would—

"What about you, Eric?"

I hear Ms. Hornwell, but I can't think of nothing to say. I can't even tell her the story I just made up in my head because everyone knows I don't know my daddy.

"Daydreaming again?" Ms. Hornwell says, her arms folded.

"He wasn't daydreaming, Ms. Hornwell. He was having visions." That's Marielle talking.

When I look her way, she tilts her head down, but her eyes are still on me. Judging from the movement of her pencil, she is just pretending to write. With her free hand, she plays with her earring, and a sneaky little smile creeps across her face.

"Like Crazy Ruth," Neil Rose says. That comes from behind me.

My neck tightens. Everyone is laughing, and it feels like the sound waves are squeezing both sides of my head together, daring me to move. I ball one fist beneath the desk, and I imagine punching Neil Rose in the face. Take that for a vision.

But I don't have visions. I dream. There's a difference. My grandma has visions. She calls them nightmares, even when they come while her eyes are wide open. Nightmares in the daytime. There's a word for that. I checked the dictionary. That's what I do when I'm bored. I read the dictionary in search of new words, right words. I'm bored a lot. That's what happens when you can't make friends. Anyway, I found the word. It's daymare, but no one uses it. I tried once and got laughed at for days. No one says daymare. Only crazy.

"Settle down, now." Ms. Hornwell's eyes send out a warning, and a hush falls over the class.

Neil Rose pretends to be innocent. "Yes, ma'am. Back to traditional literature."

"Thank you, Neil. Yes, back to the topic."

"Eric, is there anything you would like to share?"

I sit up straight and tall, like I'm about to say the worthiest thing ever. But what comes out is, "My grandma makes the best chicken salad." I was not supposed to say this out loud, but that's what came out of my mouth. The room explodes in laughter. I want to disappear.

"Man, that's just dumb," Neil says.

"Nobody's eating her food," Raheem says. "Everybody knows she's crazy."

"There it is." Neil holds his hand up and pretends to write in the air. "Introducing the legend of . . . Who's that? Crazy Ruth!"

I try to fake a laugh, but nothing comes out, not even a half smile.

The bell rings. "Tomorrow, we will finish this discussion. And there will be no teasing." Ms. Hornwell looks at Neil and Raheem.

Before I leave the classroom, I walk over to her. "I need an alternative assignment," I say.

"Alternative? But why?"

"I don't know any legends."

"Oh, but of course you do." Our eyes lock. "You just don't know it yet."

CHAPTER 2

I imagine punching Neal right in the face. His body flies up to the sky and explodes into dust. "Pulverized," I say out loud, my finger still on the word in the dictionary.

"What are you going to pulverize?"

Grandma is sitting at the table peeling eggs and slicing them. This means the chicken salad is almost done because she always tops it with sliced eggs.

"Can I have one?"

"You know you have to wait."

"I don't know why. No one ever comes over here. What's the point of decorating it?" I kick my foot against the leg of the table.

Grandma raises her eyes but not her head. "You kick that table one more time, I'm gonna pulverize you." She grabs the paprika and sprinkles it over each egg. "Don't you have homework this weekend?"

A week has passed since Ms. Hornwell assigned the family legend project, and I have yet to ask Grandma for help. Everybody in class is talking about that project. Shelia already started writing about her aunt, the bouncer, and I saw Neil showing Raheem pictures of his uncle, the Vietnam veteran. When Ms. Hornwell told us to freewrite yesterday, I wrote the same dumb sentence, "My grandma makes the best chicken salad." I think of this and frown.

"Can you tell me something about our family?"

The blade of the knife moves slowly toward Grandma's index finger as she slices another egg.

"What do you want to know?"

"What were my parents like?"

Grandma closes her eyes and takes in a deep breath. She is quiet for what feels like forever. I look at the word under *pulverize*. It's *puma*. Not helpful. Finally, she says, "Your mother was a lot like me when I was young. Stubborn and strong-willed."

"Really? What about my daddy?"

Grandma cuts her finger with the knife and lets out a low grumble. "Don't just sit there. Get me a bandage!" She goes to the sink and runs her finger under the tap.

I walk to the medicine drawer and get out the Band-Aids and anti-biotic salve. My hand is trembling. "You want me to put it on for you?"

"I can do it," she snaps. "Just get me a paper towel and go outside."

"Outside for what?"

I hand Grandma a paper towel, and when she presses it on her finger, the paper turns red with blood.

"To play." She says this like it's obvious, but it's not, because she has never sent me outside just to play.

"If I go outside, can I have an egg?"

There are two eggs left on the table. The peeled one that's already been sliced down to the yolk and now has a small bit of blood on it, and the other one that is in its shell.

"Well, let's see," Grandma says as she opens the ointment. "You had two bowls of cereal this morning, toast, and orange juice. A regular Saturday commercial breakfast. Then, you came down and grabbed a bag of potato chips, and now you want my egg. Is that right?" She pushes a small amount of salve onto the Band-Aid.

"It's just an egg."

"It's my breakfast," Grandma says. "Now, go outside and play."

She wraps her finger then points it at me. "Before I pulverize you."

I walk slowly to the door, staring at my feet because I don't want to go. It's hot out there, and I don't have nothing to do.

"What'd I tell you about holding your head up?"

"Yes, Grandma." I head outside, my head at a crazy high angle.

"And stay away from those cat people and the cats too. I don't trust them."

I get to thinking. Grandma never sends me out to play. If anything, she keeps me away from people. She don't trust nobody except Pastor Charles. She's just trying to keep from talking about my daddy, and all those things people say about her running him off are coming to my mind.

A couple of houses down, two little kids, a boy and a girl, run up and down the porch steps while the dad loads up the back of a van. The mama is standing on the sidewalk, pointing and telling him where to put stuff. I don't know their names. They have only been here a month. That's all it takes to get on Grandma's bad side though.

The first time she saw the dad, she said, "You have to watch people like that. A white man moving into a Black neighborhood? He's up to something."

I wanted to say, "Grandma, this neighborhood's not Black." But what would be the point?

We live in Mid-City, the Third Ward, which might be one of the most mixed neighborhoods in New Orleans. We have neighbors who are white, Black, Hispanic, and Vietnamese, right on our block. And this white man Grandma's accusing of being up to no good has a Black wife.

"Do you know he stands outside and watches this house. Just stares at it. I think he's a spy." Her eyes were wide, and she was peeking through the blinds when she said this. "You wait and see. He can't be trusted. White people don't move in. They move out."

Now, it looks like they are moving out after just a few weeks. They are loading up boxes in the back of that van, and everyone has a suitcase.

Across the street, Old Man Jake is boarding up his windows like a big storm is coming. I look up. There ain't a cloud in the sky. They ought to be calling him Crazy Man Jake. Always calling my grandma crazy. I walk along the edge of Grandma's flower bed, if you can call it that. It is filled with those purple leaves that sprout little pink flowers. Grandma calls them purple hearts. She says they are more real than roses. Whatever that means. A while back, she put some white rocks down under the plants, but now all kinds of little stones are there. I pick up the ones that look like they don't belong, and when I get a handful, I start throwing them one by one into a pothole filled with water.

"Don't you splash me."

It's Ms. Jackie, pushing a grocery store basket piled high with bags and cases of water. She tilts her head down, and her eyes rise above her dark sunglasses.

"Yes, ma'am." I stop throwing the rocks and slip them in my pocket.

"Your grandmother need some water in there?"

"No ma'am. We have water." Grandma always says it makes no sense to purchase water when we have a perfectly good tap.

"What about batteries?" She holds up a pack of batteries.

I try to keep a straight face, but two things are confusing about this. First, Ms. Jackie has never offered Grandma nothing before now. Second, everyone knows Grandma only accepts stuff from Pastor Charles. I must have turned up my nose and lips in confusion.

"You don't know, do you?" Ms. Jackie says.

"Know what?"

Before Ms. Jackie responds, Pastor Charles pulls up in his big, shiny black truck. He stands to his feet and stretches his arms up like a tree before walking toward us.

"Now Jackie, I told you if you need a ride from the store, just call me. You don't have to walk home with these baskets."

I like the sound of his deep baritone voice. Sometimes, when I am in my room, I stand in the mirror and practice talking like Pastor Charles.

Jackie tilts her head up. "Pastor, I know. But you were busy with the funeral this morning, and with the storm coming—"

"What storm?" I try to say this loud enough to be heard over Pastor's rumbling voice, but my voice cracks. They don't hear me.

"We all really need to get out of here."

"Pastor, you think so? I was going to weather it out. I got my batteries, water, canned goods, snacks." Each time she names something, she lifts it up and holds it in front of Pastor Charles like an advertisement. When she says snacks, she opens a big box of fruit snacks and tosses me a pouch.

"Thank you, Ms. Jackie." I open the pouch and tilt my head back to let the candy fall inside my mouth.

She smiles. "Anytime."

Pastor Charles looks up at the sky. "It's a beautiful day. But I have a bad feeling about this one." He turns to Ms. Jackie. "Why don't you give Jacob a call? See if you can go there." Jacob is Ms. Jackie's son. He left for the marines before I was born and never came back to live. She says he sends her money all the time but just never felt a need to come back home.

Ms. Jackie nods. She grabs a couple of bags of groceries and heads in. Pastor Charles picks up two cases of water and follows her. He looks my way. "Make yourself useful. Come over here and give Ms. Jackie a hand."

I pop the last fruit snack into my mouth and pick up a variety box of potato chips. We make a few trips back and forth, piling Ms. Jackie's kitchen table with water, food, batteries, and a kerosene lamp that makes me want to walk through the house in the dark holding it like one of the kids in an old movie.

Ms. Jackie leads us through the front door, straight through the living room, her bedroom, her son's old bedroom, and then to the kitchen. That's how it works in a shotgun house. Every room is connected by an open doorway, and you just walk straight through. Ms. Jackie's bedroom is the coolest place, and every time I walk through, carrying in her groceries, I slow down to take it in. A lace bra hangs over the back of this zebra print chair beside her bed, like it ain't private at all. And underneath that chair, there is something else small, lacy, and black. Pastor Charles walks through looking straight ahead, like there is nothing to see. But I see it all. The red walls. The zebra print bedding. The black lace. On her dresser, she has several pairs of sunglasses, maybe a pair for every outfit, and a glass tray filled with perfumes and makeup. That explains why Ms. Jackie always looks so fancy and smells good too.

When we make the last trip into her kitchen, she is on the phone with her son. Pastor Charles waves and points next door toward our house to let her know where he is headed. She moves the phone away from her mouth for a second and says, "Hold on, Pastor. Let me unlock the side door for you." Our houses are so close together, Pastor Charles can probably plant his feet in Ms. Jackie's side doorway and lean over to open ours.

Ms. Jackie has a deadbolt lock on her side door and iron bars, so we stand and wait for her to get the key. After she unlocks the door, she goes right back to talking to her son. "Have you heard about the storm headed this way?" We walk down Ms. Jackie's steps and cross over to our house as her voice trails off. "Pastor says I should head out and go to your place."

We enter our house through the side door which brings us right into the kitchen. Even though Grandma is afraid of neighbors being spies, she sure don't have no extra locks or iron bars. She is more afraid of getting locked in her own house than she is of being robbed.

Pastor Charles sits down sideways in a chair to make room for his long legs, and I go straight for the fridge.

"Boy, wash your grimy little hands," Grandma shouts from the other room.

"How did she know?" The words slide out of my mouth before I can stop them.

Pastor Charles laughs. "Mothers always know."

I want to say, "She's just my grandma. I don't have a mother." But I know better than to say that out loud, so I fill my mouth with chicken salad instead.

"Charles Ray, is that you?" Grandma's voice is light when he's around.

"The one and only."

"Well actually," Grandma steps into the kitchen, drying her hands on the bottom of a light blue Zion Baptist Church t-shirt. It is one from way back, and the material is thin at the bottom like she's been drying her hands on it for years. "You're Charles Ray III. Not exactly a one and only."

I laugh out loud, which makes Grandma remember I'm here.

"You mean to tell me you're going to stand there and eat and not offer a sandwich to the pastor?" The way she says "the pastor," you would think he is someone high and mighty we barely know. But he is at our house all the time. I have known him all my life. I have to finish chewing before I can say anything. With Grandma's eyes lighting into me, it feels like I can't chew fast enough.

"I'm sorry. Do you want a sandwich?"

"Would you like a sandwich, Pastor Charles Ray?" Grandma stares at me as she says these words in slow syllables like she's teaching me to read.

I make eye contact with Pastor Charles just like she taught me. "I apologize, Pastor. Forgive my lack of manners. Would you like a sandwich?"

He smiles and stretches his long arm across the table. He slaps the table with his hand. "Just what I need. I'll take crackers, please."

"Yessir."

Grandma walks over to the sink and fixes him a glass of water. When she brings him the water, his eyes fall on her injured finger.

"What'd you do to your finger?"

"Oh, it's nothing, Charles Ray. Just a little slip of the knife." She holds her bandaged finger up. "I thought you were at the funeral."

"I was. But the storm's a category 5 now. I left early. Came to get you."

"You're not gonna walk the second line? You always second line."

I place a plate of crackers and chicken salad in front of Pastor Charles, and the whole time I'm wondering why he doesn't just fix it himself. I'm tired of treating him like company. Why can't we just treat him like family? That's what I want—somebody to treat like family, besides Grandma.

"Thank you, Eric." He puts a heap full of chicken salad on a cracker and puts the whole thing in his mouth like it's the size of a peanut. For a second, it's quiet while he chews. "Ruth, the mayor called for a voluntary evacuation. We need to leave. I don't have a good feeling about this storm."

"Well, you be careful. Do you want me to fix you a few sandwiches for the road?"

"I want you to come with me."

When Pastor Charles says this, I get real interested, but I keep focusing on my sandwich, so they won't know I'm listening. I start thinking about us all being on the road together and staying in a hotel together, and Grandma being all lighthearted and nice because Pastor Charles is around. But Grandma laughs and shakes her head.

"Charles Ray, you know I'm not leaving this house. There's no telling what will happen if I do. Besides, we rode out Betsy. And what was that other one, when June was about Eric's age?"

Hearing Grandma say June makes me look up from my sandwich. June is my mother, the beautiful, stubborn, strong-willed woman I never met, the legend I'll never be able to write about.

"Hurricane Andrew," Pastor Charles says.

"Yes, Andrew. We survived that one too." She crosses her arms firmly, the fingers on each hand gripping the opposite bicep. Her arms are big and soft. Little puffs of fat rise between her fingers. "Besides, I didn't even know a storm was coming. How bad could it be?"

"Six are already dead in Florida."

"People always die." Grandma holds the word *die* longer like she wants to hold on to it or something.

"It's headed this way." Pastor Charles shakes his head. "Worse than Betsy."

I don't know how Grandma expects to have heard about a storm. Most of the time, she keeps the television and radio turned off, says she needs the house quiet to keep the demons out. Sometimes she says it's so she can hear if someone tries to break in. Every now and then she says it's to hear from God. I guess God didn't tell her nothing about this storm. Sure didn't tell me. I've been trying to figure this thing out since Old Man Jake started boarding up his windows.

Pastor Charles lifts his hand from the table and smothers his face in it. Then, letting it rest just below his chin, he says, "Ruth, I want you and Eric to come with me."

I'm real excited now, only Grandma's not, so it don't even matter how I feel.

She says, "I have an upstairs if the water rises too high." She don't even look at him when she says it. Just looks down and twirls a finger around that Band-Aid.

The only thing upstairs is my room. We have what they call a camelback house, and my room is the camel's hump. Grandma calls it the second suite. The suite has a full bathroom, a walk-in closet, and a queen size bed with a trundle bed underneath in case anyone stays overnight. But no one ever sleeps over. Other than Pastor Charles, no one ever comes to visit in the first place. Grandma don't really like people as far as I can tell, and that's why I can't get Ms. Hornwell's stupid project done. Because we don't have family, and there is no one, and I mean no one, who will tell me anything worth writing.

I fumble with the rocks in my pocket. One is completely smooth, and I roll it around between my thumb and index finger. Suddenly, I have an idea. "Pastor Charles, why don't you stay with us?"

Grandma looks up. "Is your room clean? You have the biggest room in the house, bigger than any kid your age, and you don't even keep the thing clean."

Pastor Charles looks torn. "I would, but I can't. With Mama on oxygen right now, I can't risk a power outage. I have to leave."

Grandma nods. "I understand. Ain't no way to argue with that." She rises from the table but don't move, like she forgot her plan right after she started it. Pastor Charles watches her stand, his eyes rising as she rises. Then he watches her sit, lowering his eyes slowly as she returns to her seat. I watch him watch her.

They are silent a long time. I go up to my room. At least there I can play marbles with the rocks I've been collecting. I don't like rocks. It's just something to do when I get lonely. I'm not a collector or nothing. I don't care what they look like or how they're made. None of that collector stuff. But one day, Grandma noticed rocks in my room, and the next day, she came home with this rock-collecting guide. I unfolded it and used it to make a marble ring. She won't buy me marbles, says it's the devil's game, which makes me realize she definitely ain't going to help me learn how to fight. Because what I want to do to Neil is not at all of God. I imagine him blowing up again. *Pulverized.* I like that word. But it ain't never going to happen.

I have just three rocks left inside my paper marble ring, and I'm excited that I'm getting close to the end. But Pastor Charles calls upstairs. "Eric, I need your help down here."

I run down right away. He looks at me a while before he speaks. There is something different in the tilt of his head, and it makes me feel a little funny inside, like he is trying to tell me something without saying it out loud. "Look, Ms. Jackie is going to follow me out of the city. She decided to leave. So now she doesn't need all of the stuff she bought."

I look at Pastor Charles blank-like. I don't know what he wants me to say.

"She's going to take some groceries on the road but wants the rest of it to go to you and your grandmother. Got that?"

I never move my feet from that bottom step.

"So I need you to come with me to help get everything and bring it over here."

Finally, I get what he means. "Oh, okay." I run back upstairs and slip on my tennis shoes. Pastor Charles and I go back and forth between Ms. Jackie's house and ours. This time we use Ms. Jackie's side door, so I don't get to see anything except her kitchen. We carry several cases of water and bags from Ms. Jackie's house. When I sit the box of fruit snacks on Grandma's kitchen table, it tips over the edge, and the small pouches scatter everywhere. Grandma, who is walking back and forth organizing stuff, gives me a mean look. She picks up an oversized can of green beans and stares at it a while. Then she starts shifting cans around in the pantry to keep every can organized by type and size. That big oversized can goes all the way to the back. I scramble to the floor and pick up the fruit snack pouches. Pastor Charles stacks the cases of water neatly on one wall.

"I will have the boys board up your windows before they leave. I really do wish you would leave with me."

"Charles Ray, I don't want to be boarded up in here. If there's a fire, I won't be able to get out." Grandma closes her eyes and breathes in so deep I can hear it. She walks over to the window and peeks through the blinds. "Leave me one window to look out," she says. "If someone's watching me, I want to see them."

Pastor Charles pokes his lips out like he's massaging his gums with his tongue. He sucks his front teeth and says, "I'll get the flashlights and this lamp ready. Come on, Eric." I join him at the table, and he slides two flashlights and some batteries my way. He takes the kerosene lamp apart to pour the oil in. I unscrew the first flashlight.

"How does that thing work?" I say.

"Well, you see this wick that's sticking up?"

I lean over and take a close look.

"It sucks up the oil, you see, and that makes a really bright flame."

"Can we light it?"

Pastor Charles laughs. "It needs to sit a while first. About an hour. Give the wick a chance to soak up that oil, then it will burn bright and slow. But I hope y'all don't need it."

I'm hoping we do need it. That way, I can see the lamp in action.

"We'll be fine, Charles Ray," Grandma says. "You go ahead. You got a long ride ahead of you."

Pastor Charles walks real slow to his truck like he don't want to go. When he finally gets in, he puts the passenger-side window down and leans over. "You sure, Ruth?"

Grandma waves good-bye from the porch.

I look down the street as Pastor Charles and Ms. Jackie drive away. Most cars are gone, and more houses are boarded up. Some houses, like ours, look like they look every day, not like a storm is coming. I kick a beer can that's on the ground. I know it's from Old Man Jake because at night when he gets to playing his music, dancing, and drinking, he drops a can or two on the ground. He always picks them up when he's sober in the morning, but today he's been boarding windows instead.

"Y'all ain't leaving?"

Shelia stops the can with her foot and kicks it back to me.

"Nope. Y'all?"

"Yeah. Your grandma afraid if she leave her house somethin'll happen to it?"

"Something like that."

I kick the can back to Shelia.

"I figured. I just came to say bye."

When Shelia kicks the can back to me, I just hold it with my foot and look up. That girl is tall and confusing, always acting like we're friends.

"Okay, bye."

I kick the can to my left foot and back to the right.

"You keep doing that," Shelia says, "and you'll be second lining like Old Man Jake in no time."

She laughs that soft laugh then takes off. That fast, she's in her mama's car. I shake my head and look back down at the can. I'm kicking it around when Grandma reappears at the door. I feel her before she says a word. Then I hear her.

"I know you're gonna bring that in here and throw it away."

"Yes, ma'am," I say. I walk in the house, imagining throwing the can so far it hits the back windshield of the truck and makes Pastor Charles turn around. "Eric, why don't you come?" he'd say. "Leave your old grandma here. She likes being lonely." But that don't happen, and when I look out of the window, he's too far away to see.

It ain't long before the younger men of the church come and board our windows. Grandma offers them all something to eat, but they don't know her like that (or they know too much about her). Not one of them accepts a thing other than a bottle of water for their work. She follows them around the house, watching everything they do. When they get to the last window, she says, "Leave me a space to see. I can't be in here with no way to look out."

They're all the way in my room when she finally says this. So now, she's going to have to come all the way to my room just to look outside and accuse someone of spying.

"Yes, ma'am," the one who seems to be leading says. He is tall and slim. I think he is Deacon Jackson's son. He looks like him anyway, tall and dark with high cheekbones and deep-set eyes, but he is quiet compared to the deacon who jokes a lot and makes Grandma cringe.

When they are done, it is this same one who comes to the door. His voice is calming and respectful, like he has been trained in talking to the paranoid. "Sister Ruth, Pastor called. He asked if you changed your mind. He said he'll turn around for you."

"No thank you," Grandma says. She stands in the doorway folding her arms like a shield.

---

I fall asleep to the sound of police sirens, dogs barking, and Old Man Jake playing reggae music. But when I wake up on Sunday morning, something is different. Grandma has the TV on.

"Every person is hereby ordered to immediately evacuate the city of New Orleans." The mayor's bald head shines on the screen.

Grandma is frying bacon and singing.

"Grandma, the mayor says we have to go."

"Wouldn't you know it?" Grandma's smiling, and I'm wondering what she's smiling about. "Go ahead and load up that water in the car and those groceries." She points to the bags on the table. "I already bagged them to make it easier."

"Yes, ma'am."

"And grab two outfits and your toothbrush. Lotion too. Don't want you going nowhere ashy. It makes people think they can take advantage of you."

I'm sick of hauling the same groceries back and forth, but here I go again. This time, I'm moving them from our kitchen to Grandma's car. Grandma is singing "I Surrender All," like she's holy or something, and I'm thinking she's not or people would actually like her.

We eat after I finish packing the groceries in the car, and Grandma asks me to take the leftovers across the street to Old Man Jake. He wrinkles his nose and looks in the top container real slow like something is going to jump out at him.

"You said your grandmother sent you with this food?"

"Yessir."

"Well, I'll be a monkey's uncle. Thank you!" He laughs. His teeth are brown like one of the rocks in my collection.

The sky is darker now, but there ain't no rain. I go upstairs and pack a bag with two outfits and lotion like Grandma said. When I come back down, she is standing in the door waiting for me. We walk out to the porch, and she clasps her hands together to pray. Only, she don't pray out loud. I just see her lips moving and the veins on her closed eyelids fluttering like there's a lot of action going on underneath.

"Let's get going," she says. It's like she's a different person than the woman yesterday who refused to leave.

There's a problem though. The car won't start. The lights come on, and the engine makes a light humming sound, but nothing else happens. Grandma and I look at each other. Then, we look around. Most of the cars left in the neighborhood haven't moved in years, but Mr. Chris's car is still in front of his house, and he drives that every day.

"Knock on Chris's door," Grandma says. "Maybe he can give us a jump."

Mr. Chris is a short, round man with a bald head like our mayor and a big smile like Pastor Charles. When he opens the door, he says, "Hey, Lil Man. What ya know good?"

"Nothing really. Nothing good, I mean. My grandma needs a jump."

"Oh, I got ya. Give me a minute." He closes the door a few seconds, and when he reopens it, he is putting on his belt. "Y'all gon' try to leave?" He calls out to Grandma as we head down the steps.

Grandma leans her head out of the car window. "The Holy Spirit woke me up clean out of my sleep, told me it's time to leave. And what do you know, the mayor calls for an evacuation."

I'm thinking, the Holy Spirit couldn't tell you to leave with Pastor Charles?

"Yeah, well," Mr. Chris said. "Byron and I are gonna ride this thing out though. It can't be that bad."

Mr. Chris lines his car up with Grandma's and gets out the cables. "Give it some gas," he says.

Grandma does, but nothing happens.

"You're not going anywhere today." Mr. Chris disconnects the cables and wraps the cords in a circle.

I get out of the car and see Neil Rose staring at me. He lives at the end of the same block, but he's walking his dog—a beautiful black shepherd—and he has paused right in front of our house. I guess his family decided to stay too, or they got stuck too. We just look at each other. I don't know what he's thinking, but I am thinking he is the last person I want to be left with in the middle of a storm. You stay in your house, and I'll stay in mine. Then, as if he reads my mind, Neil does a sign of the cross with his fist and points to me at the end. I will myself to look away, but before I can, he starts laughing, and the dimple in his chin deepens. *Man, you're such a jerk. I hope the flood washes you away.* That dog of his shows me his teeth like I'm the one posing a threat.

I don't go back inside right away. Instead, I go in the backyard, and I start dancing around throwing punches at the air. I imagine giving Neil a firm uppercut right in the chin. Dimple demolished.

Inside, Grandma is sitting at the edge of her recliner, leaning forward, her head almost between her knees. I turn toward the television. The mayor is talking again, and now his shiny bald head is covered with tiny beads of sweat. He's explaining that all traffic is now in contraflow, which means no one can enter New Orleans. We can only leave. The camera switches to an aerial view of traffic on I-10 East and West. It looks like six lanes of parked cars all facing the same way. Then, a news anchor comes on and says, "Expect landfall by 5 a.m. on Monday morning."

Whatever the news anchor says after that gets flooded by Grandma's voice. "Charles Ray, you can't come back. The mayor isn't letting anyone back into the city." Grandma lifts the phone from her ear, and I hear Pastor Charles yell. This is something I ain't never heard before. My stomach feels empty, but I'm not hungry. I'm scared. Fear feels an awful lot like hunger.

"If you are staying home, fill your tubs with water tonight. That way you will be able to flush your toilet tomorrow." The news anchor is reading off a list of last-minute things to do.

I look at Grandma with my mouth wide open.

"Clean your tub and fill it with water," she says. Her voice is weak. "And bring a flashlight up to your room."

I bring the flashlight up, but I do nothing with the tub. Instead, I get down on my hands and knees and play marbles until the shiny rock wins.

CHAPTER 3

S omething about my shiny rock usually makes me feel calm. Tonight, I'm rolling it around and across my fingers with my thumb, but it ain't working. I can't sleep. It's hard to explain. When talk about this storm first started, I didn't think it was a big deal, just one of those adult exaggerations. But now, I feel it. I don't mean like when the old people say, "I feel it in my knees." I mean, I feel it somewhere I can't even name. Something is wrong. That storm is coming, and it's gonna be bad.

Branches crack against my window over and over again. Downstairs something booms, and I hear shattering glass. I sit up and click the lamp on my nightstand. Nothing happens. I get out of bed, walk across my room, and flip up the light switch. Still nothing. I feel around and find the flashlight on my desk. I use this light to make my way downstairs. I'm calling for Grandma loud as I can, but she ain't answering. I don't even hear her moving around.

The stairs lead straight to the kitchen. Once I get there, I can hear the rain like I've walked outside. The wind is howling, struggling to get around something. I'm standing on the bottom step, looking around, trying to figure out what to do. The kitchen looks normal, but the sounds are all wrong. I'm thinking hard about something real simple. Which way do I go? I can turn left and go to the dining room, which leads to the living room, or I can turn right and go through Grandma's reading room to her bedroom. That's basically all of downstairs except the bathroom. The house is shotgun—one straight line—the kitchen sits in the middle.

I'm about to turn right to check on Grandma when I see a trickle of water flowing from the dining room. I turn left instead. Our oak tree, or a huge part of it, has crashed through the living room and dining room ceilings. The tree is literally inside. It's taking up so much room, I can't see the living room through the leaves, but I can see the half of the dining room closest to me. Three of the four fruit paintings have fallen off the wall. The one remaining is crooked and rocking. The table is split in two, half of it is level to the floor, and the other half is leaning into the tree. Grandma's fancy china cabinet, filled with fancy plates and cups we never use, has collapsed onto the table, one door pressed shut, the other wide open. The dishes have fallen from this door to the floor and shattered. It's raining in the house. The water is flowing toward my feet. I feel it reach my toes.

"Grandma!" I turn the opposite direction and run toward her room.

Grandma catches my shoulders in the doorway, the one between the kitchen and her reading room. I hug her so tight.

"Hold on," she says. She rubs my back and lets my head rest on her breast. "What happened?" Her nightgown hangs from her left shoulder loosely.

"The tree. It fell through the ceiling."

"My word!" She shines her flashlight across the kitchen. The shadow of the tree dances along the cabinets.

I take her hand and walk her to the dining room. The rain splashes against the front of her gown, leaving dark blue splotches on the pale material. Water pools at our feet.

"We should go upstairs," she says, as if suddenly realizing the danger. "If the rain doesn't stop, the water will get too high down here." She turns back toward her reading room. "Start bringing up the food and water. Bring as much as you can."

Grandma disappears a while, and when she comes back, she has her overnight bag and purse. By the time she steps back into the kitchen, the floor is wet all the way across. She almost slips. I drop a case of water to catch her and lean my weight against the doorway to regain my balance. When I look up, her eyes are closed, and her lips are moving.

"Come on, Grandma. Let's get upstairs." I take the bag and purse from her shoulder. "I've got this." I walk her slowly to the bottom step, where the carpet takes over and I know she can get her grip. I pick up the case of water and head upstairs, walking slowly behind her. Every few steps, she takes a break and massages her left calf. She always complains about her varicose veins causing pain. The doctor says they shouldn't hurt much. "If I could give them to him, I would," Grandma said one day. "Then, he can tell me they don't hurt."

Because Grandma insisted on having a way to look out, one of my bedroom windows is just partially covered with two two-by-four pieces crossed like an X, a way for the guys to be obedient to both Pastor Charles and Grandma. We look through the open spaces. Our oak tree is completely uprooted, and the front of our house is caved in. Part of the lower roof remains, but I doubt it's stable. It used to be that I could climb out of my window, cross over the low roof, and climb into that big oak tree. Now, there's just a little piece of roof left, and the tree is right there, almost level with it. If I was to climb out of the window now, I could take a few steps and sit on the tree.

"I didn't know that could happen," I say.

"I didn't think it would happen," Grandma says.

The tree leans as if looking into my window. Rain slashes against the shaking house. I feel the vibration of thunder in the pit of my stomach.

"I'm gonna get the rest of the food." I run downstairs. In the wet kitchen, I bend my knees and walk with my feet flat to balance. I go back and forth, carrying cases of water, boxes of canned goods, bags of snacks, a manual can opener. Every time I walk back into my room, Grandma is sitting in the window, looking out at that tree.

"What else do we need?" I ask.

"The lamp," she says. "And my photo album."

I don't have to ask where the album is. I sneak to the reading room and look in it all the time, after Grandma's asleep because that way I don't have to worry about making her mad with my questions. The thing I'm dying to know is why she only has pictures of my mama through her teen years. What happened after that? When did my daddy come into the picture, and where's the album with pictures of them together? I'm surprised she wants me to get it, but I'm glad too. We might be stuck upstairs together a long time. Maybe she'll feel like talking.

In the reading room, the carpet is damp near the entrance, but everything else is fine. The big recliner and floor lamp, the round coffee table filled with books, magazines, and at least a week's worth of the *Times Picayune* and *Louisiana Weekly*. The small brown sofa and end table with its fleur-de-lis lamp. Everything is in its place. The album is on the top shelf of a built-in entertainment center with the television we hardly ever turn on. I stand on Grandma's stool, pull the album down, and walk back to the kitchen to get the kerosene lamp and matches.

When I get back to my room, Grandma is organizing my closet. "It's a mess in here," she says. "How many times do I have to tell you: shirts with shirts, pants with pants." She has changed into flowered pajamas, and her wet nightgown is hanging in my closet, in a space she managed to create by moving my clothes around. Her hands are trembling.

I sit the album, lamp, and matches on my desk.

"The storm will hit land by 5 a.m.," I say. "Does that make it better or worse?"

She turns and looks at me a long time. "That depends. If it slows down or hits somewhere farther away, it could be better. If it stays fast like it is now and hits the city? Well, we'll just have to pray that doesn't happen." Grandma turns back toward my shirts.

I climb onto the trundle bed and watch Grandma work. She has cleared a few shelves in my closet and is using them to organize the groceries.

"It's after midnight," I say. "You should go back to sleep."

Grandma just keeps on shifting things around, tidying up my closet as if that will tidy up the raging storm.

I turn my body to the window and get on my knees to look out. When I shine the flashlight, I can see the leaves of the tree moving with the howling wind. Just when Grandma says, "Okay, that'll do," one two-by-four snaps like a wishbone, and the other flies off whole. A large piece of tin rips off Ms. Carolyn's house across the street and flies directly my way. I fold my body over the bed and cover my head with the comforter. The window shatters and rain makes its way in.

"Eric!" I hear Grandma's voice and feel the trundle bed sliding across the room. She is pulling me away from the window.

"Grandma, wait! I can walk." I'm tripping at this point because I didn't know that woman had so much strength.

She stands still a while, holding her face in her hands. Then she recovers. "Get some shoes on. We have to move the furniture across the room, and I don't want you cutting your feet."

When I get up from the bed, Grandma pulls off the sheet, folds it into a tight bundle, and ties it in a knot. She tosses it outside or drops it into the living room. I don't even know.

"There's no way to get all of that glass off. Not even worth trying," she says.

I have never seen Grandma like this—strong and quick. But here she is, helping me move the chest of drawers, the bed, my desk and chair. We move everything across the room.

"Okay, that's good. Let's get some sleep. We're safe now."

I hear her, but when I look over at the broken window, the rain is still coming in. Glass is still scattered on the floor, and nothing feels safe at all.

---

I awaken to the sound of hammering and thunder. I am on the trundle bed, and the first thing I notice is that I'm covered with a clean sheet, tucked in real tight. I have to work my way out of the thing. Next, I notice Grandma is missing. My bed is fully made as if we ain't in the middle of a storm: a fresh comforter is pulled all the way up, pillows in place. The bed is still pulled close to my closet, and rain is still pouring into my broken window. I figure someone is boarding up windows somewhere nearby. The hammering is too loud though, like it's right in the room with me. It don't make no sense.

I am hot and tired and sticky with sweat. Plus, I smell awful. The whole room smells musty. I step onto my carpet. It feels like a soaked sponge, even far away from the window. I walk to my bathroom and knock on the door.

"Grandma!"

She don't respond. I open the bathroom door and turn on the water. A few drops come out. I groan, noticing the empty tub, remembering I was supposed to fill it. I go back to my room and get a bottle of water, brush my teeth, and wash my face with it. I wet a towel, wipe my sweaty armpits, and walk into my closet to get a clean shirt. Now the hammering is real loud.

"Grandma!" I call out, but she still don't respond.

The sound seems to be coming from the back of my closet. I follow it, calling for her again. Suits line the back wall—jackets on the top bar, pants on the bottom. Grandma insists it is important to have at least six Sunday suits, plus several shirts to mix and match. The sound seems to come from behind the suits. I walk toward them. I think I am losing my mind. I push the jackets and pants aside and see a whole room back there where the wall used to be, where the wall should still be. But how? My room, including the closet and bathroom, runs the length of the back of the house. It starts above the kitchen and extends through the end of Grandma's room. That's it. Nothing else has ever been upstairs.

The kerosene lamp is on a small table in this room I've never seen, and Grandma is facing the table, her back to me. She has a hammer and something else, a small bookcase maybe, because there are books scattered on the floor around her. She is hammering at this bookcase like she is trying to take the back off. The sun is beginning to rise, and the light comes through the closed slats in a small round window on the back wall, giving the room a yellow glow. That's another thing that don't make sense. Where'd the window come from, and how come it's not boarded? So, I'm thinking I'm dreaming. That's the only thing that makes sense.

I step into the space.

"Wow! Grandma, what is this place?"

Grandma jumps, and she holds her hands up like someone caught doing some kind of crime.

"Don't touch anything."

I hold my hands up too because she's making me real nervous. Her eyes are wide like if I touch something we're going to blow up. So, I'm walking around this room with my hands up, and Grandma's watching my every move. I can't believe this room exists. It's got all kind of cool stuff inside. There's another bookshelf in the back corner on the right, filled with books, organized by size. On the left, a large cedar robe is turned catty-corner, and between the bookshelf and cedar robe is a big open leather trunk filled with photo albums and scrapbooks. I want to pick one up, but Grandma is watching me, and she keeps saying, "Eric, don't touch a thing." So, I don't, but I'm thinking hard about it.

That trunk is under the window, and now that I'm walking around, I see a fan in the window, but it's not on. Tools I don't know the names of lean against the wall, and things to clean up with—a bucket, a mop, a broom. But it's the stuff hanging on the wall that grabs my attention: newspaper articles with headlines like "Eighty-Nine Blacks Arrested," "Ole Miss Integrates, Riots Ensue," "More New Orleans Blacks Off to Ole Miss," "Crash of Black Market Adoptions." I see this map framed on the wall, and I stop in my tracks. It's all marked up with red ink and yellow and green highlights. Some stuff is circled, and some stuff is X'd out, and I'm wondering if it's the map to a secret treasure or something.

Grandma says, "Eric, come here."

I turn around and smile. "It's so cool here. What is this place?"

There's a chair pulled out a bit from the table, and I decide to sit down because that's not exactly touching anything. I just want to watch Grandma work, and I like the way the flame dances in the kerosene lamp.

Grandma yells, "Eric, no!" when she sees me sit down. She pushes me like she's trying to rescue me from a moving bus. I lose my balance and fall back, hitting my head on the floor. My foot kicks the table, and the kerosene lamp tips over. The flame goes out, and the room gets real dark. I'm feeling dizzy, so I close my eyes and hold my head. When I open my eyes again, there are more kerosene lamps all around, and people too.

A toddler hits me on the head with a plastic block or something and giggles. I'm still lying backwards in that chair with my feet up, just like I fell. A guy lifts me and says, "Shhhh, Mr. Clarence is about to read. You don't want to get in trouble, do you?"

"Who?" I say, and the guy, who can't be much older than me, looks at me real mean.

"Shhhh," he says again. He turns his head forward, away from me.

I look forward like him, trying to see what he sees, trying to see where Grandma disappeared to. Everything is different, and I remind myself this is just a crazy dream. Only, I can't wake myself up. The room is dark, like I imagine a nightclub might be, but it's quiet, except for the sound of rain splashing against the windows.

I'm guessing about thirty people are crammed in this room—a couple of toddlers, several kids in elementary school, a dozen or so teenagers, maybe ten adults, and a real old couple who sit behind their walkers holding hands. All of them are looking at this man, except the toddlers. Those two are exchanging blocks now, and the spit is glistening between them like a spiderweb.

The man is sitting on a raised stage in a big chair. His left cheek sinks in, and his bottom lip is almost completely gone. He is holding a newspaper, and there are three people up there with him: a man in a suit, a lady in a long dress, and a teenager in some black slacks and a white shirt. His shoes are long, shiny, and black. The man with half a face starts to read, and everybody leans forward. People scoot up their chairs like they want to get as close as possible. This man's voice is so deep, it's hard to hear. He keeps looking up at the window, like he's scared someone is peeking in. I follow his eyes and notice these big arch-shaped windows, like the ones in Zion Baptist Church, but they are all covered with black paper. No one can look in, and no one can look out.

"Oxford, Mississippi. Monday, October 1— Last night, James Meredith, who filed suit against the University of Mississippi more than a year ago, was finally admitted to the university after a Supreme Court ruling. The twenty-nine-year-old Negro male stayed on campus overnight with federal marshals boarding in the very next dorm room for his protection. At 7:45 a.m., he was marched to the Lyceum by armed guards, where he registered for classes. A riot followed, and more than 2,500 troops occupied the campus. More than fifty were injured; at least three were killed."

There is a sudden clash of thunder, and a baby starts crying. "You hush now," a lady says. Her voice is soft, just above a whisper, like she is right next to me. But when I look for her, I don't see no ladies that close, and I don't see no babies in the room.

The man looks up. "Let the baby cry," he says. "At least that means he's woke. We all need to wake up. Today marks the first desegregation of a public university in Mississippi, eight full years after *Brown vs. Topeka, Kansas*. And the only way Mr. Meredith can attend school is with federal marshals on sight."

"Just awful," that same whisper of a voice says.

There is a murmuring of other muffled voices.

"Sinful."

"A disgrace."

"An utter disgrace," the man says, holding on to the word *utter* a while.

The voices bounce off the walls, like they come from the room itself rather than the people.

"You see, young people, this is why we must continue fighting." The man with half a face looks right at me. I want to look away, but my eyes won't move, and my head won't budge. He's so hard to look at that I keep looking. "This is progress," he says, "but it is hardly progress at all. We have a long way to go. None of you," he pauses and looks at me again, then behind me, at the toddlers in the corner. "None of you are too young to sacrifice your very life for those who come behind you. You have to be willing to get beat up, spit on, defaced beyond recognition." He runs his open hand along his own scar tissue. "Killed . . . if that's what it takes."

The teenager on stage frowns, then drops his head. His shoulders move up and down. He is trying hard to hold back a laugh. I know what that looks like. Half-face don't notice though. He just keeps talking, but I'm distracted by the laughing teen. The next thing I hear is "Stand to your feet if you are willing to stand on the front lines."

The boy on the stage goes from laughing to standing. One by one all the kids stand until I am the only one sitting, and every head is turned in my direction. I'm nervous, thinking about the man's words: "You have to be willing to be defaced beyond recognition, killed if that's what it comes to," and I don't want to stand. My heart is beating fast, and the room gets so hot I can hardly breathe. All I see is fire. Fire in everyone's eyes, shimmers of the kerosene lamp. I start coughing. I keep coughing and coughing and coughing. I hear Grandma's voice calling me, and I stand up, ready to run to her. My feet hit the wet carpet, and I wake up.

My head hurts. I can hardly breathe. Grandma walks out of my closet, and she looks dirty. There is a grimy layer of slime on her arms like sawdust stuck to sweat. She smells bad too, something like smoke and mold, a little like vinegar.

"You slept like a brick. I don't know how you slept through the hammering."

"What?"

"I knocked all that loose glass out of your window. We can look out of it now without getting cut. Can even climb out if we have to." Grandma points across the room. There are no more shards of glass sticking up, just a clean window frame. I look over to my bed. It's made, just like in my dream, the comforter pulled all the way up. The pillows all in place.

Below the window is an ax and a crowbar. And against the wall is a piece of thin wood, like something that might cover the back of a bookcase.

"The Lord done spared us. He told that storm, you don't have to go home, but you have to get the hell outta here." Old Man Jake is outside playing a second line mix and yelling up something crazy.

Grandma walks to the window.

I walk up beside her, and we look out together. The sun is high in the sky. It's Monday morning. Old Man Jake is doing the second line back and forth in the street between our house and his. The houses lined up on both sides of the street look like spectators at a parade, but instead of arms reaching up and out, it's split wood, shattered glass, aluminum siding. Ms. Carolyn comes out of her house to see what's going on. Then Byron, who sells candles, and his dad, Mr. Chris, the barbecue man, come out. The rain has stopped.

"Come on, Old Man Jake. Get back inside. It might be dangerous still," Byron says. "No." Old Man Jake holds up a small radio. "The storm missed us. The storm went east."

"What in the world?" Grandma says, and she walks away from the window. "I'm gonna get cleaned up a bit and head outside." She goes into my bathroom. A few seconds later, she yells, "Eric Calhoun, didn't I tell you to fill this tub?"

"I forgot," I say.

Grandma reenters the bathroom doorway with her hands on her hips, her eyes narrow like darts. "I don't forget to feed you, do I?"

We have not eaten in a while, but I think it's best to not mention that. Grandma picks up two bottles of water and walks back into the bathroom with her overnight bag.

I stay by the window a while longer. Old Man Jake, a big boom box on his right side, a small radio in his left hand, is dancing like a Mardi Gras Indian in the middle of the street.

"The storm missed us," he says again. "I heard it on this here radio. It went east." He points in the direction I guess is east, but it looks like he points up and directly at me.

Mr. Chris shouts, "Got meat? Let's cook."

I run from the window and to the bathroom door. "Grandma, I'm going downstairs. I'm going to bring Mr. Chris some meat."

Grandma is singing again.

The kitchen floor is still wet and slippery. I slow down and bend my knees. Step by step, little by little, I make my way to the freezer. It's still cold inside, but the ice has begun to melt. The meat is half-frozen, the vegetables completely thawed. I pull out pork chops and ribs. I bring them out to Mr. Chris who is standing in front of his big grill. He has pulled the grill off the porch and out into the middle of the street, between his house and Ms. Carolyn's. "The Lord done spared us," he says. "Now give me that meat." I hand him the packages, and he laughs loud and deep.

Grandma comes up behind me, and she is laughing too. "Well, look at this," she says. She looks up at the sky. The sun peeks out from behind a tree, and the once gray sky is striped with a mix of yellow, white, and blue.

"I wonder who has a working phone," Grandma says.

"Mine is dead." Mr. Chris flips over the burgers on the grill.

"Someone must have a phone," Grandma says. She starts walking toward Neil's house, which is three houses down. Ms. Carolyn, Ms. Maria who is Alejandro's grandma, and Neil's mom, whose name I don't know, are gathered in a circle. Alejandro's dad, who I only call "Alejandro's dad" because Mr. Pablo don't sound right to me, passes us carrying a pan with more meat for Mr. Chris.

I follow Grandma. As we near the women, they raise their heads and their eyebrows. I read Ms. Carolyn's lips, "Crazy Ruth's coming," she says, and they all drop their heads.

Grandma bulldozes her way into the circle. "Does anyone have a phone?"

"Not me," Ms. Carolyn says.

"No tengo," Ms. Maria says. She shrugs her shoulders and says something I can't make out.

Alejandro is the oldest of five siblings. They all gather on the porch. He waves with one hand and holds back his little sister with the other. I don't have no problems with Alejandro. He sometimes laughs when people make fun of me, but I don't think he ever talks about me, or Grandma for that matter.

"Yes! Yes, I do." Neil's mom holds up her phone. She quickly dials a number and puts the phone to her ear. She's talking about how she made sure to charge her phone and had three battery packs ready in case the first went out. Neil comes outside and walks up to his mama. He pulls her long braids back to get close enough to whisper, and while he's talking to her, I swear he's looking at me. She's thin and real petite, a lot shorter than Neil, who is about 5'8" already. I'm only about 5'4", and she's even shorter than me. She's got this real smooth skin and a mole above her lip. Like Neil, she has that dimpled chin, but it looks good on her. They stand there together looking like they just stepped off a plane into a tourist expedition of a natural disaster. She has on ripped blue jeans, a fitted t-shirt, and denim tennis shoes, something close to what a teen might wear. Neil is wearing a pair of Jordans, denim shorts, and a sleeveless shirt with a hood. I look down and notice my once-white Converses are wet and grimy from walking down our side alley. My pants are wet too and rolled up at the bottom. I look a mess. Grandma don't look no better. The sawdust slime is gone from her skin, but there is sawdust trapped in the frizz of her hair and in the beads of sweat on her forehead. Neil's mom passes her phone around and lets everyone try getting one call through. She is so nice. I wonder why he is so mean. Ms. Carolyn, whose husband died last year and whose son was killed in a drive-by, says she has no one to call and passes the phone on. When it gets to Grandma, she calls Pastor Charles.

"Charles Ray, we're fine." She laughs as if she don't quite believe the words. "It's such a mess here, but we are fine. In fact, we are outside, and Chris is barbecuing." She's quiet for a second. "Yes, I'm being social today."

Out of nowhere, a boom like an explosion drowns out the music, the laughter, the chatting. Below my feet, I feel the ground vibrate. I look down, but everything looks normal. I look up. Everyone else is looking down. Grandma holds her hands out at her side as if trying to balance. "Something's wrong," she says.

"What in the world is that?" Byron says.

Mr. Chris looks up from his grill.

For a second, I think it's an earthquake, but we don't have earthquakes in New Orleans. Two explosions follow, and my mind goes to the bombing of the twin towers. I try to ask what is happening, but my throat sticks to itself and I can't get the words out. Grandma is quiet too. She looks at me, then looks around. The asphalt groans. The manhole cover on the corner pops off, and the ground crumbles into that open space. Water spouts up. Everyone scrambles, but Grandma stands still. Her eyelids fold like someone slowly pulled down a window shade.

I tug at her arm. "Grandma, let's go."

Her legs are unmoving like steel, but her lips move quickly, murmuring words I can't understand.

"Grandma, please," I pull at her arm again, and she opens her eyes. Finally, she takes my hand and starts walking toward the house, still murmuring.

Byron is helping Mr. Chris divide the meat and hand it out. Neighbors are screaming and running back and forth from the grill to home. Grill to home. I want to run too, but I can't because Grandma is walking and she is holding my hand tight.

When we pass Mr. Chris, he reaches out with a pan of meat. "Take that inside," he says.

Grandma releases my hand, so I can take the pan. "Thank you, Chris," she says, and Mr. Chris says, "Y'all get on in now."

Even though she let my hand go, I don't run. I can't leave her. I walk fast then slow. Fast then slow. Water comes from every sewerage drain. I feel it at my ankles. How can there be so much so fast? The weight of each step increases. When we get back to our house, with the fallen tree and no front door, Grandma stops again, faces the street, murmurs another prayer. Byron and Mr. Chris carry the grill back to their porch and go inside. The rest of the street is deserted except for Old Man Jake who walks in the rising water, making the sign of the cross over and over again.

# CHAPTER 4

"Someone is out to get us," Grandma's eyes are wide and wild. "Have you ever seen water do anything like that? And look at that cat."

I walk over to the window. One of the cats from across the street is standing on the steps just above the rising water, looking up at Grandma, meowing. He's almost on the porch—on about the third step from the bottom—and the water is almost touching his paws.

"He's just scared, Grandma. It's because Jeffrey and Joan, or whoever, left him. They left the cats."

"I always told you don't trust those people. Something's not right about a brother and sister living together at that age, and with cats too."

I pull softly at Grandma's arm. "Let's eat," I say, and I close the curtain to block out the cats.

"I should have gone with Charles Ray. I should have got you out of here." She lets me walk her across the room to my desk.

"It's okay, Grandma," I say. But I'm lying. It ain't okay at all. "Let's try to eat."

"I can't eat with dirty hands." She heads to the bathroom with a bottle of water. When she comes back, she lifts the photo album from my desk and hugs it close to her chest before sitting it on top of my chest of drawers. She adds my dictionary and notebook next but keeps the kerosene lamp on the desk, just pushes it back to a corner. She pulls the pan of meat forward and puts a bottle of water in each corner like she's setting a table.

When she sits back down, I hand her a rib. We say grace and eat. I think about my dream.

"You have sawdust in your hair," I say.

"I could have washed it, if you had put water in the tub."

"But where did it come from?"

"I told you, I moved all that broken glass out of your window."

"What about that board over there?" I point to the board leaning on the wall.

"I got it in case we needed to re-cover the window, in case the rain wouldn't stop."

"But where did it come from?"

"Eric, I got it from my room. What does it matter?" She shakes her head and holds her hands up. Barbecue sauce shines on the tips of her thumbs and index fingers. "I keep a few things hidden in my closet. In case of emergency."

"Oh," I say.

"Why so many questions?"

"I had a dream, that's all. It was weird."

"Tell me about it."

I tell Grandma about the room behind my closet, and she laughs. But it ain't like when she laughs with Pastor Charles. It ain't even like when she laughed outside before the manholes started exploding. It ain't a real laugh. It sounds like a question mark.

After we eat, I walk over to the window and look out. The water is flowing down the street like a river. I sit in front of the window for hours. There ain't nothing else to do. Grandma moves around a lot. She covers the ribs, wipes down my desk, reorganizes the closet shelves. She don't come back to the window, and I don't tell her when the water rises over the fire hydrant. No one has come into the neighborhood, and no neighbors have come out of their houses. Four cats are walking around on Jeffrey and Joan's porch, yowling together. I hope Grandma can't hear them.

Grandma goes into the bathroom again. After a while, the handle of the toilet rattles, and she grumbles something about me not filling the tub. The smell of feces and urine seeps into my room.

The sun is beginning to go down, and it's quiet outside like Old Man Jake don't even know night is coming. Usually, when the sun drops, his music starts, but not tonight. No music plays. No neighbors laugh. No dogs bark. No police sirens wail. It's all around eerie. I don't know how Grandma falls asleep in this silence, but she sleeps better than the other nights. As for me, every time I close my eyes, I see manhole covers popping off, shooting up in the air, the cement caving in, the fire hydrant bursting, the sewer drains exploding. Grandma's snore hums above the constant flow of water, and this sound—the sound of water rising from concrete, seeping through cracks—is more troubling than the howling wind or thundering rain from the nights before.

I get up to get a snack, from hunger or boredom or fear. It's all beginning to feel the same. I shine my flashlight and search the shelves for a bag of potato chips and a bottle of juice. I am about to leave the closet when I think of my dream again. I turn and pull back my suits. There is nothing there but a wall. I laugh a little because I am giving anyone who wants to call me crazy a good reason. Grandma's sleeping, and I don't want to wake her, so I sit right in my closet and eat. I have the flashlight leaning against the back wall, so the light makes a big circle on the ceiling. I pretend that circle's the sunshine telling me everything will be fine, and I let my body relax. I close my eyes and lean back on the wall. Next thing I know I end up back in that room from my dream.

The kerosene lamp is gone, and the room is dark, but a small ray of light comes from my flashlight. I'm half in the room and half out. My legs and feet are still in my closet. I can feel the carpet beneath my calves and heels, but my back and head are on cold hardwood. I'm scared if I just stand up, I'll be back in my closet and the wall will reappear. So, I don't stand. I scoot myself back until I feel the hardwood on my heels. I curl my body to pick up my flashlight, and when I finally have the flashlight in my hand, I stand.

Without the lit kerosene lamp and the sun shining through the slats in the window, the room is dark, dreary, and cold. The books ain't on the floor no more. They are neatly placed on a bookshelf, sorted by size. The table is now empty. It's a dark oak color and longer than I remember. Six chairs are pushed in around it. I put one hand in my pocket because I don't want to touch a thing, and I walk around, kind of tiptoeing. In the spotlight of my flashlight, spiderwebs shine. I go to the bookshelf and try to read the book titles, but the bindings are faded. I can't make out the words. The bookshelf is backless, so I can see something behind it. It's not just a wall. There's a photo behind the books. I squat down a little and flash my light up, trying to get a better look. I don't dare touch that shelf because I'm scared something crazy might happen.

I see the bottom of a dress in the photo. It puffs out in layers of thin material and trails into the green grass. I squat way down and look up, trying to see in the space behind the bookcase. That don't work, so I try standing and looking in the gaps above the shorter books. I make out an eye, an almond-shaped hazel eye, and pale skin. I gasp. This is my mother's wedding photo. I can only see the top of the groom's shoulders, not even his neck. He's too tall. I go down low, searching for some part of him. I catch a glimpse of his arm, bent at the elbow, and I follow it to the wrist and hand around her waist. He's white, even more pale than my mother. I drop the flashlight, and it thuds against the floor.

I hear something rustling, like Grandma turning in her sleep, and I kick the flashlight flush against the bookcase so that the wood absorbs its light. It dims. I stand still like a statue until I hear Grandma snoring. After that, every time I try to walk, the floor creaks. I drop down and begin to crawl, slow and steady, with my knees slightly lifted, trying not to put my full weight on the floor. Water rises beneath me, and I feel my pants getting heavy. It's getting hard to move, like I'm in quicksand, sinking.

"Boy, what are you doing?" Grandma's voice breaks the silence.

I look up, and I am back in my room, crawling across the wet carpet, Grandma standing above me with her hands on her hips.

---

It was the kind of dream that left me feeling drained and confused. Grandma says I'm probably suffering from the heat. It's Tuesday morning, and we have been stuck without power since Sunday night. The August heat of New Orleans is enough to give anyone bad dreams. She hands me a pair of dry pants. "Go and change. Today's a new day. Maybe it'll be better." She winces. "If only those cats would stop crying."

In the bathroom, I examine my jeans. They're dripping wet. The carpet in my room is only damp. I shake my head. Nothing about this makes sense.

When I come out of the bathroom, Grandma has set my desk like a table again. Two paper towels are positioned like placemats. On top of each is a bottle of water, a can of Vienna sausages, and a can of creamed corn.

"Thank you," I say.

I pick up a can of Vienna sausages and walk over to the broken window, hoping to get fresh air, but even the outside air is stale. I look out and almost choke. The water is higher, and it's still rising. All the houses are raised five or six steps, but the water covers the porches now. The cats at Jeffrey and Joan's house have climbed onto the railings, and the hair is standing up on their hunched backs. Old Man Jake has tied himself to two beer kegs and is floating in the street, his body in the middle, his arms draped over each keg. He laughs and throws his head up like he's heard the funniest joke.

I can hear Byron talking, but I can't see him. "What do you mean, 911 is not taking calls?" he yells. "We have to get out of here. We'll die here."

I walk back to my desk and sit next to Grandma. I eat slowly. It's hard to chew. The sausage is soft and salty, the corn is hard and sweet. I want to vomit.

"We should go outside again today," Grandma says. "Maybe the water is back down now, and Chris can cook again."

I don't say a thing.

"If we don't cook the rest of the meat up today, it'll all go bad. No sense in letting that happen," Grandma says.

She stands, walks over to the window, and looks out. "Oh, my word." She takes a few steps backwards, closes her eyes, and locks her two hands together like one fist.

The morning passes slowly. We sit quietly as if being still will convince the water to go away. Finally, I get Grandma's photo album and start to look through it. Grandma sits next to me, and when she sees the first picture of my mama, she sighs real big. She's a little girl gathering dandelions in what looks like a big field, but it might just be the backyard because every spring the dandelions and clovers take over for a while. Grandma calls them beautiful weeds. On the next page, the little girl version of my mama is topping a mud pie with the yellow flowers. I smile. I remember doing just that. Photo after photo, she's outside, often barefoot, and I imagine her bare feet underneath that wedding dress I saw last night in my dream. If it was a dream.

"How come you don't have pictures of Mama after she grew up?

Grandma gets up like I invited her to leave.

"Is it because of my daddy?"

"Is this about your crazy dream?"

"No, it's just that people say—"

Grandma puts up her hand. "I know what they say, but saying it doesn't make it true."

"Does not saying it make it a lie?"

I look in her eyes, and I know my words have pushed her too far. She shuts down. "Clean up this room!"

This time she goes to the window, and I'm the one trying to put things in order. It don't matter what I do, I can't get rid of the smell of the sewer. It's not just in my room; it's everywhere. Outside. Inside. In my nose. It's almost impossible to breathe. My trash can is already full, so I'm looking around trying to figure out where to put the empty cans and water bottles. I know if I get the room clean, Grandma will calm down. My goal is to get the trash out of sight, out of mind. I leave my room and head for the stairs. The smell is so much worse when I get to the staircase that I begin to gag. I can only walk down the first eight steps; the last eight are underwater. I stop and dump the trash into the flooded kitchen. Before I can stop it, I'm leaning over the stairs vomiting into the thick brown water. My eyes tear up, and my nose is running, and now the smell is also in my throat. I keep going back and forth until there ain't no more trash in my room. The last two times, I gag, but nothing comes up. It just hurts.

Grandma's still staring out of the window. I slip the photo album into one of my drawers, take out my rocks, and start a game of marbles. I feel Grandma cutting her eyes at me, but she don't say a thing, and I act like I don't know I'm breaking a rule. I just keep playing, and when I'm done, I lie on the trundle bed and roll the shiny rock between my thumb and index finger.

The sun goes down, and Grandma pulls out potted meat and crackers. She starts setting the desk like a table again.

"Don't we have peanut butter?" I walk back to the closet.

"Sit down. You don't have the luxury of being choosy. You can have peanut butter tomorrow. Because if we don't finish this potted meat now, it will spoil. Then it will smell. And I don't want to smell another spoiled thing."

Grandma lights a candle, vanilla scent, and puts it between my potted meat and hers. The odor in the room changes to something like syrupy sweet bowels. She falls asleep before the sun sets, which isn't like her at all. I walk to the window again. Old Man Jake, still floating on the beer kegs, is farther away, about half a block, and his head is down so that he looks like he has fallen asleep. No one is outside, not Ms. Carolyn, or Neil and his mother, or Alejandro and his whole family. Byron's and Mr. Chris's muffled voices hang in the air, like they are yelling from far away. Neil's dog is howling on his rooftop, and two cats are yowling from the porch railing across the street.

I look back at Grandma. She is sound asleep. Then I run my hands along the windowsill. She got out all the glass alright. I lift myself up, just as I had done so many nights before to climb out to the tree, but now I just sit in the window. My feet rest on what remains of the dining room roof. I look to my left. Mr. Chris and Byron are sitting on top of their roof, which is next to ours, but a little lower.

Mr. Chris lifts his head and looks my way. "Be careful, Lil Man," he says. "That roof might not hold you."

I sit still. "How are we going to get out of here?"

Mr. Chris looks at me a long time as if he is trying to think of a clever response, but the only thing that comes out is, "We're gonna die here. That's how." Then he folds his face in his hands.

Byron looks at Mr. Chris a second then back at me. "Nah, Lil Man. We're not. Somebody'll see us. Somebody'll save us." But his voice lacks the authority of his father's, who is older and wiser and usually very much in control.

I go back into my room, open my chest of drawers, and pull out the photo album again. I light the kerosene lamp to free up my hands. When the flame dances, I think again of my dream—the first one—when flames lit everyone's eyes. I want to forget it, but it keeps coming back to me. There is something so familiar about it. I can't focus on the album. I put it back and get my backpack, which Grandma moved into a corner of my closet. I fumble through my notebook and come across a folded article: "The Legacy of James Meredith." It's an article Ms. Hornwell had us read in one of her lessons on family legends. I had forgotten all about it, but it seeped into my dream. That's it. No magic. No secret room. Only a dream.

Forget there was sawdust in Grandma's hair or that my jeans were drenched when I woke up. Those are coincidences. I walk over to my chest of drawers and pull down the dictionary. *Coincidence: a remarkable concurrence of events or circumstances without causal connection.* I roll my eyes. What does that even mean? I flip forward several pages. *Concurrence: two or more events happening at the same time.* I try to put this together in my mind. It so happens I had a dream in which Grandma was working with wood, and when I woke up, she happened to have sawdust in her hair. That don't mean the sawdust came from the room in my dream. Besides, she even said she got the wood and stuff from her room. Coincidence. Now, my jeans. It so happens I had a dream in which I crawled across a floor with rising water. When I woke up, my pants were not damp but drenched. My carpet was only damp. So how did my jeans get so wet if I didn't crawl in rising water? Coincidence?

I climb back into the window. The sun is almost completely down. I turn on the flashlight. The water is still rising. Grandma's maroon car is somewhere under the dark green water. I look down the block where I had seen Old Man Jake last, but there are only two beer kegs and floating debris, stuff like roof shingles and wood and lots and lots of paper. I don't see the old man.

"What happened to Old Man Jake?" I turn my head toward Byron who is alone on the roof now.

"He got tired."

The water is higher on the other side of the street, and Ms. Carolyn's door has fallen in against its weight. Shelia's mom's flowerpots are floating down the street, and the For Sale sign in front of the Nguyen's old house has made its way to Old Man Jake's porch. Jeffrey and Joan's cat (I only see one now) walks back and forth on the railing, just above the water. At the end of the block, Neil sits on his rooftop, his face turned away from me.

"They're going to let us die," Byron says. Then, he drops back down into the attic, and I hear things crashing around, like he is throwing furniture or something, having some kind of tantrum.

Just like that, I am alone in the darkness, and I stay in the window imagining Old Man Jake playing his music and doing the second line in the middle of the street.

That night, I don't sleep. I don't want to dream.

CHAPTER 5

By Wednesday morning, it's hard to remember where the porches used to be. The cats are all gone now. Alejandro's dad is outside, steering his refrigerator through the front door onto his porch, only the porch looks more like a lake. Alejandro walks through the front door, guiding the other end of the fridge. His grandfather comes out, and he's waving his hands in the air like he's fussing about something. Alejandro's dad backs up toward the sidewalk, and the water rises, waist high, chest high, then shoulder high. He stops and lifts himself on top of the fridge. He crosses over to the other side and climbs down onto one of the porch steps, but I can't see which one. The three of them stand crammed side by side between the porch railings. The water is just a little below Alejandro's waist, hip level on his grandfather, thigh high on his dad. Alejandro pushes his hair away from his eyes.

There is no way out, not without a boat or plane. We're stuck.

Mr. Chris climbs back onto his roof with a can of beer. "Hey, Lil Man." He throws his head back and chugs the beer like water. When he's done, he makes this loud exhale, almost like a groan. "Is your grandmother still alive?"

The words roll out of his mouth like an everyday greeting, like, "Hi Eric. How's your grandma?" Except they are slurred, and I figure he's drunk. I look at Mr. Chris a long time. He sits there shirtless in gray sweatpants wet from the knee down and a pair of stringless tennis shoes with the tongues flapping forward. I ain't never seen him like this, not the barbecue man.

I climb back into my room. What kind of question was that? I kick my backpack, which I had forgotten to put back in the closet. I kick it hard as I can.

"Watch yourself," Grandma says. Her voice comes out in a low, deep rumble. She's sitting up on the bed, her legs dangled over the side, her feet bare. She still has on those flowered pajamas.

I look at Grandma, but I don't say nothing to her. I just kneel down, pull the shoestring from my shoe, and make a circle on the floor. I pull out my rocks and play marbles until there are no more rocks in the circle, and I don't care if Grandma says it is the devil's game. I'm thinking about Mr. Chris and his stupid question, and for a second, I think if she was dead maybe I would have some friends. And maybe, just maybe, I could do enough digging around to find out something about my parents. Maybe my daddy would come back when he learns she's not here to run him off with her hateful ways.

Grandma is rambling on and on about levees blowing up, and the white man coming to kill, steal, and destroy, and us being left here to die. I don't see what the white man has to do with anything, especially now. The only one taking something from us is God himself, taking our street, our houses, even our neighbors. I want to spit, but I know better than to spit on my carpet, even if it is already wet and smelly. I climb back onto my window, but this time I go all the way out and stand up tall on what roof is left. I look at that stupid tree, and I look through the leaves and into the dining room with its shattered plates, and I gather as much spit as I can in my mouth, and I spit right onto those stupid leaves.

"You better get back in the window, boy," Mr. Chris says. "That roof is barely holding up."

I look at him long and hard. "Yeah, my grandmother's still alive," I say, and I spit again.

Ms. Carolyn is floating out in the street on her refrigerator, and Old Man Jake's two beer kegs are still floating in the same spot like something is holding them in place. At the end of the block, Neil's mama is with him on the roof. Three days ago, they looked untouched by the storm, but now, Neil's wearing a dingy white shirt, his curls are large and unruly, and his mother has on a tank top and short shorts that look like underwear from a distance. Her long braids are bundled up on her head.

Mr. Chris stares at me. "Yeah, well, I guess I shouldn't have asked you that like that. Everything just feels like death around here. But you be strong, Lil Man."

"It can't be much longer now," Byron says. His hair is matted, and his eyes are bloodshot. A black beaded necklace with a silver cross hangs from his neck, sharply visible against his black shirt. He cut the sleeves off, or maybe he ripped them off, and a few loose threads fall from his shoulders.

A helicopter flies overhead. At first, the sound is a distant whizzing, but the helicopter dips down a little, and the blades chop against the air. We all wave our hands and yell. It circles around three times but never stops.

"Damn it!" Mr. Chris says. He throws his beer can into the lake where our street used to be.

"Eric!" I hear Grandma screaming, and I bury my head in my hands. "Eric!" She sounds frantic.

"You'd better go," Byron says, tracing Jesus's body on that silver crucifix with his finger.

I scramble back inside and find her moving around my closet, calling my name, totally disoriented.

"Grandma, I'm here!"

"Oh, Eric," she says, and she points to the wall. "I thought you—". Then, she stops and gives me a big tight hug. "I didn't know where you were. I thought something happened to you." She pulls me real close and squeezes so tight I have to open my mouth to breathe.

---

For three days, I climb out of my window and sit on the sill until the sun goes down. Byron and Mr. Chris take turns coming out, but they stop sitting together. The same thing is true for Neil and his mother. Sometimes I see him, sometimes I see her, but I rarely see them together. Alejandro's three little sisters are sitting on that refrigerator, and his father has tied a rope around it, securing it to the porch rail. He has stepped down deeper into the water so that it is now chest high. Alejandro's grandparents are on the porch steps. His grandfather leans against the railing. His grandmother rests against him. The water is a little above his waist, slightly below her breasts. Alejandro and his brother sit on the porch railing, their feet under the murky water. Ms. Carolyn still floats outside on her refrigerator, looking like she regrets ever climbing on board. The fridge, unanchored, has moved out to the middle of the street. She is too far out to come back in without swimming.

Old Man Jake's beer kegs have moved farther away, down into the next block, past the corner store. I'm thinking of the old man—the light that used to dance in his eyes, the smile that never skipped a beat, and those legs, always moving, always headed to the next destination. I stare out at the beer kegs, remembering when he first brought them home. He sat them on his porch, one on each side of the steps. Ms. Jackie asked him what he was doing with them. "I'm gon' plant me some flowers," he said. And Ms. Jackie frowned and told him that was the most trifling thing she ever heard, and furthermore, she did not want to see two big beer kegs sprouting flowers every time she went outside. "I'll plant them inside then," Old Man Jake had said, and he pulled those beer kegs into his living room. I never saw them again until the day I saw him floating, one arm over each keg. I had thought it was a brilliant idea at the time: both the beer keg planters and the beer keg floaties. But what do I know?

When the sun goes down, I go back into my room where Grandma and I slurp green beans from a can and scoop Spam with our fingers. Grandma has taken to crying every night. She does sleep though, and after she drifts off, I wander into my closet and feel around the back wall and wonder if there is really a hidden room back there. I don't find anything but solid wall.

This is our routine for several days. Grandma stops worrying about washing up. She stops organizing cans. She no longer puts anything back in its place. Her body is wet with sweat and beads of perspiration dot her forehead all day and all night. Her hair is frizzy and lacks form, like a dark gray cloud. She has stopped singing, and when I go out to the roof again and stand up, she don't even call my name.

I am on the roof when another helicopter comes near. A man using a bullhorn leans out and speaks through the sound of blades striking the wind, "Are. You. Alone?"

I lean down and brace myself on the window to keep from falling. "No. My grandmother is here. Inside."

"Okay. I. Am. Going. To. Get you. Out of there. Tomorrow."

"Man, you gon' leave us here to die?" Byron yells.

"No," the man says. "There is more help. Coming. But we are getting. The women. And children. First. I will come. Back."

He flies over to Ms. Carolyn and slowly lowers a basket to the refrigerator. The man reaches for Ms. Carolyn, trying to steady the basket and close the gap between the refrigerator and its side. Ms. Carolyn's arms tremble and her knees buckle when she tries to reach him.

They lock arms, and the basket hits the side of the fridge then rocks away from it. Ms. Carolyn's legs slip off the fridge, and her shins hit the basket.

"Jesus," I say. And I ain't using his name in vain. I am calling out for help.

The basket keeps shifting position, but the man holds steady. The helicopter hovers in one spot until Ms. Carolyn is in the basket and seated. Then the basket is slowly raised until it reaches the open door of the helicopter, and another man helps Ms. Carolyn get inside. It takes a long time, like she can't figure how to move her legs or something, but finally, the man pulls her up and in. As soon as she is inside, I realize I've been holding my breath, and I gasp for air. The helicopter flies over to Alejandro's family, and the basket comes down again.

I rush back into my room. "Grandma, we are getting rescued tomorrow."

"By who?"

"A man in a helicopter. He has helpers, and they come down in a basket. They just got Ms. Carolyn."

Grandma don't say a word. She just gets up and starts packing up groceries.

"What are you doing?"

"We're not going to leave this food. There's good stuff left in here."

I have to explain to Grandma three times why we have to leave the food and our clothing behind. Finally, she agrees that we will each bring one bag with as much as we can fit and carry. I grab my backpack, and Grandma picks up her overnight bag. I empty everything out of my bag, except my notebook and some pens, and when Grandma ain't looking, I take the photo album out of my drawer and slip it into my bag. I have to fit my clothes around it, so I don't add much: just a pair of jeans, a shirt, and some clean socks. I pour my rocks into the small part of my backpack and add my old shoestring. I pick up my dictionary, but I have no room for it, so I sit it in the drawer I just moved the album from. Grandma don't have nothing clean to pack, so she packs her dirty nightgown, soap, shampoo, toothpaste, toothbrush, and pain pills. She takes her wallet out of her purse and puts it in her overnight bag. She opens the drawer and sits her purse inside.

That night, I sit in the window again and look out at the sky. It's streaked with gray clouds. There ain't one star, but the moon is full. It feels like I might fall into those clouds or into that moon or into the tree and disappear forever. I am too tired to stay up all night again. I climb inside onto the trundle bed and fall asleep.

I awaken to the sound of Grandma singing. The sunlight is brighter than it has been in days, so bright I see red light before I open my eyes. Grandma greets me with peanut butter and crackers. "I thought this might make you smile," she says. And I do smile.

When I finish eating, I go back to the window and wait for the helicopter to return. Behind me Grandma cleans and sings, like she is preparing the room for a guest.

Hours go by before the helicopter comes back. For the first time in days, everyone is outside at the same time, like everyone wants to be seen. Byron and Mr. Chris, Neil and his mom, Alejandro, his dad, grandpa, grandma, brother, and three little sisters. His two youngest sisters are curled up on the floating refrigerator sleeping. His grandpa covers them with what looks like a thin, wet sheet and waves his hand as if trying to cool them. The other girl is sitting up, reaching for her father. He reaches into a bag that is sitting on the fridge and holds something pinched between two fingers. He shoves it in her mouth. The little girl chews a little and then stands to wrap her arms around his neck. This causes him to stumble, and he slips deeper into the water. He pushes her away, and she starts crying. I wonder why Alejandro's grandma and sisters are still there. I thought the helicopter picked them up yesterday.

The helicopter blades snap in the air, and its engine whirs. When it gets close enough, the pilot hovers low, close to the window, and a man peeks out from the cabin. "Go inside," he says. "I need. To send. A basket down."

I nod, and he moves back up into the air.

"Grandma, the helicopter is here," I say.

When the basket comes down, there is a man inside, just like with Ms. Carolyn's rescue. The basket keeps hitting the side of the house, and the man keeps trying to grab hold of the windowsill. I walk over to help, but he shoos me away. When he finally grips the windowsill, he says, "I can take one of you at a time. Help your grandmother in first."

"What?" Grandma's eyes are wide and wild again. "I'm not going without him. No. We don't separate."

"Ma'am, I understand your fears." The man's fingers are sliding off the window frame, and he keeps repositioning them. The basket sways in the wind. "I'm just going to bring you up, then come back to get your grandson. The basket will only hold two of us at a time."

Grandma folds her arms and shakes her head. "I don't move without him."

The man's fingers slip from the window frame and the basket swings out a little then crashes into the house. He tries again. This time, when the man finally grabs the windowsill, he throws in a rope and asks me to pull it hard. I do, and that anchors the basket to the house. The man climbs in through the window. Grandma pulls me close to her and backs up.

The man puts his hands up like someone under arrest. "Ma'am, look, I am only here to rescue you. So, here's what I'm going to do. Since you won't separate from your grandson, I am going to put both of you in the basket. You'll go up together. Then I'll go when the basket is lowered again. Will that work?"

Other than Pastor Charles, I ain't never seen nobody treat Grandma with so much patience. This man's got one of those special callings or something. He's dressed in olive green with black shoes, a puffy black vest, black gloves, a green-and-black helmet, and black sunglasses. His lips are the only thing visible. They are thin and tan, the skin around them smooth.

Grandma nods and loosens her grip. The man takes the rope from me and holds it tight. Grandma and I walk over to the window and sit our bags in the basket. My bedroom windows sit low, but the basket is resting on what is left of the dining room roof, so it is a bit higher than the windowsill. Grandma tries lifting her leg over the side but loses her balance. I catch her, lean over, and let her put all her weight on my back while I lift her leg up. "Lord, have mercy!" she yells.

Grandma grips the side of the basket with both hands and lowers herself slowly. When she is finally sitting, she pulls her bag to her lap. She reaches forward to move my bag too.

"I can fit," I say quickly. "Don't hurt your back."

I climb in the basket before Grandma can lean forward again. The man throws the rope back into the basket and lets it go. The basket rocks back and forth as it is hoisted back up to the helicopter. Grandma grips both sides and sits forward. I do too, so our foreheads almost touch. As we are lifted over the house, Mr. Chris and Byron wave. Alejandro and his brother wave, so do his dad and grandpa. Neil's mom waves but not Neil, and I wonder why we're going and not them.

When we reach the helicopter, the side is wide open, and another man dressed in the same green-and-black uniform reaches out for the basket, secures it, and helps us climb in. He says something on a walkie-talkie and sends the basket back down. He motions for us to move back, away from the door. We do, and I am glad because the wind from the propellers makes me feel sick and dizzy. When our rescuer gets back inside, the two men pat each other on the back. Then, they secure the rescue basket and close the helicopter's door.

Through the window, I see only the top of Ms. Carolyn's roof and Old Man Jake's. The water is just below the windowsill of my bedroom window and just below the roof of Mr. Chris's house. Pieces of houses, siding, tin, and shingles float in the water.

"You'll get them too, right?" My face is pressed against the glass, looking out.

"I will. Or someone will." The man who rescued us sits back and takes off his helmet.

He is so young. His hair is surprisingly long.

"How come you didn't get those little girls on the refrigerator and their grandmother yesterday? And Alejandro and his brother? You said you were getting women and children."

"They wouldn't separate from the men. We have to wait for a bigger helicopter or a boat. This one is too small."

Another helicopter flies into the neighborhood as we fly out, and a white boat with a big black motor comes down the street.

"What's today?" Grandma asks.

"Saturday, September 3rd," the man with long hair says.

"My, my, my." Grandma lets her back fall against the cushioned seat. "A whole week!"

I look down at our house as we fly away, and I swear I see a little round window where the back of my closet should be. I gasp, and for a long time, I look away.

When I look out of the window again, we are out of our neighborhood, and I see only the blue tops of street signs. There are people on rooftops, and once, exactly once, I see a boat lined up next to a roof, and a man is lowering a little girl into the boat. She won't let go of the man's neck.

A Walmart Supercenter sign rises above the water. A few minutes pass, and I see people on a flat rooftop, holding up a sign that says "Save Us: Children. Dog. Cat," and the dog is barking frantically, running in a small circle. I think of Jeffrey and Joan's cats and Neil's dog, and I wonder where that dog's been and where the cats have gone. At some point, we get to where the water must have gone down or maybe never rose because I see what looks like thousands of people moving around. I have no idea where we are and no idea where we are going. The pilot lands in a parking lot with two other helicopters, both red, not black like the one carrying us. One helicopter is preparing to take off, and mechanics are working on the other. Two men—one short, one tall—dressed in jeans, white t-shirts, and rubber work boots like they are prepared to rake leaves, come over, and as soon as our rescuers open the helicopter door, they reach for Grandma's hand.

"Come on, ma'am. We've got you."

Grandma gets up real slow, and I try to help her. It's hard to feel my legs. They are wobbly and weak. Grandma stumbles when she puts her foot on the ground. The short man wraps his arms around her waist, and the other helps her get her other foot on the ground.

"That's it. You're safe," the tallest one says.

Grandma holds on to the man who wraps his arms around her a long time. The tall man reaches for my hand, and I let my weight lean into him to gain my balance. When my feet hit the ground, I nearly fall, and my body bumps against the man's. For a moment, I grip his hand tighter. Grandma is still hugging the short, stubby man. I slip in between them, beginning to feel control of my legs, and I ease her away from him.

"Come on, Grandma," I say. Another helicopter is preparing to land. "He has to help someone else."

"Where are we?" Grandma asks.

Wherever we are, we can see the ground. Garbage lines the streets, not just along the curb, but the middle of the streets, and the sidewalks too.

"Across from the Convention Center, ma'am. Just head over that way where you see those people gathered. Someone will direct you to the right line."

When the man points, I realize the trash might not be trash. It might be people surrounded by trash, carrying trash bags, dressed in dirty clothes. But that can't be people. Can it?

"That way?" I point just as the man did.

"That's right." He turns and walks to the helicopter pilot to tell him something before he takes off again.

When we get closer to the building, I see lots of movement. People are carrying stuff, mostly boxes and trash bags. And when a whole lot of people are carrying a whole lot of trash bags and are surrounded by a whole lot of trash, those people, it turns out, look a whole lot like trash. And now here we are, lost in the mass of people. Lost in the trash. Lost like trash.

A man holding up a toddler with a sagging diaper and a pot belly, yells, "She need food. Her mama died. Somebody help me." The toddler squints in the sun and wiggles his fingers and toes.

"The buses are coming," someone calls out. I have no idea where that voice comes from, and I don't see no buses. I also don't see nowhere to sit down. Grandma will need to sit before long.

This lady starts talking about how it's a shame the Superdome is already at capacity and they are trying to move people out because the sewers are backed up and part of the roof was ripped off by the wind. She's rambling about women being raped and people stealing and the city gone mad because we were all left to die. And now we're here, still waiting. "Where they want us to go?" She throws her hands up. "Look around." Her eyes get real big. "Ain't nowhere to go."

There are so many people, more than I've ever seen in one place, even right before a parade when people fill the streets, waiting to throw their hands up and say, "Throw me something, mister."

"I don't want a handout," the woman says. "But if I had the money to leave, I woulda been gone. Where I'm supposed to go without a car? All them school buses, all them RTA buses, gone. Gone! And we out chere just waitin'." She looks at me a long time and leans in. "To die."

Grandma pulls me away. "Come on," she says. She holds me real close to her, almost too close to walk right.

We walk over to a man who's handing out bottles of water.

"Excuse me," Grandma says. "Where do we go for the buses?"

"Everyone here is trying to get on one of those buses," he says. He gestures to the thousands of people surrounding him. Everyone is filthy. No one's hair is combed. People are closing in around us, trying to get closer to the bottled water. Grandma swats at a fly on a little girl's head. An old man wets his pants; his eyes grow big and a faint smile creeps across his face as the urine travels down his leg. Grandma's still distracted by the fly.

I look back at the water guy. "But when the buses do come, where will they park?"

"Down there. At the corner of Calliope and Convention Center Drive." He points and shakes his head. "But I'm telling you, everyone here is waiting on those buses."

Grandma's still shooing away the fly on the little girl's head, but it just keeps coming back.

I tap her arm. "Let's walk to the corner. The buses will park in that area when they come."

Grandma looks at the distance, and I hear a small whimper in her throat. But she starts walking.

The heat is awful and the air thick with humidity. The stench is the same one I have smelled for days, like mold, sewage, and vinegar all mixed together.

When we finally get to the corner, there ain't no one there to help. No one giving out water or offering directions. Just a bunch of people as stuck and desperate as us. I see a man with an old woman in a wheelchair, and I think maybe she can be company for Grandma. So, I walk over to him, prepared to get Grandma and the old woman talking. Only when I get there, I realize the woman is already dead.

I step back. My chest is so tight it hurts.

"Mama," the man is saying softly. "Mama, come on. Wake up." He puts his ear near her heart and places his fingers on her wrist. "No, Mama. You can't die like this."

"Oh, Lord have mercy!" Grandma says. Her eyes are not wild and wide. They're narrow and soft and shiny like tears are stuck on her eyeballs.

The man lies his head in his dead mother's lap and cries. All around us people dodge death. They just keep walking, shuffling, crying, arguing. But this woman is dead.

After a while, when the sun finally goes down and evening comes, the man whose mother has just died removes her from her wheelchair and drags her body to a wall of the Convention Center. He leans her against the brick and crosses her hands and feet. She looks asleep when he's finished.

He walks over to Grandma. "Ma'am, would you like to sit in my mother's chair? She'd want you to."

Grandma looks at the man and takes his hands in her own. "I'm so sorry," she says. Then she sits down, and I think it is less because her legs hurt and more because the man needs her to sit, needs someone to sit in his mama's chair. He starts to walk away, but I stop him. I reach right out and grab his arm.

"What's your name?" I say.

"I'm Leonard. My mama is Linnie. She named me after her. Sort of."

"Maybe we'll meet again."

"Yeah, maybe," he says. I let him walk away that time.

Grandma rocks back and forth, massaging her calves and saying, "Lord, Lord, Lord."

Leonard leans his back against the brick and holds his dead mother's hand. I watch him cry, and I realize I cannot find my own tears in this sadness.

# CHAPTER 6

After walking inside and smelling the stench of sewage soaking the Convention Center's carpet, Grandma and I decide to go back outside. The smell is worse than it was at home, which I didn't think was possible. I turn around and cover my nose with one hand. With the other, I am pushing Grandma in the wheelchair. I see graying bodies lined up against the wall near the exit. These people are dead. There are actual dead people just propped up against the walls. It takes everything I have not to vomit on Grandma's head. I'm gagging like crazy, but I don't point this out. I drop my eyes and push the wheelchair through the doors and back into the outside heat.

The crowd is unbelievably big. Everywhere I look—on the sidewalk, in the street, against the building, inside the building—people are waiting to be rescued. A pregnant woman passes out before my eyes, and a man lifts her head from the ground and yells, "Somebody help me." The next thing I know people are chanting, "Help. Help. Help. Help." The chant catches on and gets louder and louder until finally we hear a horn blowing and see a big tan Hummer-like vehicle driving slowly down the street. People start pushing back, making room. The vehicle parks, and four National Guard soldiers get out. They unload cases of bottled water and meals that remind me of the dry soup in the grocery store. Two of them ask people to form lines, and some people complain that they haven't had food out here in more than four days.

"Man, we had to steal water and juice from the Riverwalk," a man says. "Just to survive. What took y'all so long?"

It's the man who was passing out water bottles when Grandma and I first arrived.

The soldier's trying his best to explain that they had to wait for the water and food to arrive. "We just got it," he says. "We got here fast as we could."

"Bless you, man," a man with a black cap walks up and shakes the soldier's hand.

One of the soldiers picks up the pregnant lady. "We're going to get her to the medical helicopter," he says. "Come on." He motions to the guy who was holding her head up off the ground, and they start running back the direction we came from in the first place, where the helicopters are landing and taking off. Now, people are waving down the soldiers trying to tell them who's sick.

"Help is coming," they say.

But after the National Guard soldiers unload the food and water, they leave. We are left to finish giving it out ourselves, and that's when the man in the black cap takes charge. He tells us to form lines, so we can make sure everyone gets fed. It's thousands of people, but the word spreads and lines really do form. He recruits people to help distribute. Another guy who has a bunch of kids sitting in two grocery store baskets takes his kids out of the baskets and tells them to sit still on the ground. He brings the baskets up to the new leader, and together they fill them with food and water. Then, the volunteers push baskets down the street and pass food from the people at the front to the people at the back. But the man with the kids goes back to his kids and sits on the ground. A little girl climbs in his lap.

I sit on the ground next to the wheelchair and eat the dry soup meal. It's really meatballs and spaghetti, but it has this little heater in it that works when you shake it. I stir the thick red sauce and wrap the spaghetti around my fork. I'm so hungry, I can't wait to taste it. It smells so good. I stab a meatball, so it hangs on the tip of the small fork, and I open my mouth wide, ready to savor the taste. Almost immediately, I gag. The meatball tastes nothing like meat. It's like chewy dust. I chew slowly and wash it down with water. Now, I'm eating real slow, like one noodle at a time. I'm too hungry not to eat at all, but it's too nasty to eat fast.

And suddenly I'm really missing Grandma's chicken salad.

I have no idea how or when I fell asleep, but I wake up to something different in the air. The food is gone already, and people are back to complaining. There's nothing left to steal. A few blocks away, we can see buses, but they're not coming our way. They've been sitting still for hours.

The guy in the black cap goes down to the buses and finds out the drivers are scared to drive in. They've been told people are out of control, and they are waiting for the National Guard or the police or both to come in before they start picking people up. "So, I told them we'll all get in line, and we won't fight. You feel me?" The man in the black cap explains. "This is how we get out of here."

People line up again, just like they did for the food. This man in the black cap is like Moses from one of Pastor Charles's sermons. It's like he says something, and the people listen, like he's got a magic staff or something. The volunteers are back at work, making sure no one is blocking the street so the buses can come on through. After a while, people start organizing, putting older people, children, and the disabled at the front of the lines while keeping families together.

Grandma looks older than she is. Her hair is a silvery gray. The hair around her temples and at the nape of her neck is soft and frizzy like wool. She has crow's feet in the outer corners of her eyes and deep bags below her bottom lashes. On the left side of her lip and along her cheek is a deep scar, like a small trench. Sitting in the wheelchair, rocking back and forth massaging her legs makes her look even older. We end up at the front of a line.

The sun is beginning to set when the first bus finally pulls up. The man in the black cap is working like it's his job. He motions for one person to come at a time. Each time, he checks to see if the person is alone, and if not, he calls up those who are with them. Grandma and I are in the third line, so we're just watching everything. When the first bus leaves, another bus comes. The buses roll in one after another. One exits, another arrives. That's how it goes. The lines are so long, it takes two buses to carry a line of people. We don't get on a bus for another two hours. It's getting dark, and we're told this is the last bus loading tonight because it's too dark to see, and it's dangerous.

"Who's it dangerous for?" I ask Grandma once we get on the bus.

Grandma rubs my hand like she can't find the right response.

"The bus drivers waiting to drive in or the people waiting to ride out?"

"The bus drivers are afraid, Eric."

"Of what? I don't get it."

"Of the people, baby. Of us."

"But why?"

Grandma rubs my hand again and turns to look out of the window.

The driver stands in the center of the aisle. His shirt is perfectly ironed, and his pants sharply creased. He wears shiny patent leather shoes and a matching captain's hat. There is a badge on his chest that looks official, but I am too far away to read it.

"Today is Monday, September 5th. It's 8:42 p.m. We are departing the New Orleans Convention Center and heading to the Astrodome in Houston. We will make no store or restroom stops during this trip. There is a toilet in the back."

He pauses and looks around like he wants to say more but can't get up the courage. His lips have a look like there is something pressing against them from the back of his throat. He toys with his hands a little then tips his black captain's hat before sitting.

Grandma taps my hand and points out of the window. It's Leonard. He's waving bye, and she waves back. I wave too. As the bus pulls off, he hugs himself like he's sending Grandma a hug. She nods then sits with her back flat against the seat, her head facing upward, eyes closed, lips moving. I rest my head on her shoulder while she prays. I think about asking Grandma to switch seats so I can look out of the window, but I decide I've seen enough. I'm tired. I don't want to see. Instead, I close my eyes, and before long, I'm in a deep sleep.

In my dream, I see people waving bye: Byron and Mr. Chris, Alejandro's family, Neil and his mom, and even Old Man Jake, who is standing on one beer keg, second lining to the other with a cat on his shoulder. I wave back, and the cat meows so loud it hurts my ears. I put my hands on my ears, and everything starts spinning real fast until I'm back in front of my closet door. I put my hand on the knob, but before I can turn it, a cat rubs against my leg and hisses.

I jump up then, and my entire back—my actual back, my butt, the backs of my thighs—is wet. Grandma laces her fingers around mine.

"You slept a while," she says.

I turn my face to look out of the window, but it's still dark, and a hint of my own face stares back, ghostlike.

# PART 2

# EMBRACING
# THE REFUGEES

CHAPTER 7

W e step off the bus, and at first it looks like we're back at the Convention Center, except the building looks more like the Superdome. Thousands of people stand in long lines, still dirty, still carrying trash bags and backpacks and boxes that look like they might fall apart any minute. The only thing better than home is that the streets are basically clean, no piles of debris and trash as tall as people. There ain't no water closing in on us like Noah's flood either. And one other thing, one other really big thing. For the first time in days, I can breathe in air that smells clean. I raise my armpit and smell myself. I still smell awful.

The luggage area of the bus opens, and people rush in to get their stuff—trash bags, duffel bags, boxes. One man even has clothes tied together with rope. We kept our bags with us on the bus in the overhead compartment, but the wheelchair is with the luggage underneath. I'm waiting for everyone to get their stuff so I can get the wheelchair and we can get in the long line. I have my eye on it, but then a man just walks up out of nowhere, squeezes himself into the crowd of people unloading the bus, and picks up the wheelchair like it's his. Just like that, and then he just keeps walking like he ain't done nothing wrong at all.

"Hey!" I say. "That's my grandma's." The man starts running. Grandma squeezes my arm. When I look at her, she is shaking her head at me, not at the man.

"But Grandma, he took your wheelchair."

"It wasn't mine anyway. It was a gift."

"But he took it."

"Maybe he needed it."

I want to yell that he is running, so obviously he don't need that chair, but I'm too tired. If she don't care, I don't care either.

We turn our backs to the bus and follow the crowd. We're herded into lines, and a man is giving out bottles of water and saying, "God bless you." I wonder if he had to steal the water like the man in the black cap back home. Grandma puts her bag down and massages her calves.

"Grandma, are you okay?"

"I will be." She hums a song I can't make out.

We walk down almost a block away from the building just to get in line. From the end of the line, I see the silver rounded roof of the Astrodome and windows all around the side of the building. It looks like there's some kind of fencing too. I can't figure out how close we are to the entrance because the line curves up ahead. It's like we're taking a step only once every ten minutes. After an hour, I feel like I'm in the same place. Grandma keeps massaging her knees, and I take her bag to make it easier for her to stand. But even my legs are hurting, and my shoulders are too. I shift the bags back and forth. I move my weight from one foot to another. This goes on for hours. People in line are basically quiet, just talking a little to those nearby. One lady says she had to leave her two dogs; another has nothing with her except a chicken in a small cage, and she says she couldn't leave her behind. My mind goes to Jerome and Joan's cats, Neil's dog.

When we finally get to the entrance of the Astrodome, a lady in a red-and-white American Red Cross vest meets us at the door. She says her job is to help track down family and gives us both a form to complete. It's only half a page. I leave the line labeled *Father's Name* blank. I write in *June Calhoun* next to my mother's name and the word *deceased*. Under *Race*, I check the box next to the word *Other* because suddenly I'm thinking I don't even know. And why is it important anyway? I write in *human* on the line and hand my form back to the lady. She's looking over my form, and her eyebrows rise. She gives me my form back.

"Fill it out accurately if you want real help," she says.

Grandma looks over my shoulder and points to *African American/ Black*. I think she's about to fuss, but she don't say nothing. She just points and then moves aside to let the person behind us pass. *Human* ought to be good enough, at least that's how I feel, but I guess it ain't. I check the box next to *African American/Black*, and while I'm at it, I go ahead and write *Pastor Charles Ray* next to *Father's Name*.

The woman in the Red Cross vest and thin-framed glasses looks over my form again. "Your father's a pastor?" The expression on her face says she don't believe me one bit.

Grandma's eyes dart into my neck. I place my right hand over my throat and my left hand over my right one, like they're bullet-proof protection for what Grandma wants to do to me.

"Well—" I say.

But before I can get any words out, the woman places a check mark in the upper right-hand corner. "There are no more cots. Go to Section 127, Row AA." Then, she hands Grandma a small card and calls out, "Next!"

We walk forward, and I see that we are at Section 126 already. I take in a big breath of relief. We keep walking, but somehow we end up at section 128.

"What in the world?" Grandma says.

"Can I help you?" Another Red Cross worker walks up to us with a huge smile on her face.

"Yes, we were told to sit in Section 127." Grandma points to the slip of paper handed to her at the door. "But that was 126 and this is 128. So, where is 127?"

"Oh, yes ma'am. That's very confusing. This side of the stadium is even numbers. You have to walk around to the other side. That's where you will find the odd numbers." She moves her finger from left to right real slow when she says around to the other side.

"Can't we just sit here?" Grandma asks.

"No, it's all full or already claimed," the lady says. "Everybody has an assigned place to keep it safe and make if feel as much like home as possible."

"Can I just see?"

"Why sure." The lady with the Red Cross smile walks us into Section 126. There are people sitting in almost every seat and people's stuff in the empty seats. Thousands of cots fill the stadium floor from one end to the other, except along the side walls. Closest to the walls, different colored tents (the pop-up kind, like Mr. Chris sometimes set up for block parties) have lines of people in front of them.

"What are those lines?"

"Stations," she says, like that's an answer to everything. She walks away to help someone else.

Grandma and I look at each other, and we both shrug. We start the long hike to Section 127. People move in both directions. Grandma smacks me in the back of the head.

"Ow! What's that for?"

"That's for staring at that man."

The man has a big belly, no shirt, and suspenders holding up his jeans, but I didn't realize I was staring.

Then, she pinches my arm. "And this is for lying and saying Charles Ray is your father. What's wrong with you?"

"She told me to complete the form. I was trying to follow directions."

"By lying? Is that what Charles Ray would do?"

"I don't know. He knows his father. He could fill out the form just fine."

"Did you write down me as your mother?"

"No. My mother's dead."

"Oh, Eric," she says. Her voice is soft, but her eyes are distracted. She is staring at something behind me.

I turn around. A toddler with a sagging diaper is walking alone with a Cheeto in her hand, crying. The Cheeto has that wet spongy look, like it's been sucked on a long time. The little girl's face is crusted with orange crumbs. Grandma walks past me, picks up the little girl, and holds her close.

"We're not taking another step until this baby's mother finds her." She backs up to a nearby wall and bounces the little girl up and down on her shoulder.

"Get out my wipes."

I dig in Grandma's bag and pull out a packet of alcohol wipes. Grandma takes a wipe and rubs the little girl's face and hands. She curls the Cheeto up in the wipe and hands it to me. I frown. What am I supposed to do with it? Then, when she sees a woman entering the bathroom across the hall with a little boy and a diaper bag, she says, "Stay here. I'm going to get this little girl a clean diaper."

I lean against the wall and Grandma carries the toddler into the bathroom. I slide down to the floor and watch people pass. A lot of people seem to be with big groups, and I wonder if they came together or found each other. Some are clean, others dirty. And I'm thinking I want to be clean. Where did they bathe? For the first time in days, I see very few people carrying bags and boxes. Where are people putting their stuff? Do they even have stuff? I hear more muffled announcements, but I can't make out the words. I want to know what's going on, so I walk from the hall toward the stadium seats and dip down into

Section 101 so I can see the floor again. There are so many people. Even more people than at the Convention Center. Way more people. The scoreboard says: "Thomas Anthony looking for Marguerite Antoine. Call 504-477-8906." I wonder if anyone is looking for us.

"Eric!" I hear Grandma's yell.

I run up the steps and back out to the hallway. Grandma is still carrying the little girl, but she is spinning in circles screaming my name. People have paused all around, staring at her.

"Grandma, I'm here."

I am ready for her to tell me how wrong I am to disappear like that, but she just pulls me close and kisses the top of my head. Her lips vibrate against my scalp. "Don't you ever leave me like that."

The little girl starts crying again, and Grandma takes a wet brown paper towel and wipes her snotty nose.

"The scoreboard has messages on it." I point to Section 101. "On the floor, I mean. We can use it to send a message to her family."

Grandma walks back to where I just ran from. I follow.

Now the board says, "Angel James looking for Patrick Kilpatrick. Call 713-748-8203."

Grandma screws up her face like someone in pain, and I remember her legs. She is getting tired of walking. I count in my head from 101 to 127, odd numbers only. We still have twelve more sections to walk past.

"I can go down and find out how to get a message up there."

Grandma shakes her head. "I don't want you wandering around a bunch of strangers. We'll just keep walking. Maybe we'll find one of those Red Cross people to help get the message out."

We start walking again. What I can't figure out is how we walk so far without finding this little girl's mother. How come no one is looking for her? I have my bag on one shoulder and Grandma's on the other. I'm getting tired, but I don't say so. I look up. Section 109, nine more to go.

We make it all the way to 121 before we see a police officer.

"Look!" I point and start moving toward the man at the same time.

Grandma is right behind me, and when she gets to the officer, she explains that she found the little girl all the way back at Section 101. He says there's been an all-call looking for her.

"We have a location on that missing toddler."

A raspy voice comes through the receiver. "What's your 20?"

"Section 121. Subject is with an elderly woman and small boy."

"Elderly?" Grandma frowns.

"Small?" I mumble under my breath.

"Ma'am, I need you to stay here with the child. We have an officer bringing the mother to you."

"Can I take a seat?" Grandma says, her face turned up again.

The officer nods his head toward the seats in 121. "The back row is empty for officers. Go ahead."

We sit down. Grandma lets the little girl stand on her lap, holding her fingers. "Your mama's coming, baby."

But it seems like forever. I watch the scoreboard change three more times. The third time, the message is "Missing thirteen-year-old boy. Kevin Andrews. Report to the NAM mission center."

Suddenly, I am glad Grandma didn't let me wander off.

Section 121 is loud. A group of shirtless guys is playing loud music on a big boom box, and I wonder how they even got that out of the city. A Bob Marley song comes on, and a couple of the guys let out a big yell and then start dancing on the steps. It looks a whole lot like second line dancing, but there's something different, a little bounce in place, almost like a squat. The little girl stops crying. She's staring at the dancers instead. I'm staring at the dancers too. My mind goes to Old Man Jake, second lining in the middle of the street with chaos all around.

"Maliya!" The little girl's mother reaches up and the little girl reaches down. "Oh my God. Thank you!" She looks so young, maybe not even out of high school. When she has her daughter back in her arms, she presses her cheek against the girl's. "I was so scared. I thought I lost you."

"Mama," the little girl says, and she puts one of her mother's braids in her mouth.

An officer stands on the side of the woman. "Toddler reunited," he says, talking into his walkie-talkie.

"10-4," the reply comes back.

Little more happens on our way to 127. We just keep passing people moving back and forth. In the background, muffled announcements never stop. Waves of laughter or shouting take over now and then, like when two sisters who spotted each other ran in front of us to hug and cry and laugh.

When we finally get to our seats, there's luggage and bags filling the row, except for two seats way at the other end. We scoot past the stuff—two suitcases, two backpacks, a garbage bag, and a box—to get to the only empty seats. We don't have nowhere to put our stuff down, so we sit down all stiff, holding our bags in our lap.

"Grandma, why don't we just go to another row."

"Our card says Row AA. We need to follow the rules."

"But there's room here," I look back to point behind us. Another family steps down, holding a card, and I hear a woman say Row DD. They wave at us with bent arms like they're scared to speak and sit down. It's six of them—two women and four teenagers. Grandma waves and turns back to her stiff position.

Finally, the people who own all that stuff in the seats come back. It's just two people. Their names are Wilbur and Charlotte, like something from a storybook. Mr. Wilbur is deaf but pretty good at reading lips, and he likes to talk. I can't understand him though, so Ms. Charlotte tells me everything he is saying and even what she thinks he is thinking. When he smells the food being served, Mr. Wilbur's eyes light up, and Ms. Charlotte says, "He's thinking that smells like fried chicken." It is. Our first meal in the Astrodome is fried chicken with red beans and green salad.

We have to stand in line to get our food, but we don't have to go all the way to the floor. The food lines are at all the vending stations, where they usually sell hot dogs and pretzels during the games. We go to the line closest to Section 127. While we're in line, Ms. Charlotte tells us about how Mr. Wilbur was the first to know the levees were about to break.

"He felt it," she says. "Before I ever felt the ground shake or saw water break through that fire hydrant, he signed that it was time to go inside. Water was coming. Then boom. Just like that, water was everywhere. It came up so fast, we couldn't even get back inside before it was already up to here." She points to her calf.

Mr. Wilbur nods, taps three fingers on his chin, and then brings both hands down toward the ground and back up real fast. "That's flood," Ms. Charlotte says, and she repeats the motions.

The other six people near us stay to themselves. Even when Ms. Charlotte turns to one of the ladies and says, "Imagine that!" The woman just looks at her and don't say nothing. I look back at the teenagers because Grandma, Mr. Wilbur, and Ms. Charlotte are talking, and I'm left out. I'm thinking maybe I can talk to the kids, but they're busy talking to each other and playing hot hands. I stare at them a long time, waiting for the chance for eye contact. It's two girls and two guys, and one of the guys finally looks up. I nod my head and wave, but he looks away fast like I just creeped him out or something.

We only move from our area to go to the food line and the restroom. The restroom is always crowded, except when it is roped off for cleaning. I go in right after it's cleaned, and it's not clean. I miss the at-home kind of clean I'm used to. Back home, Grandma was constantly tidying up, lighting candles, mopping floors, cleaning toilets. I mean, I cleaned a little, but not like Grandma. She said I gave everything a quick lick and a promise, and she always had to come behind me to do the real cleaning.

We spend nearly a week in the Astrodome, getting to know Mr. Wilbur, Ms. Charlotte, and the lady who lost her little girl. Her name is Scarlet, and I call her just that. She looks so young. I don't think she is much older than me, and Grandma must think the same because she never tells me to say Miss.

Scarlet stops by to see Grandma every day. On the third day, her little girl has on brand-new pajamas with tiny purple hearts all over.

"Well, those are pretty," Grandma says. "Where'd you get them?"

"The mission station. I got this too." She pulls out a long, flowered dress. It's cotton and has short sleeves. "It's for you, Ms. Ruth." Grandma hugs it and smiles.

"But I can't put clean clothes on a dirty body," she says.

"Oh, Ms. Ruth. You need to come with me. There's a place to shower." Scarlet gestures for Grandma to come. "Get your bag. Let me show you."

Grandma picks up her bag and beckons for me, Mr. Wilbur, and Ms. Charlotte. We all follow. Scarlet leads us out of the building and to a line in the parking lot.

"We're going to catch the shuttle to where the showers are."

The shuttle looks like a long van. There's three of them, and they are coming back and forth constantly. Not that many people are waiting, and before I know it, we're on the shuttle. The ride is short, just a few minutes. When we get off, we're outside something that don't look like much of a building at all. It's only one floor and looks like metal on the outside, like something I've seen in a book about farms—where they keep those big tractors or horses. When we get to the door, it's just an opening, and there are open stalls on both sides. Some of them are covered with hanging sheets that are tied to the iron bars between the stalls. I guess those have people in them, but the triangle shaped signs that hang overhead have pictures of cows, horses, and even pigs on them. Scarlet walks past several and brings us all the way to the end like she just walked us into her home. There's a black hose tied to a faucet and wrapped around a bar on the wall. The floor is shiny, dark gray concrete, and the water on its surface looks slimy, the way my spit looked on that leaf outside my window.

Grandma backs away. "This is where they clean animals."

"It's not so bad, Ms. Ruth. And when I put this sheet up," Scarlet pulls a sheet out of her bag and reaches high to tie it to the silver bar running across the top of the doorway, "no one can see you." She ties a second knot. "See? You can get clean real fast, put on your pretty new dress, and then go get some new clothes from the mission booth."

Mr. Wilbur nods.

"I don't know either," Ms. Charlotte says.

"I'll wait until we can shower somewhere else."

Grandma turns and starts walking back to the open doorway, past the draping sheets.

Scarlet follows Grandma. She takes a few quick steps to get by her side. "I didn't think it was so bad, Ms. Ruth. It felt good to get clean."

Grandma stops dead in her tracks and grabs hold of Scarlet's shoulders. "Don't never let nobody treat you like an animal."

Scarlet hangs her head and follows Grandma back to the shuttles.

We're quiet on the shuttle, and the few minutes feel real long compared to before. When we get back to the Astrodome, Scarlet takes Grandma's hand.

"Will you at least walk the floor with me? Let me show you where I got the clothes."

The floor of the stadium is crowded with makeshift barricades and narrow aisles made by pushing people's belongings in two different directions or spacing cots an extra four feet apart. From upstairs, we couldn't see this. Since we were able to get food without coming all the way down, Grandma avoided coming. I don't know if it's because her legs hurt or because she just didn't want to leave our stuff. I'm guessing a little of both. Anyway, it's the first time we're walking the floor, and it's so crowded it's almost impossible to walk without bumping into people. Children wander around alone, and Grandma keeps taking out alcohol wipes and wiping snotty noses.

But I'm glad we finally came down because we find stations for almost everything—food stamps, emergency welfare, housing, pharmacy, doctors, dentists, counselors, a charging station, and even a phone bank where we can make free long-distance calls.

"Look, you can charge your phone there," Scarlet says. "And there you can make a long-distance call for free. Don't you have someone to call, Ms. Ruth?"

Grandma gives me her phone and says, "You sit right there and try to charge this." She points to the charging station, which has just one more available spot. I sit on the floor and plug in Grandma's phone. From where I sit, I can see her every move, and I feel her eyes on me. She ain't letting me out of her sight. Grandma walks straight to the phone bank. Scarlet and Maliya join Grandma in the phone line. Mr. Wilbur and Ms. Charlotte get in the housing line.

Grandma dials Pastor Charles but gets his voicemail. "Charles Ray, it's Ruth. Eric and I made it to Houston. We are at the Astrodome in Section 127. My phone is dead, but Eric's trying to charge it now." She pauses a long time. "Love you, Charles Ray."

When Grandma hangs up the phone, Mr. Wilbur and Ms. Charlotte wave her over to housing, and the people behind them let her skip. The phone is only at 11 percent, so I stay seated. Grandma and Scarlet sit down in two chairs in front of a lady with bright green glasses, pale skin, and the reddest hair I've ever seen. Grandma points to Mr. Wilbur and Ms. Charlotte. The woman behind the table looks up and pulls her glasses down. Ms. Charlotte waves and smiles. Mr. Wilbur points first to his head then uses both hands to point to Grandma. The woman behind the desk shakes her head. She writes something down. I wonder what that was all about.

Grandma can't stand being downstairs on the floor. It's too crowded, and she don't like bumping into people. So, I sit at the charging station just a little while each day, while Grandma goes to a kiosk and checks the status of our housing application. Every day when I start charging the phone again, it has already lost some of its charge. Three days of this, and I am only at 27%. Grandma tries to call Pastor Charles every time we go the charging station, but his phone keeps going to voicemail. That worries her. I can see it in her eyes. They look kind of vacant, except for when Scarlet and Maliya come around. Then she smiles, and her eyes light up a little. Even when she talks to Ms. Charlotte who is always bubbly, she sometimes just nods blankly like she's not really listening.

So the morning we wake up and learn that Scarlet has been approved for Section 8 housing is what Grandma calls bittersweet.

"You'll come see me, right, Ms. Ruth?" Scarlet's eyes are teary, and Grandma is biting her lip like she's chewing words.

The next morning, Grandma walks to the kiosk with Ms. Charlotte and Mr. Wilbur. I go to the charging station like usual. Only this time a smile creeps across Grandma's face, and Ms. Charlotte lets out a big shout. We have all been approved for housing. Grandma and Ms. Charlotte are so happy they stand in the middle of the floor and hug. They exchange addresses and promise to call. I'm watching this all unfold, and I'm thinking of Pastor Charles who I always thought was only a phone call away but who we haven't been able to reach in days. That makes me think we won't be able to reach Mr. Wilbur and Ms. Charlotte when we need them, and I start feeling kind of sad when I know I should be happy. But I don't say this out loud.

Grandma signs something to Mr. Wilbur that makes him laugh, and Ms. Charlotte says, "He thinks you called him fishy."

"I said it's finished. I meant, we're getting out of here," Grandma says.

Mr. Wilbur reads her lips and puckers his lips like a fish. He laughs again.

"No," Ms. Charlotte says. "You definitely called him fishy."

They all laugh, but I can't find my laugh because I'm too busy thinking we won't see them again or Scarlet or even Pastor Charles. And things will go back to being lonely and boring. My mind is all over the place. I'm thinking I won't make friends, and every kid is going to ignore me like those four teens who were on Row DD for two days and refused to speak, or the dancers who never invited me to join in, or Neil who refused to wave bye when we got rescued.

CHAPTER 8

After we get approved for housing, Grandma is told we can leave right away or stay for one more meal. Every day, food is only served twice. Early in the morning, it's something like grits or oatmeal. In the evening, it's spaghetti with meat sauce or beans and rice or some kind of soup. In the middle of the day, we are on our own, and that usually means we drink a carton of juice Grandma slipped in her bag after breakfast or eat the fresh fruit I slipped into mine after dinner the night before. For some reason, I feel hungrier now than all those days trapped in my room. The Astrodome ain't home, but it feels like its own little safe city. I think that's why Grandma chooses to eat one more meal in the stadium before leaving. Because where else are we supposed to get food?

Tonight, dinner is vegetable soup. I eat the vegetables first, and when they are gone, I place the bowl at my mouth like a cup and drink the soup like I'm drinking orange juice. Grandma slaps me on the back of the head.

"If you're hungry, go and ask for seconds."

Grandma knows there ain't no seconds. We run out of food every night. I look at a family eating just a few feet away from us—a mom, dad, and three small kids, two of them boys. The dad is using his roll to soak up the soup left in his bowl. He breaks a roll in half and hands one half to each son. They do just like him, slide that bread around the bowl and soak up all the juice. That seems like a good idea to me. I imagine sitting with my own daddy, eating soup, and breaking bread. I pick up a roll and use that to soak up the soup left in my bowl. When I finish eating, Grandma says the bowl looks like it's already been washed.

"It's impolite not to leave a trace of food in the bowl," she says.

So first I get slapped for drinking my soup even though it's a liquid, and now it's rude to clean my bowl with the bread. And I can't help but wonder if my daddy was here and he did the same thing, would she slap him in the back of the head? Just thinking about it makes me mad, 'cause now I'm thinking it is all her fault. Ain't nobody lying on her. She did run him off. I'm hungry and mad. I'm confused too. Back home, she always told me to eat all my food. I do that, just like a man who looks like a mighty good dad, and she's slapping me like trying to be a man is a sin.

When we step outside, the sun is beginning to set, but somehow it's still hot on our skin. I run my fingers up and down my arms like I can wipe off the heat. Outside is buzzing with slow-moving traffic and people walking around. We walk across the street to a bus stop. A pregnant lady sits on the bench rubbing the bottom of her stomach. Her feet hang out of dark pink slippers two sizes too small.

"Do you know how to get here?" Grandma asks, and she points to the address on the housing slip.

"You can't catch the bus there," the woman says. "That's in the suburbs."

"So, what do I do?"

The woman points back across the street where a line of taxis sits beside the Astrodome, waiting for people to come out of the stadium.

Grandma peers across the street like she's reading small print. "How much will that cost?" she says.

The woman shrugs. "Never took a taxi before."

We cross the street again. Cabs line the curb. They are yellow, black, white and black, red, red and white. There's even a black-and-white-checker-printed taxi with a red light on top. A man gets out of that one and calls out to Grandma.

"You need a taxi?" he says with a huge smile, waving his arm.

"No," Grandma says. She leans down and whispers in my ear. "We're gonna get in a yellow one because that's the color of the taxis in that movie. You know the one?"

I look at her blankly, and she pats the top of my head. "I guess you're too young."

We walk over to a yellow car with the word TAXI printed on the side in all caps and a light-up sign that reads TAXI on top. "Now, this is a taxi," she says, and she knocks on the window.

The driver is sleeping inside like he sleeps there every day, like his bed is in his car and there ain't nothing at all strange about sleeping on the side of the road. He wipes the side of his mouth and puts his window down.

Grandma peeks in. "We need a taxi," she says.

The man unlocks his doors. I look around and see other drivers hopping out and opening doors for their customers. The man in the checkered car is putting a suitcase in his trunk, and a man in a suit and tie who looks like he don't even belong in this chaotic scene hands him a crisp bill. I can't see how much.

Grandma opens the door of the yellow cab and motions for me to slip in. I sit down, and air that smells like stale cigarette smoke rises from the leather seat.

Grandma takes out an alcohol wipe and starts wiping the seat. I have no idea how she even has wipes left.

"Where to?" the driver says.

Grandma gets in and hands him the address. He nods.

"This far," he says. "Out in Cy-Fair. Fifty-minute drive."

"How much?" Grandma takes her wallet out of her bag and looks inside. She pulls out a few crumpled dollar bills.

"I live out there," the driver says. "I give you free." And he pulls out onto the street.

I look out of the window and see people walking away from the stadium and toward the taxis. A big man with one shoe drags his left leg as he walks to the bus stop. That's the last thing I see before we pull out into traffic. We go real slow, and Grandma sits back on the seat and lifts her head like she's just taking in the quiet. It's the first time in days we don't hear a bunch of voices at one time. I'm enjoying the quiet too, and the look outside the window makes me think of home a little. We pass stores and tall buildings and big billboards with pictures of lawyers and dentists on them. The driver pulls around a curve, past a place called Louisiana Chicken, and under a bridge. Suddenly, it gets real dark. I close my eyes, and they relax because there's no light seeping through for a moment. It's the first moment like that in a long time because in the Astrodome there were always lights on, and it was hard to sleep. I feel the taxi speed up when he pulls out and onto the interstate. His doors click and lock. I'm dozing off when suddenly I feel Grandma's grip on my thigh.

"Where are you taking us?" Grandma asks, and I see the wild in her eyes.

"Suburb," the man says. He raises the glass that separates him from us.

Grandma panics and tries to open the back door. The doors are on safety, but the man sees her attempt.

"Lady, what are you doing?"

We are on the interstate now, but I don't know a thing about Houston, so I have no idea where we are.

"Why am I locked back here?" Grandma says. She is frantic now and bangs on the glass.

On each side of the glass are bars that separate us from the driver. Grandma grips the bars and pulls at them. The man is driving over 70 miles per hour on the interstate, and his eyes keep darting back and forth between us and the road.

"Lady, I take you to suburbs. Calm down."

"Why are these bars here? Are you arresting me?"

"No arrest. Taxi used to be police car. Bars and glass keep me safe." He looks through his rearview mirror. "From crazy people." His lips stay parted like there is an extra word resting between his lips.

"Grandma!" I say. "We are in the yellow cab, remember?"

The cab driver looks at us through his rearview mirror. "Crazy lady," he says under his breath, but I read his lips. I'm familiar with the words even when they are not spoken aloud.

Grandma digs in her bag and pulls out her phone.

"Hello."

I hear Pastor Charles's voice through the phone and feel the muscles in my shoulders relax.

"Charles Ray, it's Ruth."

"Ruth! Where are you?"

"We are in a taxi headed out to—" Grandma's voice is frantic. Her hands shake as she searches her bag for the address. Just when she finds it, her phone dies. Grandma groans and throws the phone back in her bag.

"I have to get out of here," she says. Her head turns from left to right like she's considering jumping out of either window. "Something's not right."

"At least Pastor Charles answered this time," I say.

Grandma bites her lip. Her grip on my thigh is so tight I'm wondering if I'm bleeding. "Get me out of here." She's back to yelling again.

"Lady, we in the middle of the freeway. I take you to suburb. Calm down. I let you out here, you die."

"Grandma, we're in the cab," I say again. I pry her fingers off my thigh and hold her hand real soft and gentle. "Remember, we're going to the new house, the one on the card, and this is just a cab."

"But the bars—"

"Old police car," the cab driver says again.

"Grandma, it's okay. You're not being arrested."

We pull off the interstate and drive down a service road. I feel Grandma's hand relax a little, but she's craning her neck like she's planning an escape. We turn right and enter a neighborhood that looks like a construction site. We ride past a block with nothing but mounds of dirt on both sides of the street to a block with houses on one side and mounds of dirt on the other. The driver turns into the driveway of the third house. It is a brick house with one floor, sandwiched between two houses with two floors. The two-story houses have wood at the top that reminds me a little of home, only the houses are far apart. At home, whenever I sat on the roof, I could almost reach out and touch the roof next door. Not here. And maybe that's why I have a strong urge to climb to the top of the roof and sit down.

"This is house," the driver says. He unlocks the doors.

"How much?" Grandma asks.

"I told you, I live out here. I give you free."

"I owe you money," Grandma says.

"I take no money. Just go."

I look at the meter in the cab: 29.5 miles. 42 minutes. $58.75. No way Grandma has that. The wad of bills in her hand looks like crumpled up one-dollar bills, and it ain't that many.

"But, I owe—"

"Grandma," I say, "he's letting us go. Just come on."

"That's what they do, Eric." Grandma's eyes are wild again. "They tell you they got you, but they don't. It's a setup. We don't pay and tomorrow, they're knocking at our door, dragging me out by my hair and throwing you in a sack."

"What?" I can't even get another word out.

"Just go," the driver says. He gets out and opens the door on Grandma's side.

I can't tell what the man is thinking, whether he feels sorry for us, is being nice, or is spooked by Grandma. As soon as we step out of the vehicle, he jumps back in and backs up. He don't even wave bye, just backs up and speeds off. He's out of sight before we make it to the door.

Grandma stands at the door a long time, like she's thinking of knocking, as if someone is going to come and open the door.

"Do you have a key?" I say.

"Yes."

But Grandma lingers at the door as if it can't possibly be home.

---

We walk through the front door and into a foyer. To our immediate right is a door and in front of us an open doorway. We walk through the door on the right and end up in a small room with another open doorway. Through that doorway, we can see the kitchen. It's small but has a shiny silver refrigerator with a matching dishwasher and stove. I run over to the dishwasher and open the door. It still has tags inside, and everything sparkles. Above the stove is a built-in microwave. I had no idea that was a thing. I stand on my tiptoes and look inside. Sparkling new. The floors and the walls are white, but there are little specks of gray in the tiles on the floor and behind the sink. The countertops are gray with silvery flakes, and they are shiny too. Grandma stands in one place and looks around. Her mouth opens slowly, and she puts both hands on her head like she is about to smooth back her hair. Only, she don't. She just stands there with her mouth slightly open. In the middle of the floor is a counter with cabinets underneath and a dark glass stove in its center. Grandma turns a knob, and a section of the stove turns red. She waves her hand over it, and her mouth opens slightly wider.

The kitchen has a wall of windows, and next to that wall is another one with two doors and a window between them. I go through the door on the right and end up in a laundry room with a silver washer and dryer and the same white walls with specks of gray and gray counters with flakes of silver. On the countertop is a small bottle of detergent and a box of dryer sheets, like a gift put there just for Grandma. Through another closed door is a very small bathroom with a toilet and sink and again the matching white, gray, and silver.

I walk back into the kitchen, "Grandma, there's a washer and dryer and detergent in there."

But Grandma has walked off through the other door and is standing in the middle of the backyard, her hands in a posture of praying. I stand in the doorway and look up. I don't like the feeling of the dark. It makes everything look like rising water. I turn away from the yard and walk through the wide-open doorway to my right. This room is a large open space with high white ceilings, white walls, and light wood flooring. Two windows in this room face the backyard. I walk through a closed door, and my foot lands on soft carpet in a small hall with doors to my right and left. I turn left and end up in a big room with a full bathroom, a big Jacuzzi-style tub, and a shower.

When Grandma comes back inside, she says, "Can you believe this? This is where we'll live?"

I am still carrying my bag, and I begin to feel the weight. "I think this is your room. I wonder what mine looks like."

"Well, let's see," Grandma says.

I shift my bag to the other shoulder and follow her back into the hall and through the other door. It's another bedroom, and the bathroom attached to it has a small shower behind glass doors and no tub. Again, everything is white, gray, and silver.

That's the whole house. It is smaller than home, but it is new, safe, and dry. I sit my bag down in the middle of the floor in my room. There's no furniture, but the floor is carpeted, and that beats sleeping in the stadium seating at the Astrodome. In Grandma's room, a big window seat pushes out to the street. Grandma presses the cushion. She sits her bag in the window and pulls out a few oranges and an apple. She hands them to me, and I go straight to the kitchen. There are no bowls, no dishes at all, so I sit the fruit on the counter. I open the fridge, partly out of habit, partly out of hope. The shelves are empty and still have tape and a bright green sign about energy savings. I open cabinets one by one. All are empty. In the bathrooms, there's no tissue, and the gift of detergent makes less and less sense.

"Eric!" Grandma calls.

I run to her, expecting panic. "Yeah?"

Grandma puts her hand on her hip. She's calm and even smiles. "Yeah?"

"I mean, yes," I say.

"We can shower." She smiles and holds up the soap she took from home. She's been carrying it around for days, refusing to use it because she was scared to even sit it on the sink in the Astrodome restrooms. I know because I asked, and she said the restrooms weren't clean enough. My skin is dry from using alcohol wipes, and I feel every movement of my eyes and mouth. Even my hands feel like sandpaper.

I step in the shower, and suddenly I just freeze. For days, I have wanted a shower. But now that it's time, I just stand there staring at the tiles on the shower floor and wall. The floor has the same oversized white tile as everything else in the house. This is so different from home. I fumble with the glass shower doors, another thing I've never seen, and slide them closed. I make the water as hot as I can stand it because that keeps me from mistaking it as rain. I never want to mistake anything for rain. But there's something about being here in this new, empty, much-too-quiet house that makes me think about the flood, makes me see the flood, makes me feel the flood all over again. And for a moment, for a very short moment, I want to go back to the Astrodome, that small, safe city inside a building that made everything wrong feel almost okay.

The shower must have done the same for Grandma because when she calls my name again, there is panic in her voice. Panic like when I disappeared at the Astrodome or out onto the roof during the flood. Only this time, I'm not annoyed. I want to reach out and touch her too. I turn off the shower. "Coming!" I say. Then, I put the one clean outfit I have on my soaking wet body and run out into Grandma's arms.

I stay in Grandma's room until she falls asleep, but I have trouble sleeping. The carpet ain't bad. It's soft enough to fall asleep on, but the house is too quiet. Back home, on any night, depending on where I was in the house, I could hear Old Man Jake playing his music, Ms. Jackie laughing, or Byron and Mr. Chris debating, and if I went down to the kitchen, I could hear it all at the same time. On some nights, Old Man Jake's music drew other neighbors out of their homes, and I could hear dancing and laughter. But here, it is quiet. Too quiet. And that makes me think too much, about the storm, the flood, Old Man Jake's beer kegs floating without him in the lake that used to be our street.

I leave Grandma's room and feel my way down the dark hall to my own. I turn on the light, grab my backpack, and sit on the floor. I take out my album and start looking through the photos. My mother is beautiful at every age. I'm tired, so I flip through the pages quickly, glancing, just trying to get sleepy enough to fall asleep. But then one photo grabs my attention. My mother is sitting in a pew next to Grandma inside Zion Baptist Church. She's no more than a toddler, maybe two or three. Grandma is sitting on the pew looking solemn, a scowl on her face. Behind her a man is clapping, raising both hands high, his head lifted to the ceiling. I notice him for the first time. His cheek sinks in on one side. What is left of his lips is scarred and swollen. It is Half-face, the man from my dream.

# CHAPTER 9

The window to my new room looks out into the backyard, which is not much to see. The yard is closed in by an unpainted wooden fence that hides the first floor of the house next door. Close to the fence is a tree so young it is tied to two wooden stakes. I think it's an oak tree. The leaves look like the one at home. The grass around the tree is a crayon green.

Grandma clears her throat from the doorway, and I turn my head in her direction. She's wearing the long cotton dress from Scarlet. "Good morning," she says.

"Hi."

"There's someone I want you to meet."

"Have you heard from Pastor Charles?"

Grandma frowns and shakes her head. "Not yet."

I follow her to the kitchen. A lady with a gray dress and heels greets me with a smile. She's sitting in a chair made of blue cloth. It's the kind of chair you might bring to a block party or picnic. She rises and holds out her hand. I shake it just like Pastor Charles taught me to.

"I am Francine Nicholls. I have been assigned to your case," she says.

I don't have nowhere to sit down because we don't have furniture yet, and that makes it hard to figure out what to do with my hands and feet. It's awkward, standing in front of this stranger in an empty kitchen with nothing but the chair she's sitting in. I put my hands in my pockets and cross my legs.

"My case?"

"Yes. You see, my job is to make sure students displaced by the storm transition back into school properly." She's standing, and she leans in close to me and says the last part in a softer voice, like it's a secret. "Especially those who are separated from their parents."

"Displaced?" My eyes fall on a mole above the woman's lip that moves when she talks.

"That just means—"

"I am his parent." Grandma's voice cuts in. She locks her elbow in mine and pulls me back a little.

"I realize he's your grandson—" Ms. Nicholls begins.

"Realize I am his parent." Grandma's eyes narrow.

"My apologies. I'm only doing my job." The woman sits again, leans over, and lifts a black folder out of a purse-like briefcase. She ruffles through papers and pulls out a form. "It says here your father is Pastor Charles Ray III." She hands me the form. It's the one I completed when we first got to the Astrodome. My stomach tightens. "Can you tell me when you last saw him?"

Before I can respond, Grandma lets my elbow go and wraps her left hand around her right fist. "Are you kidding me? You said you were here to help us get Eric enrolled in school." She paces the floor, walking away from Ms. Nicholls and back. Her voice gets louder, and I wonder if people can hear her outside. "Now, if you had questions about Charles Ray, you could have asked me directly."

Ms. Nicholls pulls the black folder close to her chest. "I'm sorry to upset you, Mrs. Calhoun. It's just that there are people abducting children during this crisis, and we're just trying to protect them."

Grandma backs farther away from Ms. Nicholls. I look back and forth between the two. Grandma's fists are clenched at her side. Ms. Nicholls has her arms folded in an X across her chest. Her fingers grip the top corners of the folder.

"I'm sorry, I—" My hands are back in my pockets, and I rock back and forth on my heels trying to figure out how to fix this. But I don't have a chance to say a thing before Grandma is at it again.

"Is that why you put me in this house? So, you can spy on me?" She walks to the kitchen cabinets and opens several doors, slowing to look in each one. "Is this house bugged?" Grandma has that wild look in her eyes again, and I'm praying she calms down because now, for the first time, I'm worried someone might take me from her, and I realize I don't want to be with anyone else. Not even Pastor Charles, not if Grandma's not around anyway.

Ms. Nicholls stands and folds her hands in front of her lips like she's praying. "Let's just start again, why don't we?" She looks at me and goes back to that soft voice, like she's talking to a toddler. "Eric, will you please give your grandmother that form in your hand?"

I hand Grandma the form.

"Your grandson did not list you as a parent or guardian," Ms. Nicholls says. Her words come out slow like she has to think between each one. "Therefore, he went into our system as an unaccompanied youth."

"But I listed him as my child, and he has been with me his entire life. He has never been unaccompanied."

"It's a precaution."

Grandma looks at me and throws up her hands. "You see what trouble you caused."

"I'm sorry." I turn to Ms. Nicholls who is frantically writing notes. "I been with Grandma all my life. I don't know my parents."

"I see," Ms. Nicholls continues writing. "And this Charles Ray. He is?"

I sigh and rock on my heels. "Pastor Charles is Grandma's best friend." I put my head down and mumble the rest. "He's kind of like a father, I guess."

Ms. Nicholls looks up from the paper she's writing on. Grandma is bent slightly, rubbing her calves.

"Oh dear, Ms. Calhoun. Forgive me. Do take a seat." She reaches beneath the chair and pulls out a red-and-black folding chair. Ms. Nicholls unfolds the chair and sits it down so that it faces her blue seat.

Grandma pulls the chair back, away from Ms. Nicholls, like she's trying to get all the way back to the wall, as far from Ms. Nicholls as possible. When she finally sits, she leans against the thin material uncomfortably like she's sitting on a hammock.

Ms. Nicholls wipes her forehead with the back of her hand. There's a ring of sweat under the arm of her gray suit. "Well, now that we have all of that straight, let's talk about getting Eric back in school and a few vouchers that will help you get on your feet while waiting for your insurance claim."

I turn to walk back to my room. I'm ready to play a game of marbles while these two talk it out, but Ms. Nicholls says, "Eric, this is good for you to know too, so why don't you have a seat?"

Grandma moves her chair just a little closer to Ms. Nicholls but keeps a few feet of distance. I fold my legs and sit on the floor beside her.

Ms. Nicholls starts with school registration. I learn that I'll be going to a big high school with more than 4,000 kids. We only had about 1,200 in my school at home. Other kids from New Orleans will be there too, and the counselors will be available to talk about the flood if we need to. I'm thinking that's the last thing I want to talk about, but she sounds so excited about the counselors that I don't tell her what I'm thinking.

"There will be some teachers from New Orleans, as well. All of our schools are hiring displaced teachers to help with the bigger class sizes."

"You keep saying that word, displaced. What does it mean?"

Ms. Nicholls nods. "I guess that would be a new word. It means you were forced to leave your home because of the flood."

I stare at a string of hair sticking out of that large mole above her lip.

"You had to move quickly from one place to another without expecting to. That's the difference in being displaced and relocating."

I nod and Ms. Nicholls goes on. She fills out the registration packet for school with Grandma. Grandma says she don't have my social security number because she never memorized it, and the cards got left in the house. "They're probably ruined," she says. "And before you ask, I don't have his birth certificate either." Grandma exhales.

Ms. Nicholls continues reading off her list of questions.

Grandma wrings her hands in frustration. "No, I did not bring the shot record with me. And we don't have a primary care physician here."

When Ms. Nicholls asks if she can list herself as an emergency contact, Grandma looks at her like she's lost her mind.

"I don't know you like that," she says.

"Yes, but there is no family here yet, and you don't know anyone else either."

Grandma shakes her head. "Put down Charles Ray. He's my emergency contact."

"Where is he now, Ms. Calhoun?"

"I don't know yet." Grandma stares out of the window. "But he's still our emergency contact."

Ms. Nicholls gathers the papers together. "Well, you may get a call back from my supervisor on that one, but for now Charles Ray it is."

Grandma nods.

When the registration paperwork is complete, Ms. Nicholls gives

Grandma a card that has the school's name and bus information. Then, she walks to the window and points to the corner to show me where I will catch the bus every day. I look outside. Across the street, there ain't no houses, just dirt and construction equipment, rounded piles surrounded by large concrete pipes. In my imagination, I'm filling in the space with our house from back home while Ms. Nicholls's voice drags on in the background. A cat walks up a dirt mound, sits, and licks his paw. He looks just like Jeffrey and Joan's tabby cat, the last cat I saw on the railing before all the cats disappeared. I go back and sit next to Grandma.

Ms. Nicholls is sitting again, and she pulls out an envelope with an emergency food stamp card, a Visa gift card, and a voucher for clothing at the Salvation Army. Grandma's eyes fall on a space beside Ms. Nicholls, and she chews at her bottom lip. Maybe she's staring out of the window, and I wonder if she sees the cat.

Ms. Nicholls looks at Grandma lowering her eyes to her fingers.

"I'm sorry. This must be so hard. Is there anything I can do for you right away?"

Grandma rocks back and forth in the chair. "I guess I need a phone charger."

After Ms. Nicholls looks at Grandma's phone, she says, "I'll tell you what, I'll leave you with mine. That way you can get charged up before you try going to the store. She walks over to a wall outlet and plugs in the phone. "And while that's charging, let's go ahead and contact your insurance companies."

I dip out of the room at that point, and no one stops me. I think about looking in the photo album again, but I'm afraid Half-face might not really be there. So, I just get the rocks and my old shoestring. I set up a marble ring and begin to play. Above the mumbled sound of Grandma's and Ms. Nicholls's voices, I hear a cat. I look outside my window, and the cat is sitting in front of the young tree. He sees me and hisses. I close the blinds but peek through them a few seconds later. He is gone.

---

An hour or so after I leave the kitchen, Grandma calls me to let me know our insurance company is putting us in a rental car while they work on the claim. Ms. Nicholls brings us to the rental car place, but she don't come in. She leaves Grandma her phone number in case something goes wrong. Grandma's phone is at 52 percent, so she has more charge than before. Only, for some reason, she don't want to call Pastor Charles yet. She says she'll wait until we get back to the house.

The rental car place is crowded, and I'm guessing most of the people there are in our situation. Though there's this one guy in a starched business suit with a briefcase who keeps checking his watch and complaining that he should have been served over thirty minutes ago. He says he's a VIP. I'm pretty sure he may be the one person not here because of the flood.

Everyone else looks tired and desperate. There's no one thing that makes me think this. It's a combination of things, like uncombed hair or mismatched shoes, untied laces, or plain white t-shirts like the ones so many people got at the Astrodome, sweatpants cut off into shorts, or sandals with dirty toes peeking out. These are the things that made me think *storm victim*. I look at myself and notice my own unlaced shoes.

The guy in the starched suit finally gets served and demands an upgrade to a Lexus with tinted windows because he had to wait.

Grandma clicks her tongue, "My, my, my."

When it's Grandma's turn, she says she'll accept whatever vehicle is available. "I only need something small. It's just the two of us."

We leave in a shiny black sedan.

Our first stop is the grocery store. Grandma has that food stamp card, but she's still saying no extra snacks and no buying anything that's not on sale. I convince her microwave popcorn is not only a healthy snack but an economical price. That's a school word, and it wins her over. She gets the microwave popcorn plus yogurt instead of ice cream and rice cakes instead of chips. She loads up on meats, rice, pasta, beans, potatoes, and vegetables. When I see the fresh chicken breasts, I smile.

"You're going to make chicken salad?"

"Yes, I will," Grandma grins all the way to the mayonnaise aisle.

When we pass the crackers, I ask for a box of Ritz instead of the store-brand saltines, and Grandma surprises me and puts the Ritz crackers in the basket.

In the checkout line, she starts complaining about the hurricane taking a toll on her legs. She bends to massage her calves but then complains about her back.

"I should have asked Ms. Nicholls to leave one of those chairs," she says.

"Oh dear. Did I hear you say you lost everything in Katrina?" The voice comes from the lady behind us who is wearing a big straw hat like she's on the beach.

Grandma says yes, but God has blessed us with a new place to live for a while. Only we still don't have furniture, and she's constantly standing or sitting on the side of the bathtub or on the windowsill to give her legs a break. "They sure aren't what they used to be."

"Well, that can't be," the woman says. She opens a big purse and pulls out a pad and a pen with a big flower on top. "You write down your address, dear. We are going to get a good recliner right over to you. You can't stand on your feet all day. No, indeed."

"Oh no," Grandma says. "I couldn't accept something like that from you."

"Well, yes you can. You just write down the address, and we'll get it right over."

But Grandma refuses.

"Oh honey," the woman says before she and her husband walk away, "Don't you wish she'd let us give her the chair?"

The husband is a short, round man with no hair and dry lips. "As she should," he says. "But dear, we can't force it."

The couple walks out, but the lady keeps looking back. I watch her watch us until she drops down into their car in the parking lot.

When we get back to the house, Grandma checks every cabinet for bugs before she puts groceries in it. "I just don't trust that Ms. Nicholls."

We're putting up groceries when the phone rings. We both jump. We haven't heard the phone ring in over a week. Grandma looks at the phone. "It's Charles Ray," she says. Her eyes light up.

"Hello, Charles Ray?" Grandma walks away to her bedroom.

I want to follow her, but I know better, so I just keep putting up the groceries, and I find myself checking for bugs too. When Grandma comes back from the bedroom, she's still on the phone with Pastor Charles.

"He wants to talk to you." She hands me the phone.

"Hello, Pastor Charles?" I can hardly hold back my smile. His deep, baritone voice is the best thing I've heard in weeks.

Just a little while after I start talking to Pastor Charles, the doorbell rings. Grandma looks through the peephole. "It's that lady and her husband," she says. "What are they doing here?" She looks around frantically, like she's trying to find something to block the door.

I look through the peephole. "Grandma, they have that chair. Why don't you open the door?"

"What chair?" Pastor Charles says.

"You ask yourself why a perfect stranger wants to give us a chair? You don't know what they put in it."

"What would they put in a chair?" I feel my chest tighten, and my voice is louder than it should be. I try real hard to soften my tone.

I'm so tired. "Grandma—" I take her hands. "We don't have anything anybody wants right now. It's just us. Take the chair."

"What chair?" Pastor Charles is louder this time.

I tell him about the couple at the store. The doorbell rings again.

"You don't understand," Grandma says and shakes her head.

"I understand your legs hurt every day, and we have nowhere to sit down. I understand that."

"Put me on speaker," Pastor Charles says. When I do, he says, "Ruth, calm down and open the door. People are just in the spirit of giving right now."

Grandma mumbles that if something happens to us, it'll be on his hands, but she lets me open the door.

The woman has changed hats. This one looks like a huge tulip. "Oh, I am so sorry to barge in on you like this, but we just have to give you this chair." She gestures to the chair, and Grandma gasps. She literally steps back and away.

"Grandma, it's your chair." I'm so shocked, I can't even close my mouth. The not-so-new recliner is identical to Grandma's velvet recliner from back home.

The man takes Grandma's stepping back as a sign to come in, and he carries the chair inside.

"Where did you get this?" Grandma's voice is accusing.

"Why dear, it was ours for a long time. Now, it's yours."

"How did you know where to find us?" Grandma's eyes are wild.

"Ruth," Pastor Charles calls her name, but she don't respond to him at all. She just keeps going.

"But I had this chair. This is my chair."

"No Grandma. It can't be. Your chair flooded. Remember? This is a chair like your chair."

"How did you know? Who are you? Who sent you here?" Grandma's spitting questions out rapid-fire.

"Ruth," Pastor Charles calls her name again.

"Oh, let's just take the chair back," the man says.

"No, dear. We're going to leave it right here. She needs a chair."

"She doesn't want it," the husband says.

"Ruth? It's Charles Ray." This time he practically yells.

"Charles Ray, something's wrong. Something's not right."

"Ruth, I think it's okay. Just God restoring. That's all. Take the chair."

"You just can't help some people," the husband says as he heads to the door.

I follow them to the door and watch them walk to the car. The wife circles her index finger around her ear. "She's crazy," I hear her say. "That poor kid."

"Hello?" Pastor Charles calls out.

Grandma is quiet, eyeing the chair.

"We're here," I say. "The people left."

"Did they leave the chair?"

"Yessir. It's right here."

"Ruth?"

"Yes, Charles Ray," Grandma darts her eyes at the phone like she wants to shoot him.

"That chair is a sign of God's restoration. Not a spy."

"How do you know?"

Pastor Charles don't answer that question though. I wish he would because I'm wondering the same thing. Grandma storms off to her empty bedroom, and I sink down into the chair. I'm thinking restoration feels good, even looks good. I never liked Grandma's recliner back home, but now that it's in Houston, brown sparrows in twig-sized branches against a slate blue sky is the most beautiful velvet pattern I've ever seen.

I tell Pastor Charles about getting stuck then getting rescued, meeting Scarlet, Mr. Wilbur, and Ms. Charlotte, catching a taxi to the new house, our shiny black sedan, and finally having groceries. I leave out the stuff about Ms. Nicholls having me on a special list because I lied and wrote down that he was my father. I wonder if Grandma told him. If she did, he don't say a thing about it. I don't tell him a thing about the hidden room from my dream either. I wouldn't know where to start.

When I say Grandma's making chicken salad tonight, he tells me he wishes he were closer, but he's almost three hundred miles away in Baton Rouge with his cousin, Charlese.

"I'll be there soon," he says.

After we hang up, I wish Pastor Charles was already here. He's just about the only person Grandma listens to. I think I can add Mr. Wilbur and Ms. Charlotte to the list now, but we ain't heard from them since we left the Astrodome. So, maybe not. If Pastor Charles was here, I could ask him about that picture of Half-face, but I can't ask Grandma. Not yet anyway. Maybe not ever.

# CHAPTER 10

The Salvation Army is crowded. I'm surprised to see several teenagers shopping with their parents, holding the same yellow voucher I have in my hand. Everywhere I go I find people who escaped the flood and are trying to get back on their feet. I thought I'd feel embarrassed shopping at a store that only sells hand-me-downs, but it don't feel so bad with so many people doing the same thing. One guy, who I think is my age, walks with his head down and both hands in the pockets of a pair of cutoff sweatpants. His mother tells him to try on a pair of jeans she has in her hand, but he says he don't want to try on nothing here and just wants to go home. After a while, they leave, and I see them talking outside in front of the store, the mother's hands flailing in the air.

I decide to give shopping here my best try because I don't have no good reason not to. What's the point of saying no? Eventually, that kid who walked out will walk back in, and he'll just have less to choose from. So I start looking through the jeans. Behind me, a girl with shiny straight hair is looking through skirts. We bump elbows when we both lift a hanger at the same time and turn.

"I'm so sorry," I say. I wince because I hit my funny bone, and I feel that tingling pain running up my arm. I wonder what she's feeling.

"It's okay," she says.

She has the most beautiful gray eyes I've ever seen—big and round. Her reddish-brown hair hangs over both shoulders. "I'm going to try this on." She holds up a denim miniskirt. "Will you tell me how it looks on me?"

I stand there staring at her a few seconds. She has a thin nose, full lips, and a long, slender neck. The shirt she has on drops down into a V-neck, and I can't help but notice her breasts.

Grandma walks up, puts her hand on my shoulder, and clears her throat.

"Oh hi," the girl says. "I'm Layla." Then she looks at me, "Come on. I need you." She skips off to the fitting room, which is just a few feet away.

I take a step in that direction, but Grandma squeezes my shoulder. Her eyes are wide and wild again. "Whatever you are thinking about that little white girl, don't think it."

"I don't even know her," I say. "She just asked me to let her know how she looks in that skirt."

"In that miniskirt," Grandma says and clicks her tongue. I try to wriggle away. Grandma grips my shoulder tighter. Her eyes glaze over like she's seeing something in her head. "That's how it starts, and the next thing we know your whole world is upside down."

I'm trying my hardest to keep a straight face. I know if I frown, Grandma will end up on one of her rants, and that's the last thing I want in public.

Layla steps out of the fitting room. "Ta-da," she says and does a slow turn. "What do you think?"

Her legs are perfect. I nod and smile. Because I can't get the words out of my mouth, I give her a thumbs-up. After that, we end up shopping together, mostly for my clothes because Layla has a full basket already. Only Grandma keeps pulling my ear or pinching my arm every time Layla turns her head.

Layla finds me a pair of jeans that were mixed up in the girls' section. "These'll look good on you."

I take the jeans from her just as Grandma slips a pair of dark green corduroy pants in my hand. "These'll look better on you," Grandma says.

Layla's smile suddenly reminds me of Marielle's sneaky little smile, the one that came out whenever she brought up Grandma's crazy. Now I want to disappear. I put both the jeans and the corduroys in the basket without trying them on.

"Thank you," I say.

"You're not going to try them on?" A tiny dimple forms on the left side of Layla's mouth.

"You know you're skinny as a twig," Grandma cuts in. "You have to try everything on and let me see. I'm gon' have to add tucks to the waist by hand."

I cover my hand with my face and speak into my palm. "I hate shopping."

"It's better with company," Layla says. She grabs my hand and almost drags me to the dressing room. On the way there, she says real soft, "That's your Grandma, right? Don't be so hard on her. She's trying to help." Right away I'm thinking I can love this girl. I look back at Grandma before walking into the fitting room. She's standing with her arms folded, shaking her head.

When I come out of the fitting room, Layla gives me a thumbs-up on the jeans. Grandma says they're too big. "You're sagging," she says. "Like some prison rat." Then she pulls the jeans up so high they suddenly become highwaters, and she tugs at the waist and pinches the denim near my butt. "Looks like I can put tucks though. Go ahead and get them."

Layla turns her head for a moment, and I can tell she's laughing. I'm so embarrassed my chest hurts, and I'm feeling dizzy. When she turns back to face me and Grandma, she points and says, "The corduroys, please." She covers her mouth, and I know exactly what she's doing. She's trying to hide her laugh, and she's laughing at me.

That fast, I'm thinking I can hate this girl.

The corduroys are the opposite problem. They are so tight, they are pushing up my testicles, and I want to put my hand in my pants and figure out how to get comfortable. But Grandma says these are just right.

"Oh, yes," Layla says. "These make your butt look so fine. The girls will be looking at you twice all day long."

Grandma looks like she wants to just slap her, then turns back to examine the pants again. "Maybe they are too tight," she says.

Layla winks at me and mouths, "I got you."

I don't know how I feel about this girl, but she definitely saved my day.

Grandma takes a trip to the restroom, and Layla and I speed shop while she's gone. "That was pretty smooth," I say.

"Hey, you're not the only one with grandparents. They can really lay on the old school."

"Yeah? Where are your parents?" I look down. "If you don't mind me asking."

"It's embarrassing," she says.

"Why?" I say. "Whoever they are, wherever they are, you're still you, not them." I don't know where these words are coming from. It's like I've heard them a million times but can't remember when or from who or if I just dreamed them up. "I mean, you don't have to carry your parents' stuff."

Layla looks at me a few seconds and nods, but she don't offer up no real response. "They're not here," she says. "They never wanted to be here."

I know what she's saying, and she's not saying they don't want to be here in Houston or in the Salvation Army. She's saying they never wanted to be here for her. Like wherever here is, wherever she is, they don't want to be. She's saying they don't want her.

Layla don't ask about my parents, and I'm glad because it's not an easy answer. I can say my daddy never wanted to be here, just like she said, but I can't say they because my mama didn't have no choice. Every time I have to explain that my mother died when I was born, I think of saying, "I killed my mother." That's how it feels, like I killed her. Bringing me into the world, took her out of the world. What else do you call that? But that's not something you just say out loud. So, I don't volunteer no information. I just nod and say, "That's tough. Sorry to hear that."

I go to the register with three pairs of jeans, six shirts, and a pair of beat-up Converse—nowhere near as much as Layla has in her basket. My legs are long, and I'm skinny. It's hard to find anything that fits. I don't like the shoes, but Layla says you can wear Converse dirty and still look good.

"Anyway, I like them on you." The way she has her hand on one hip and her head nodding, she looks like some fashion guru approving the clothes for a photo shoot. And that pretty much settles it in my mind, at least enough to put them in my basket.

The cashier is an old lady whose eyeglasses sit on her nose like they have rested there for years, even in her sleep. "You have a voucher too?" she asks.

"Um, yes ma'am." I take the folded-up paper out of my pocket and unfold it.

"Did you count your items?" She chews on her bottom lip like it's bubble gum, and I wonder if she even has bottom teeth at all. "It says here you get up to five sets. That's five shirts, five pair of pants, five socks, five pairs of underwear."

"I, I don't want—I mean, I couldn't find anything else."

"Uh-huh," the woman says, and she pulls her lip in and holds it, her eyes peering over the thick gray frames on her face.

"Well, you don't get to go to another location to finish. Once you turn in this voucher, that's it." She looks at me again. "Do you understand what that means?"

"Yeah, I guess so."

"Well, did you at least get a pair of shoes?"

I hold up the ugly Converse, and the old cashier stamps my voucher with the word void. "Next!"

Layla has too much stuff.

"Can you just put two of her skirts and one of her shirts on mine?"

"Yours is used already," the woman says, and she rolls her eyes like a kid at school.

So, now Layla is trying to figure out what to keep and what to get rid of, and suddenly there is a line behind us. Layla's grandma walks over. Now this woman looks old, real old. Her face is covered in tiny wrinkles and dark spots.

"What's the problem?" she asks.

"Are you her guardian?" the cashier asks.

"She's my granddaughter. What's wrong?"

"It says right here, she can get no more than five matching sets. That's five shirts, five pair of pants, five socks, five pairs of underwear. She has too much stuff."

"Well, she doesn't have any underwear." Layla's grandmother

frowns when she says underwear, like it's a bad word or something. "Can't you swap out something for that."

"Five sets, ma'am. That's all she gets."

Layla folds both hands around her face and shakes her head. "Just forget it. I don't need anything." She starts walking away.

"No, I won't forget it," her grandmother says. "You need—we need everything." She turns back to the cashier. "Just give me five of the bottoms and five of the tops." She looks at the long line of people, alternating which leg their body weight rests on. "Any five."

The cashier lifts five of each carelessly. Layla's grandma sees the miniskirt and pulls it out. "Not this one," she says and cuts her eyes at Layla. The cashier picks up a long, ruffled skirt and adds it to the bag.

A t-shirt that reads "I'm a Survivor" still sits on the counter.

"Wait," I say and pick it up. "This one. She needs this one."

The cashier squints and reads the shirt. Then she looks sideways at me and says, "I'm putting that one on your voucher."

---

Layla and I end up at the same school, but I don't see her until lunchtime on the third day. We don't have any classes together, and I have no reason to expect to see her. Except I do, across the cafeteria, sitting alone at a table. Layla's reddish-brown hair is pulled back in a ponytail, and her head is down. It's hard to see her clearly, but the shirt gives her away. I slide into the seat in front of her, carrying a plate with some kind of taco bowl and a cup of pears on it.

"Nice shirt," I say.

"Thanks. I mean double thanks. Good lookin' out. I almost didn't get this one."

"Well, you helped me out, so—"

"Can I sit here?"

I recognize Neil's voice immediately, and even though it is Neil,

there's something about having someone here from back home that
feels good.

"Sure," I say.

Neil sits down, and he don't say one mean thing. His hair is longer
than it used to be, and his curls are sort of loose and wild. His eyes
look vacant, but he still has that same dimple in his chin that deepens
when he smiles. He don't smile at all now though. I keep waiting for
some sly joke, some mean comment, but he's quiet.

"This is Layla," I say. I can't bring myself to look up. I'm scared I
might find her staring at him instead of me.

"Hi," Neil says. I hear him unwrap his plastic fork. "Nice shirt. I'm
a survivor too, I guess."

"Then we all are," Layla says. "Eric picked out this shirt."

"So, you two know each other?" Neil asks.

"We met yesterday in—"

"The shopping center," I say, suddenly not wanting Neil to know I
got my clothes from the Salvation Army. "We met shopping."

"Okay." Layla hesitates, and I can feel her eyes on me. I don't want
to look at her, so I focus on my taco bowl. "How did you two meet?"

"School," Neil says.

"That's cool. I don't know where any of my old friends are."

I look up because I'm wondering what makes her think we're friends.
Neil is staring at his pears, spinning them around with the fork.

"Did you get out on a helicopter too?" I ask.

"No, a boat came."

"Where'd it take you?"

"I don't know. Like we went kind of far until the water wasn't high
no more. Then we had to get out and walk the rest of the way."

"You walked to the Convention Center?"

"Lakefront Arena."

We sit for a while, eating quietly. In the background, I hear a boy say, "Get off me, man. Bring your monkey-looking self back to New Orleans. We ain't got room for you here." Two boys are braced shoulder to shoulder like neither really wants to fight. One of them reminds me a lot of Raheem, only he's bigger, not fat but muscular, and his dreadlocks are longer.

"That's not right," a girl with long, silky black hair says. "Just sit down, Paco. Leave that boy alone."

When I look back at Neil his eyes are closed like he's praying.

"Your mama found housing yet?"

"My mama gone," Neil says.

"Wait, what?"

"Slipped under the water. They was trying to find her, but they found Old Man Jake, pulled him right up out of that water. He was all puffy and kind of purple, and his eyes sat back real deep. I ain't never gonna get that image out my head, man. But they ain't find my mama."

"I'm so sorry," Layla says. "That sucks."

I put down my fork and look at Neil. I never really looked at him so closely before. Before the storm, I wouldn't dare look into his eyes. Now, I'm staring at him, and I ain't trying to threaten him or nothing. I'm trying to figure out how to say I know what that's like. Kind of. Losing your mama. I know something about that.

"She was there, man. She was right there, trying to get into the boat, and she slipped. I reached down, tried to grab her. Then I tried to jump in the water, but Mr. Chris was holding me back. Byron and some other dude jumped in looking for her, but they ain't never let me look."

He looks mad and empty. Something about this storm did that.

The five-minute warning bell rings, and Neil wolfs down the rest of his pears and guzzles his milk.

"Are you with family?"

Neil shakes his head. "Not yet. But my grandfather is on his way."

"So we're all with grandparents then," Layla says. "Almost like a club."

Neil kind of grunts, but he don't disagree. We rise and walk to empty our plates. I'm trying to figure out how to walk with Neil and Layla at the same time, so I take long strides—my legs going forward, trying to keep up with Neil, but my hand reaching back trying to tell Layla to come on.

"You at a shelter?" I ask.

"Yeah, at a church. There's a bunch of us. Kids with no parents."

"Are the others here? At this school, I mean."

"I don't think so. Maybe. Most seemed younger. Like in elementary or junior high school. No one else came here with me this morning, so I think I'm the only one who will be here."

Layla catches up with us and grabs hold of my hand. Even though I'm reaching back for her, I don't expect her to actually reach for me. When her soft, moist hand folds into mine, I feel a bit lightheaded.

"Ms. Hornwell's here though," Neil says. "I saw her in the office yesterday."

"What's she teaching?"

"I don't know. Not me though. I went to English already."

"Me too," I say.

"Hornwell? I have her for English. It's two teachers in there. Her and some old guy," Layla says.

"Lucky you." Neil and I say this together. I think if we were happy or if we were friends, we would have said jinx and started laughing right away. Instead, we turn in separate directions and head for the next class.

My next class is biology, and the teacher is a man named Whittaker with long, slick hair. He's kind of round too. Whittaker starts this lesson on recessive and dominant genes by slapping a family photo on the screen. His parents both have curly hair.

"These are my parents," he says. "Why do you think my hair is straight?"

One person says he must be adopted, but mostly people just shrug their shoulders like they don't care.

"I'm not adopted," he says, and he laughs at that. "My parents must each carry the recessive gene for straight hair."

He's drawing a grid on the board to show us what he means. "Let's say capital C is the dominant curly gene, and lowercase c is the recessive straight-hair gene."

The whole time he's talking, I'm feeling my curls and thinking about that wedding photo of my parents and the rumor about my daddy being white. By the time Whittaker finishes explaining his grid and the possible combinations of genes for curls, I'm thinking there ain't no way my daddy has all straight-hair genes. But what I'm really wondering about all of a sudden is how this gene thing works for skin color. As soon as he asks if we have questions, I raise my hand.

"What about dark skin? Can someone dark have two parents who look white?"

A few people laugh like I just asked the dumbest question ever. But Whittaker smiles like my question makes his day.

"Now that is a fun one to explain. He draws an even bigger grid on the board. Just when he starts explaining, all us storm kids get called to a special assembly in the auditorium. I'm the only one in my biology class who has to leave, and all eyes follow me out of the room. I can feel it. Worse, I can hear Whittaker continuing answering my question even though I'm leaving.

When I get to the auditorium, they make us spread out, saying they don't want us sitting too close together and getting in trouble. The next thing I know they're breaking down the rules, one by one. No tardies. No hitting. No pushing. No sneaking food in our pockets. Zero tolerance. By the time the principal's done, I'm thinking I can be put out of school just for sneezing in class. That's when I realize, this principal thinks we're all notorious just because we lost everything in the storm. *Notorious: well-known for some bad quality.* I don't guess he realizes losing everything in a storm ain't a quality at all. It's just a fact. It happened, and every day keeps reminding us that it happened. I don't even have a bed at home yet, and I wake up when debris flies my way in a dream. Neil stuffs his pockets with fruit and cookies because that's the only way he can have a late snack. And this principal is warning us that any little outburst can get us put out of school?

After the assembly, I head to the bathroom before going back to class. Only I can't even use it. I open the stall, and I see Old Man Jake sitting there on a beer keg all bloated and gray, his eyes set way back like a zombie's. I run out of the bathroom fast, and a teacher stops me in the hallway and sends me straight to the office.

I'm thinking I'm about to get put out of school, but Ms. Hornwell saves the day. She happens to be in the office filling out a form when I walk in with an infraction slip that has a check mark next to the word *running*.

"Eric Calhoun?" Ms. Hornwell's hair ain't as put together as usual, but she still has the same warm eyes and comforting voice.

"Ms. Hornwell!" I don't know what comes over me. I just fall apart at the seams and hug her so tight. Next thing I know, I'm crying and telling her about how I saw a big bloated Old Man Jake in the restroom on the third floor.

"And you want to put this child out of school?" Ms. Hornwell has her hand on her hip. "These kids need support not ridiculous discipline."

So I end up in the waiting room outside the counselor's office instead. But I never make it in to see the counselor. Bell after bell, I'm just waiting with a whole group of other storm kids. I know that's who they are. I can see it in their eyes. I can hear it in their voices.

After school, I'm about to get on the bus when Layla and Neil grab my arm.

"Come on," Layla says.

"Where are we going?"

"To Ms. Hornwell's writing club."

We make our way to the main staircase, where a principal—there are lots of them at this school, not just one or two like at home—stops and asks for a pass. I struggle to find words and search my pockets, trying to pretend I misplaced the pass.

"Here they are," Layla says, a smile across her face.

"Writing club?" The principal frowns. "When did we add a writing club?" Then he lets us go and mumbles something about no longer having control of the school, displaced teachers and students taking over everything.

"Where'd you get three passes?" I ask.

"Ms. Hornwell. Where else?"

The room is at the top of the stairs off to the right. The walls are cluttered with stuff. Nothing that looks like Ms. Hornwell. No inspirational quotes. No posters of current authors. Just things like lists of dead words, transition words, graphic organizers shaped like hamburgers, and rules. The room is overcrowded too. Even with only four kids sitting in a circle, I can see this. The circle has been carved out of rows of desks, so the rest of the desks in the room are still in rows.

"Eric! Neil!" Ms. Hornwell smiles her pre-Katrina smile. "I am so glad you're here." Three kids slide their chairs back to make more room. Layla, Neil, and I pull up three chairs. "Eric and Neil are two of my students from New Orleans," Ms. Hornwell says.

"Cool," a guy with spiked hair says.

"Let's do introductions."

Layla starts, explaining that she lived in St. Bernard parish and her entire house ended up completely underwater. Not even the roof was visible. They left before the waters rose though, so she don't know what it's like to get stuck. She just knows what it's like to not be able to go back.

The Raheem look-alike is there, only his name is Bryson. He lived in the Lower Ninth before the storm. His family was brought to dry land by some men in a boat, and then he hot-wired a car at a dealership. They drove out of the city.

"I'm Eric," I say. "I'm from the Third Ward. We lost everything, I think. I haven't been back yet. But I think we lost everything."

"Not each other," Ms. Hornwell says, pointing my way.

"I lost my mom," Neil says. I suddenly feel like total crap for saying I lost everything. Ms. Hornwell has to pass the Kleenex. Layla reaches out and grabs Neil's hand. I watch her fingers curl over his knuckles. I want to reach out to pat his shoulder and kind of let him know I understand, sort of. But I don't.

Spiked hair is called Jake. He moved from California right before New Orleans flooded, so he was the only new kid a few days before the refugees came in. I cringe when he says that.

"Evacuees," Ms. Hornwell says. "Let's agree to say evacuees."

"Why they keep calling us refugees?" Neil has a scowl on his face.

I notice we have dictionaries under our seats, so I grab one and look it up. It feels so good to have a dictionary in my hands again. I read the definition aloud. "Refugee: a person who has been forced to leave their country in order to escape war, persecution, or natural disaster."

"See? Man, I ain't no refugee. I'm a United States citizen." Neil slumps down in his seat.

A girl named Aleja explains that she moved to the area over the summer, from Cuba. "I actually am a refugee," she says.

Layla's eyes light up. "What if we turn the word refugee on its head? Give it a new twist."

"Like people did with the word nigger?" Bryson says.

Layla's and Jake's faces draw a blank.

"Ah, yes," Ms. Hornwell says. "Gloria Naylor has an essay about that: 'The Meaning of a Word.' We'll have to read it."

"I guess?" Layla wrinkles up her nose.

"It's like this," Bryson says. "White people used the word nigger to put us down, but then our people flipped it and started using a form of it, nigga, as a term of connection, love, and respect."

"My nigga," Neil reaches out to Bryson, and they dap off. Neil smiles, and the dimple in his chin deepens.

That makes me smile because it's the first time I've seen Neil smile all day.

"So, I can call you nigga?" Spiked hair raises one eyebrow.

Neil and Bryson answer in unison. "Um, no. Don't do that."

Layla pops back in. "But if we do that same thing with the word refugee, we can make it work instead of hurt."

"You're on to something," Ms. Hornwell says.

I'm thinking hard. "Refugee: a citizen of a country who has found himself at the mercy of a natural disaster, suddenly incapable of independence, suddenly at the mercy of the government."

Aleja chimes in. "That doesn't work for me. For me, the real definition fits."

Neil has his arms folded and his head down. "What if we keep the first definition but instead of saying forced to leave their country, we just say forced to leave home."

Editing the dictionary definition as I read, I say, "Refugee: a person who has been forced to leave home in order to escape war, persecution, or natural disaster."

"That works for me," Aleja says.

Everyone except Jake nods. "Can we add job loss or something? We moved from California because my dad got laid off. We lost everything. He couldn't find another job back home. That's why we're here."

"Wow," Aleja says. "I'm sorry that happened."

Everyone nods.

"Yeah, I'm glad you're here though. Cause, you know, we can get to know each other and stuff."

Jake looks up at Bryson. "Appreciate that, man."

"Well, then, that settles it. That's who we are," Ms. Hornwell says. "This writing club will officially be called The Refugees. Now—" She looks around the circle, taking the time to make eye contact with each of us. "Let's talk about writing."

# CHAPTER 11

E ver since The Refugees started meeting, I don't catch the bus home. Instead, Ms. Hornwell drops me off. Layla's grandparents offered, but Grandma said that would happen over her dead body. That's what she said to me anyway, but on the phone with Layla's grandma, she said, "No, thank you. I'll make sure he gets home." Then she turned to me and said, "I told you be careful with that little white girl. Besides, didn't you say your old teacher Ms. Hornwell is running this?"

It turns out Ms. Hornwell lives two subdivisions over and passes our neighborhood on the way home. Neil's grandfather accepted Layla's grandparents' offer. So, now Layla and Neil are together without me every day after school. I wonder what they talk about.

Sometimes, the ride home with Ms. Hornwell is awkward. We're just quiet. That's when she turns the music up. She's always listening to jazz. No words, just instrumentals. Today is one of those awkward days, but I'm loving this song and snapping my fingers to the beat. Ms. Hornwell looks my way and smiles. When she turns on our street, I notice another house is complete, and a young couple is moving in. I'm looking at them unload a fake tree from the back of a big truck when Ms. Hornwell says, "You have company today."

I turn my head and see a shiny black truck in the driveway. "Pastor Charles!" I open the door of Ms. Hornwell's car before she even stops.

When Ms. Hornwell parks, I jump out and run into the house. Grandma is standing in front of the kitchen window, looking outside. Pastor Charles sits at the table, his chair turned to the side, long legs sprawled out like he's giving them a good stretch. "Pastor Charles!" I practically jump into his lap and wrap my arms tight around his neck. He laughs a big burly laugh.

"The one and only," he says, patting my back.

Grandma clears her throat but keeps looking outside.

"Well, the one and only Pastor Charles Ray III." He laughs.

I pull out the chair next to him and take a seat. "What took you so long?"

"Eric!" Grandma turns and gives me a sharp look.

He puts his big hand on my head like he's petting a puppy, but I don't even mind. He takes a long look at me. "Is that hair on your upper lip?"

"You see it too?"

Pastor Charles laughs, strokes his upper lip, and nods. "You know a funny thing happened at the church I've been volunteering through." He gives me a sideways look. "I was trying to help place evacuees in housing when the pastor walked in and said, 'Reverend Ray, I need to see you in my office.'"

"Well, what was that all about? Sounds serious." Grandma turns and leans her back against the counter.

"That's what I was wondering. We get in his office, right? And he says, 'I see you have a son. You didn't tell me about this.'"

"Oh no." I put my head down.

"Lord, have mercy." Grandma gasps. "What happened?"

"I told him no. Said I never been married. Never had any kids. Then he slid a form my way. First thing I saw was Eric Calhoun. The address was filled in at the bottom in the same box I had been filling in for other people." I can feel Pastor Charles looking at me, but I don't look up. "Now that I think about it, I didn't even explain. I just got up and left, made my way here."

"That form ended up all the way in Baton Rouge?" Grandma darts her eyes my way. "Charles Ray, I'm sorry. I don't know what got into Eric."

I'm wishing I could disappear.

Pastor Charles looks at me a few long seconds, right in the eyes. "Well, you are the closest thing I've got to a son."

I try to hold back my smile by focusing on the tips of my fingers, but it don't work. The smile creeps out just before Pastor Charles looks Grandma's way.

"But you knew we were here already. You didn't learn that from the form," Grandma says. "What took you so long?"

I really want to say, "Grandma! How rude!" But I just sit and listen because that's exactly what I want to know.

"I wanted to finish helping out there first. I kept thinking it would be just one more day, but people kept flooding in. Besides, I needed to make sure Mama was okay staying with Charlese without me a while."

"Oh, your mother loves her. You know that."

"Ain't that the truth? But Eric's form just made me realize how much I miss you." He looks Grandma up and down kind of slow before turning back to me. "Both of you."

Grandma turns to face the window again. "You close your eyes too long around here and a new house is up and filled with people. I've never seen anything like it. Houses coming up fast like that. New neighbors every day."

"It's an investor's paradise." Pastor Charles slaps the table. "I'm in the wrong profession." He laughs.

"I'll tell you what, these are the houses that Jack built. You can't touch a thing in here without it falling apart." She points to the sliding door that hides the pantry. It's off track and leaning against the frame.

"Figures. Build fast and cheap. Sell fast and high. Do you know they sell these houses before they're even all the way built?"

That explains why we seem to have a new neighbor every other day.

Grandma sits in the one chair that's left. It's the only one with a cushion. When she sits, she closes her eyes a moment and then lifts her head and exhales. "This chair sure is comfortable. Ugly little thing, but it does feel good." Grandma looks at Pastor Charles. "What about you, Charles Ray? Are you going back home, or are you going to buy a house in Baton Rouge?" She wrings her hands. "Or maybe here?"

I'm thinking here sounds like a great idea.

"Tell you the truth, Ruth. When the city is ready, I want to go back home. Get Zion up and running again. Meet the needs of the people."

"I get that," Grandma says.

"Don't you want to go back home?"

"Oh, I don't know. Too many demons to fight there."

"That's true everywhere. You know that."

I don't know what it is about Grandma, but demons always end up in the conversation.

"Why don't you just stay here until it's time to return?" Grandma says. "We don't have much furniture, but we can come up with another air mattress."

I think they've forgotten I'm here, so I just stay real quiet and look around. From the kitchen where we sit, I can see the entire living room.

It's almost empty except for that recliner from the couple at the grocery store and two brown velvet wing chairs Grandma got free from Gallery Furniture. In the entire house, we have those three chairs, a trash can, a laundry basket, two air mattresses, a small kitchen table, and the three mismatched chairs we're sitting in now. Mine has unleveled legs, and I'm trying hard not to wiggle because they make a knocking sound on the tile when I do.

"Now, you know, Ruth, as soon as I come over here to stay, the rumors will start flying about. The next thing you know, you'll be pregnant and nesting."

Grandma huffs. "Well, the rumors can't hurt me no more than I've been hurt already. But I guess you've got something to lose. I might laugh myself. Pregnant for Pastor Charles Ray? If that ain't a Sara story." She pauses and gives a little half smile. "You would make a good Abraham."

"I'll tell everyone you're my sister."

Grandma and Pastor Charles stare at each other a while. The whole conversation makes me feel real silly, and a giggle escapes my parted lips. They both look my way.

"I'll tell everyone you're my daddy," I say, joining the fun.

To my surprise, they both laugh. "Well, you already did that," Grandma says.

She's always nice whenever Pastor Charles is around. Maybe if he comes to live with us, Grandma will be nicer to Layla and her grandparents too. Then, I can ride home with her and Neil, and Neil won't be with Layla alone all the time.

Pastor Charles taps the table and moves his eyes in my direction. "How's school out here?"

"Too big," I say. "But I joined a writing club."

"Who is she?" Pastor Charles raises both eyebrows.

"I said I joined a writing club."

"I know, and I asked who is she? There's always a girl when a boy in ninth grade joins something like a writing club."

"Pastor!" Grandma laughs. "You ought to be ashamed of yourself."

"Well?"

"Her name's Layla. She's really smart." I want to say, and she don't call me dumb or my grandmother crazy. But I just add, "Her eyes are pretty too." I say eyes, but I'm thinking legs.

"And she's white," Grandma says, tightening her lips.

Pastor Charles looks at Grandma. "Now Ruth, don't go casting the sins of one person on another."

"One person?"

"One family. Either way, this girl has nothing to do with any of that."

"Any of what?" I ask.

Grandma looks at me and back at Pastor Charles. Then she leaves the room, walks straight into the living room and through the door that leads to our bedrooms.

I look at Pastor Charles. "Is what they say true? Did Grandma run off my daddy because he's a white man? Is he white?"

Pastor Charles bites his top lip and closes his eyes. "There's a lot of lie in that story. A whole lot of lie."

---

Pastor Charles found a church in Houston to partner with and arranged a bunch of mission trips to gut out houses and clean up debris in New Orleans. Grandma wasn't eager to go back, but she said I could go down and help as soon as I got a break from school.

It's November 19, and I can finally go. Pastor Charles has already been down twice with several deacons from the church in Houston and our church back home. They gutted out the first floor of houses in the community and hauled debris to the road: wet carpets, sheetrock, warped and rotten wood, all sorts of papers and photos. Now, they're ready to put sheetrock in the houses and gut out Zion. Grandma says Pastor Charles should have done the church first, but he says the people are the church, so the church did come first.

Grandma rolls her eyes and says, "Charles Ray, you know what I mean." She's sitting on a sofa we just got from Goodwill. More velvet. More slate blue. "Are you sure it's safe for Eric to go down there? I don't want him sick."

Pastor Charles says it's high time I learn to serve, and now's a better time than ever. Then he asks if there's anything Grandma wants him to try to salvage.

"Just the photos. I left my photo album in a drawer in Eric's bedroom. And in my bedroom, there's a safe with important documents, birth certificates, things like that."

Pastor Charles just nods and sucks his teeth. "All right then. Let's get going."

At the door, he gives Grandma a long hug, even rests his chin on the top of her head a while. Then we get in his truck and pull off. It's just the two of us at first, but when we get to the church, we meet up with a caravan of seven more pickups with four to five guys in each and a church van filled with young men ready to help gut out houses. Pastor Charles gets out of the truck and walks over to a short man with a balding head and round belly. The short guy draws a map in the air. Then the two shake hands. Pastor Charles moves his arm over his head like he's making a lasso as he walks back to the truck. This must be a signal to get going because all the trucks begin to line up behind ours. Being alone with Pastor Charles in the lead vehicle makes me feel proud.

We don't talk much on the road. The whole time he's taking phone calls and connecting members of Zion with other pastors. People are still moving around, trying to find a place to settle while our city struggles to get back up again. One of those phone calls is from Ms. Jackie. "Pastor!" I hear her yell through the phone. "Your voice is a sound for sore ears!" She's still with her son in Mobile, Alabama. She got a job out there and wants to send her tithe to Zion to help get the church up and running again. Pastor Charles tells her he's working on making tithing easy while everybody's scattered because members have been calling and asking how to give. But for now she can send it to him directly, care of Revered Joe Green at Greater Pleasant Hill in Houston.

A little while after we cross over into Louisiana, we stop at a small Cajun restaurant, Boudreaux's Fresh Catch, to eat—all thirty-eight of us—and when the hostess tries to figure out how to seat everyone, she looks at Pastor Charles and says, "I'll keep you and your son together." Pastor Charles is what the ladies at church call regal but what the boys just call buff, and the girls call one fine old man. The men just call him Reverend and pretend they don't know everyone's gawking over his looks. And Grandma, for her, he's just Charles Ray—which makes some of the women say she has some audacity with her crazy self. Anyway, this hostess assumes I'm his son, and that makes me feel kind of regal too. She starts directing the other guys on where to sit: six over here at this table, four in that booth, sixteen in the party area, ten on the outside patio. Pastor Charles and I get the one table that is left after everyone is seated.

"What can I get you to drink?" The waitress smiles wide like she gets paid extra for showing her teeth.

"Just water," Pastor Charles says.

The waitress turns to me. "Let me guess, you think your father's lost his mind just getting water, and you want a southern-style tea all syrupy sweet." She spreads that smile across her face again.

This is one of the things that's different about being with Pastor Charles. With Grandma, I always end up having to acknowledge my mother's death because she looks so old. "Eric, this must be your grandmother," teachers say. "And your mother? Is she at work this evening?" No matter how hard she tries to slick back her hair, it always ends up curling forward, making a silver halo around her head. She has crow's feet in the outer corners of her eyes and a deep scar on the left side of her lip that looks a little like a zipper. Sitting alone with Pastor Charles, I realize I feel ashamed of Grandma. I'm realizing this for the first time because what I feel with him is so different. I can just pretend I'm with my daddy, and Pastor Charles just lets it go. I like that.

Pastor Charles and I sit at a small light oak table with Cajun French words painted all over it in bold black print. There is a glaze over the words, so the table shines and feels smooth like glass. We are surrounded by the clattering voices of hungry men.

"Looka here," I hear Deacon Jackson say, "a frog leg tastes just like a chicken leg and alligator does too." Deacon Jackson is one of our deacons from Zion who ended up in Houston.

"No, man. Alligator tastes good, but it's chewy, not tender like chicken. And frog legs are just nasty." I don't know this voice. Maybe it's someone from the Houston church.

"Well, let me tell you, when I met my wife, it was at a fish fry down home. And my boy, Henry, ran out of fish and fried up some frogs. Caught them right there in the canal—the whole frog—and my wife sat there and ate that whole frog, and that's how I knew she was the one."

The men burst out in laughter. Someone says Deacon Jackson's a real trip, and someone else says they wouldn't touch a woman that ate frog like that. Pastor Charles chuckles a bit, but he don't comment.

"How did you meet my grandma? Was it when you started pastoring the church?"

He sits back and looks at me quietly a moment. "Well, this story could take me all day to tell."

I drop my eyes. "We can talk about something else."

"It's no trouble. I could talk about Ruth all day." Then, he smiles, and there is something different in his smile. He don't look like a preacher at all. "When I met your grandmother, we were young, not much older than you. Fifteen."

"Fifteen?"

"Yeah." He splits a boudin ball in half and puts it in his mouth. His eyes roll up to the ceiling. "That's good stuff." After he eats the second half of the boudin ball, he says, "It's probably hard for you to imagine your grandmother a teenager, but she was. Once upon a time."

I try to imagine this. I have seen pictures of my mother, but in all of these it seems Grandma is missing. She must have been the one behind the camera. I never really wondered what she looked like when she was young. In my mind, she is always old, and if I try to picture her young, it comes out like an old lady wearing little girls' clothing, a misfit in a crowded hallway of real teens who laugh and tease her. I can't imagine her in the kinds of things teenage girls wear, not even back in her day. I quickly do the math; she would have been a teenager in the '60s. I think they wore miniskirts back then, but Grandma in a miniskirt? No way!

"Was she nice?" I ask Pastor Charles.

"She was." Pastor Charles nods and taps the table lightly with his big hand. His thumb sits right under the word *lagniappe*.

"But how did you meet? Was it at school? Was she in the hallway bossing people around?"

Pastor Charles moves his tongue around so that the area above his lip puffs out a little. "Well, I do suppose it'd be hard for you to imagine, but she used to be a real teenager. She had a sense of humor too." He stares over my head as if looking at the wall behind me. "She had a real attitude sometimes though. But I liked her."

"You liked liked her?"

"I still like her. We're best friends."

The waitress sits a shrimp po'boy in front of me. The two halves of French bread are wide open. I pick off the pickles one by one.

"We met at the church, back when my daddy was the pastor."

I look up at Pastor Charles. His eyes seem far away. I think maybe he's looking at his daddy somehow, remembering when his daddy used to be the tall man in the pulpit with his hands stretched out like the hands of God, making everyone feel safe.

"Yeah, I remember that day well. I met your grandmother about a week after my family moved to New Orleans. We came from Atlanta. My dad's church there was big and buzzing, always busy. There was an auxiliary for everything. Everything. That was back when you couldn't even think of being a pastor before having a wife, and my mother was the model first lady. She had her own women's auxiliary, and they were the movers and shakers in the community. Nobody, not even my daddy, did anything without talking it over with her."

"How come you can be a pastor and not be married now?"

"I don't know. But I do know when God says you will pastor, that's all there is to it. I wanted a wife though. Just never worked out."

"You never loved anyone enough?"

Pastor Charles pauses like his words are scrambled and he has to pick them up and put them back together again before speaking. He moves his lips to one side, and his left eyebrow goes up. "I did love someone enough."

I sit up in my seat and lean forward.

"She didn't love me back." He puts a mouthful of étouffée and rice in his mouth and chews as if it's steak. When he finally swallows, he says. "At least not like I loved her."

For a moment we sit in silence. Then Pastor Charles slaps his hand on the table and says, "About the day I met your grandmother. Your grandmother's uncle, Mr. Clarence, was president of the New Orleans branch of the NAACP. He was the one who called my daddy and asked him to come down to New Orleans to lead Zion Baptist Church. I was mad because I had friends in Atlanta, and when we moved, we left more than a bigger church. We left a whole support network, and I might as well tell you, I liked our house in Atlanta better too."

"So you didn't like New Orleans?"

"Not at first anyway. Then, I met Ruth."

I smile. Listening to Pastor Charles say this makes me feel happy.

"We were at the first NAACP meeting after my daddy started pastoring. All of us were cramped in the small back room of the church. All of us meant twelve adults, fourteen or so teenagers, a few kids in elementary school, a couple of toddlers, the founders of the church, and of course my daddy, mama, and me. I had to sit on this raised platform which was awful because that meant all eyes were on me, at least that's how it felt. Mr. Clarence was reading the newspaper aloud under the dim light of kerosene lamps. We couldn't put bright lights on when we had meetings."

"Refill on your drink, darling?" The waitress holds a pitcher of tea in one hand, water in the other. Pastor Charles lifts his glass, and she fills his cup with water. "What about you?" She turns to me and lifts the tea pitcher a bit. "It's all the way sweet, sugar." I look at Pastor Charles for approval. Grandma never lets me get refills, but Pastor Charles nods.

"Yes, ma'am," I say.

The waitress fills my cup to the brim. "You two aren't from around here, are you?"

"No. We are just passing through on our way back to New Orleans."

"New Orleans? That's where I'm from. But I settled here in Lafayette after the storm. I don't know if I'll ever go back. It just breaks my heart. Did you lose everything? We lost everything."

"We didn't lose each other," Pastor Charles says. "So, no, I don't suppose we lost everything."

"I guess that's the right attitude to have." She wipes a puddle of water from the table. "But I don't think I'm ever going back." She continues talking as she walks away, her voice fading in my ears, "No indeed. Not ever going back."

Suddenly, I feel scared about going. I push the last fourth of my po'boy aside.

Pastor Charles raises an eyebrow. "You're not finishing that?"

"I'm sorry. Grandma says I should eat everything on my plate. There are starving children in other countries, and—"

"You should be grateful and eat what the Lord has provided," Pastor Charles finishes the sentence. "You still okay with going? I mean, if it feels too hard, you don't have to go. The boys can go on without us."

I feel like Pastor Charles is calling me a baby without saying it, and I don't like that feeling. I feel embarrassed now and kind of angry. "I'm not scared," I say. "I can go."

"Okay, okay," Pastor Charles says. "But I want you to know it was hard for me to go in the first time, and even the second. It's okay to not be brave all the time."

Pastor Charles looks around. The men traveling with us have all finished eating. Everyone is just sitting and talking. He puts the last spoonful of étouffée in his mouth and says, "Let's get back on the road then." When he stands, the men around him stand too, even though they sit at different tables. It's like they have all just been waiting for him to give the signal. I want power like that when I grow up. Pastor Charles starts walking, and I follow. When I look back, there's a long line of men behind us, zigzagging around tables. I pretend they are following me, and I hold my head up high. I lean a little to the side like Pastor Charles, and I nod at the hostess when I pass her and say,

"Thank you for the service. Have a nice day," in the deepest voice I can get out.

Pastor Charles looks back. "Whoa, where did that come from? You growing up on me?"

Back in the truck, Pastor Charles says, "You know, that waitress interrupted my story."

I don't say nothing. I'm wishing he never heard me imitating his deep voice. Now he thinks I'm just a little boy pretending to be a man. And I don't know if that makes me mad or sad or embarrassed.

"When I was your age," Pastor Charles says, "I sang boy-soprano in the church choir."

I look at him sideways.

"Yes, I did. I took the lead in 'Happy Birthday, Jesus' at thirteen years old."

"That's a girl's part." I laugh, "You're just messing with me."

"No, I'm not. My voice was so high back then. You're one up on me. You're a tenor easily. I was a tenor by the time I met your grandmother, but at fourteen? Nope. I was a boy-soprano."

I laugh at this. When I look up, I see a sign that says I-10 East – New Orleans Business District. Pastor Charles pulls into the right lane.

"So how did you meet?"

"Man, for a pastor, I'm really bad at telling stories."

"No, you're not. I like your stories."

Pastor Charles lets his eyes leave the road and looks at me a few seconds.

"Mr. Clarence was sitting on the platform, with my parents and me, reading. He sat in this big, gold wing chair. Now, he had a deep voice, but he was short. So, his head barely peaked over the top of the chair. But that voice rumbled and shook when he spoke. I used to try to talk like him when I was home alone. His voice was deeper than my daddy's. That room was dark. We had black felt covering all of the windows so no one could look in."

"Black felt?"

"It could be dangerous. We didn't really get it then, but the adults were organizing protests and pushing for integration. Anyway, we were supposed to be listening to Mr. Clarence read."

I'm thinking about my dream, and that boy who said, "Shhhh. Mr. Clarence is about to read."

Pastor Charles keeps talking. "The adults sat closer to the platform, and they kept scooting their chairs up, trying to lean in and hear. The teens were inching back, rolling their eyes, mouthing messages to each other, swapping smiles. There were these two toddlers sitting on the floor playing with something."

"Blocks?"

Pastor Charles looks at me a second. "Yes, it was blocks. I still remember those toddlers because they were the beginning of my friendship with your grandmother."

"The toddlers?"

"You have to picture it. These two toddlers were sitting on the floor in a corner near your grandmother. They started taking turns putting the blocks they were playing with in each other's mouths. It was a boy and a girl. The boy pulled a block from the girl's mouth and went to put it straight in his own mouth."

Now, I'm seeing those toddlers from my dream and that dim room with covered windows and nothing but the light from kerosene lamps. The truck feels real hot inside, and my head is spinning. I'm squinting and scrunching up my lips, and Pastor Charles figures it's because I'm imagining the toddlers swapping spit. In a way, I am. But I'm not really imagining it. I'm remembering it.

"Exactly," he just keeps talking. "I dropped my head right there on the platform and started laughing, which I was not supposed to do. When I looked up, Ruth was shaking her head, warning me to get my act together. But then she kind of started falling apart herself. She folded her arms across her lap and let her head drop a little. I saw her shoulders rising and falling and knew she was laughing too. I locked my face into a fake smile and tried to cover my laughter with head nods as if I agreed with everything Mr. Clarence was saying. When your grandmother looked up, she smiled at me and mimicked my head nodding. 'Ruth,' Mr. Clarence said, 'I am so glad you are excited to join our cause. Who else will join Ruth in standing on the front lines of full desegregation?'" Pastor Charles shakes his head. "She had no idea what she signed up for, and neither did I. But when Mr. Clarence said, 'Stand if you will join Ruth,' I was the first to stand. Well, everybody started standing then. Later, after the meeting, she walked up to me and said, 'What did I sign up for?' I told her I had no idea, but whatever it was, we were in it together."

"The integration of Ole Miss." I just whisper it, and Pastor Charles don't hear me at all.

"We had fooled around there and agreed to continuing the integration fight at the University of Mississippi."

I'm real quiet. Just thinking about my dream, trying to pull up the face of a teenage girl. But all I can remember is the couple on the stage and Half-face in that gold chair and the teen boy with his shiny black shoes. "Pastor Charles." I whisper again, but he hears me this time.

"You okay?" He looks my way, reaches out, and touches my forehead. "You feel hot."

CHAPTER 12

I feel the seat vibrating beneath me and hear the chop of the helicopter blades over my head—*chk-chk-chk-chk*. For a moment, I think I'm on the helicopter again. But really, I'm just dreaming, which I realize when I open my eyes and see Pastor Charles exiting I-10 East. It's funny how the memories flood back at random. I look out of the window, half expecting to see thousands of people standing outside, hungry and thirsty, just waiting. I see the trees lining City Park Avenue. Only the trees are leafless as if it's already winter, and the grass is brown. The stench of the storm remains, and I wrinkle my nose, disappointed. When Pastor Charles turns right on Canal Street, I see one front lawn after another piled high with debris.

Everywhere I look the houses are marked on the front siding or on boarded windows with big red or bright orange X's and numbers and sometimes words, like *Help us.* Pastor Charles drives down to Carrollton Avenue, and I realize we are headed to Zion. There are hardly any people moving about. A man walks out of a blue shotgun house with an X spray-painted between two windows. There are codes written inside the four spaces of the X. On the left are the letters *TFW.* At the top *10/9.* On the right, *RATS.* At the bottom, 3 with a D underneath.

He adds a photo album to a large pile of trash. He puts it down then picks it up again, holds it to his chest, then kneels and sits it on top of the pile. He rests his head on the album.

Pastor Charles looks at me and says, "I hope we can save your Grandma's album. It's upstairs, right?"

"We moved it upstairs," I say, looking out of the window. I don't explain that I already brought the album to Houston and really it's in my luggage for this trip. I'm thinking I can sneak it back in, then just pretend to save it. Maybe I'll just tell him the truth though.

Two men pull a deep freezer to the road in front of a peach-colored house with yellow shutters. It's the first thing pulled out to the road, and it makes me think they are just getting started with clearing out the house. But it's November, three months after the floodwaters destroyed our home. The waterline on the house is above the doorknob. When we pass the next house, which is sort of a faded, tan-looking gray, I see what looks like a dead dog under a leafless hedge. His ribs are showing, so he looks striped, but his jaw is swollen like someone blew air through his nose.

I blink my eyes and squint, but we're already too far away for me to take a closer look. Maybe I just imagined the dog.

The church is near the corner of Carrollton Avenue and Ulloa Street and has a huge parking lot to the right. There are houses across the street but none next door. Not really anyway. We pull into the parking lot, and the trucks following us pull in too. The men start taking out work bags, crow bars, drills, and some things I can't identify. Everyone has on jeans and rubber boots, caps, masks, and gloves.

"You'll need this," Pastor Charles says, and he hands me a mask and gloves too. "The smell is bad inside. There's mold and sewage. You need to protect your hands."

The men are buzzing around, and Pastor Charles runs up the concrete steps to unlock the sanctuary doors. When he gets to the upstairs porch that leads into the sanctuary, he turns around to face the men who are rushing up the concrete steps behind him. Then everyone stops to listen. Standing in the doorway with his hands raised like that, Pastor Charles reminds me of Martin Luther King Jr. In my mind, I imagine the twenty men are a hundred, then hundreds, then thousands.

"Before we go in," he says, "I just want to say thank you." He thanks everyone who came before and those who are here for the first time. "Together, the men of Mount Zion have already emptied and gutted 158 houses. That's a lot for a group this size, and I want you to know, I don't take this lightly."

I can't see Pastor Charles closely, but there is a weakness in his voice, a cracking, almost like mine does sometimes for no reason at all. This is new, and it makes me feel like crying, but I don't because I'm imagining a thousand men around me.

"It's okay, Pastor," Deacon Jackson says. "We're in this together."

"We decided to save the church for last," Pastor Charles says, "and to be honest, I thought we'd get help from a missions group before now. But everyone has been spread so thin. No one has made it here yet. We're on a list. Several lists. But we have to get started before the damage is irreversible." He turns and unlocks the door. He opens it slightly and immediately closes it back as if someone sprayed tear gas his way. He shakes his head. "You'll need your masks."

Then he starts organizing. He calls on Deacon Jackson and Deacon Anders to go in first, set up something called dehumidifiers, and open any windows that can open.

"No problem, Pastor. Whatever you need." They both make their way in, one walking to the left of Pastor Charles, the other to the right.

Pastor Charles asks the rest of the men to break up into four groups: one for the main sanctuary, one for the restrooms upstairs and downstairs, another for the fellowship hall, and the fourth for the kitchen.

"After we finish these areas, we'll divide again and tackle the classrooms. I don't expect us to get that far before tomorrow."

The men nod as if one body and begin to group themselves. Four groups form real fast, each with about nine people, but I'm stuck in one spot with no idea what to do and a real strong desire to run back down the steps.

Pastor Charles sees me and waves his arm. "Eric and I will be cleaning out my office if anyone needs to find me."

Pastor's office is downstairs in a room below the sanctuary and behind the fellowship hall. I follow him to his office. He unlocks the door, but when he tries to open it, it just falls off its hinges and into the room. A couple of guys show up to ask him a question, and for a second, they just stand there looking from the door to Pastor. Pastor Charles don't give no orders or nothing. He just stands there, but the men take action. They drag the door back out and haul it to the road. Whatever they planned to ask Pastor Charles goes unsaid.

I'm expecting Pastor Charles to walk in, but he turns around and walks away, clean across the parking lot, and leans on his truck. Now I'm standing motionless again, trying to figure out what to do. I lean against a big column and try to turn my head toward a better scent, but there ain't nowhere that smells good.

The men come back, and one of them, a tall, thin guy with long sideburns, says, "I don't think Pastor doing so well."

"Nah, I expect not. Let's just try to tackle it without him. He can't do this. It's like burying your own child." These words come from Deacon Jackson's son who everyone just calls Lil Deak because he looks just like his father.

Sideburns looks at me. "Lil Man, what you wanna do? You wanna go over there with Pastor or try to help?"

"I want to go to Pastor," I say, but when I get there, his eyes look real hollow, like I ain't never seen. "Are you okay?" I ask, and I see a knot in his throat and tears streaming down his face.

"Yeah, I'm fine. Just need a moment."

I take that to be a way to say leave me alone awhile, so I make my way back to Sideburns and Lil Deak. They have let the other guys go on to the fellowship hall and kitchen, but they are focused on Pastor's office. When I get there, I not only smell the mold, I feel it. It gives off a thickness and heat that makes me feel tired and heavy. My eyes burn the moment I step inside. There's a big orange machine that kind of looks like a fan in the doorway leading to the hall. I think it's a dehumidifier. The whole office looks like it's covered in a thin layer of mud, but in the corners and around the baseboards and door frames, there's a dark fuzzy growth, and this is in some random places too. The carpet is caked up with something like mud but has spots that look like the algae in the swamp at the zoo. Pastor's bookcases have fallen forward and dropped their books just like Grandma's china cabinet.

"Can you grab the other end?" Sideburns is holding up one end of a bookcase.

I grab the other side, and he tells me to back up to bring it outside. It's heavy, and I'm straining, but I don't say that out loud. Sideburns is stepping over the books and trying to maintain his balance. We lie the bookcase on top of the door at the road and go back inside. Next, we get a trash bag and start bagging once-wet, now-dry books with warped covers and swollen pages.

"Can any of these be saved?" I ask. I have a copy of *Strength to Love* in my hand, and he has a copy of something that looks like an encyclopedia. There's a full set of these, dark green hardback books with gold lettering on the spine, only most of the lettering has washed away and I can't make out the words.

"No, it's too dangerous. They're all contaminated with mold spores now. Everything has to go," says Sideburns.

I want to run back out to Pastor Charles, but I keep working until we have the books and the bookcases all at the road. Then, we take down the pictures on the walls. I pull down a certificate. I can't make

out all the words, but I see *Cert___ion of O___nation* at the top
and near the middle in much smaller print, the words *of the Gospel* are
clear. The rest of the print is all distorted from the water, and there's
even mold growing under the glass.

We tackle the desk next, and that's when Pastor Charles shows up
at the door and just looks inside with his hands in his pockets. Sideburns pulls at the middle drawer, and the whole desk collapses like a
house of cards. Lil Deak looks over his shoulder from across the room
where he is taking down the last painting, a scene of Jesus baptizing a
woman in a sea with children watching from the shore. There's a man
in the painting up on a hill in the distance. He has an umbrella, but
there's no rain, and he's obviously dancing because one foot is raised
in the air, and his back is arched back. The painting makes me think
of Old Man Jake again, and the man in the painting gets all swollen
and gray.

Lil Deak frowns and moans at the sight of the collapsed desk. Pastor clicks his tongue and shakes his head.

"Pastor is there anything we're supposed to try to save?" Sideburns
looks up.

"No, Nic. I just gotta start over. The Lord giveth and the Lord ta-
keth away." He picks up a piece of the desk and walks it to the road.

We have to take the desk out in pieces. The papers in the drawers
are all stuck together, but it don't matter no way because all the ink
has smeared and some of it even disappeared. I'm throwing papers
in the trash when I come across a photograph of Pastor Charles and
Grandma when they were young, and Pastor Charles Ray II, First
Lady Ray, and my grandmother's parents, who died before I was born.
Grandma and Pastor Charles are holding papers up, but I can't read
them. Their smiles are big. I want to keep it, but I know I can't. Still, I
keep putting that one picture to the side. I just can't trash it.

About the time Pastor Charles comes back to his office, Deacons Jackson and Anders come from upstairs bringing out carpet from the sanctuary floor.

Pastor takes a deep breath and closes his eyes a long time.

When he opens them, he says, "I'd like you to excuse me a while. I am going to take Eric to his grandmother's house to work upstairs. Maybe should have sprayed bleach in there, but I was thinking up-stairs'd be fine."

"You want some of us to go with you? It's a lot to tackle for just you and the boy."

"No, not today," he says. "I need you guys here."

Pastor Charles don't go straight to our house though. He drives to the Marriott, a big hotel on Canal Street, checks in a room, carries his luggage upstairs, and takes a shower. When he comes out of the bathroom, he lies on the bed, right on top of the comforter and stares at the ceiling.

"I thought we were going to our house." My voice trembles a little, but it's not like I feel afraid. I'm just confused.

"Tomorrow." He crosses one foot over the other and closes his eyes. "Go ahead and shower."

---

Morning comes slowly. All night, I'm listening to Pastor Charles breathe and the sounds coming from outside—sirens and faint voices but no dogs barking. That gets me thinking how nothing is the same, not even Pastor Charles. In the middle of the night, he calls Grandma, and I pretend to sleep, but I hear every word.

"I just need to hear your voice," he says. There's a long pause. "I don't know how you do it. You just keep getting back up, no matter what." He takes a deep breath and turns in bed. "I'm so tired, Ruth."

I hear Grandma singing through the phone until he falls back to sleep: "I don't feel no ways tired. I've come too far from where I started from."

I don't remember falling asleep, but I wake up to Pastor Charles singing that same song. Now, he's handing me a plate of eggs, toast, bacon, and grits.

"Go ahead and eat," he says. "Today's going to be a full day of work."

I'm wondering if I dreamed up the whole conversation with Grandma, just like the hidden room behind my closet, or whether I'm just losing my mind.

At first, when we start driving, it looks like everything is better. The stores downtown are open. The streets are even clean. But once we drive out of the business district, the damage is everywhere we turn. Sometimes, several houses in a row have the exact same spray-painted codes, except with different bottom numbers in the *X*. Sometimes it's zero, sometimes one, two, three. I have even seen numbers as high as seven. Sometimes there's an *A*. Sometimes a *D*. Sometimes, the word *dead* is spelled all the way out, so I know the letter A means alive.

When Pastor Charles turns onto our street, I see *9/22* on the three houses leading to ours, and all zeros in the bottom of the X. I exhale and let my shoulders relax. But then I see Neil's house, and the words *Dead Dog* painted next to the dark green shutter, and my shoulders tense up again.

When we get to our house, the fallen tree is no longer there. It has been removed, and the front of the house is just this big wide-open space. I can see inside, but there ain't no walls, no rooms to actually see. All the walls have been removed. The carpet is gone too. There's just wood on the floor. It's like the opposite of watching the houses come up in Houston, like home is a house being unbuilt.

The front porch is there, but it's not actually attached to the house. It's a set of steps and a concrete slab on cinder blocks in the middle of a space with a half-of-house nearby. We don't even have markings painted on the front of our house because we don't have a front to paint on.

I turn and look across the street. The beams on Old Man Jake's porch are intact, but his door is down as if someone has broken in, or as if it fell in like Pastor's office door did when he tried to open it. Many of the wooden shingles are missing from the siding of his house, so the markings are on his windows, the letters close together to force fit them on the plywood: *9/22*. A code I can't understand. A zero. And on the other window, something else, a note: *Jake, where are you? 504-478-7905*.

"He's dead," I say. "Should we call and tell them?"

Pastor Charles is quiet a few seconds. "How do you know for sure?"

"They pulled up Old Man Jake's body when trying to find Neil's mom." It's the first time I am really thinking about this.

Pastor Charles puts his arm around me and squeezes a little. "This is a tough way to suddenly grow up," he says. "I'll call. By now, they may already know, but I'll call to make sure."

Old Man Jake's house looks sad, like actually sad. The siding has faded from loud orange to a pale peach that is even lighter below the brown waterline. I turn around and face our house again. Despite not having a front, the house seems to stand up straight, unlike Mr. Chris's house next door, which leans to the right as if the cedar blocks slipped from one side.

We walk down the side alley that leads to our kitchen. The markings are painted on the side of the house. Another spray-painted *X*. On the left *CJA*, at the top *9/22*, on the right *MMS*, and at the bottom, a zero.

"What does all of this mean?" I point to the *X*.

"Signs of rescuers coming in. They were checking houses, trying to make sure no one was left inside."

"Is 9/22 the date? September 22?"

"Yes, I think so."

"What's all that other stuff?"

"I don't know what it all means. Some kind of code."

I point to the zero at the bottom of the X. "I think this is the number of people found in the house. Zero means no bodies were found."

Pastor Charles nods.

"On the way in, I saw some with numbers and an A or D. I think that's about who they found and whether or not they were living."

Pastor Charles takes off his cap and rubs the top of his head. He sighs. "I'm sure you're right."

When we reach the kitchen door, Pastor Charles takes out his key and strains to unlock it. The key won't turn. "It's jammed," he says.

"Can't we just walk in the front? I mean, it's all open anyway."

Pastor Charles kind of chuckles, and I laugh too, because even though it's sad, it's also kind of funny. We walk back past the markings and into the wide-open space with nothing but wooden beams. The smell's not so bad because the carpet has been pulled out and the walls gutted and sprayed with bleach already. It's really damp though.

"I'm gonna need to get a tarp and cover that opening until we can get it fixed. It'll never dry out like this."

We make our way up the bare stairs, which have been stripped down to their wood. The wood creaks beneath our feet. When we walk into my room, it's clear someone has already been here. The smell is bad but not exactly horrible, compared to the church anyway. My furniture is gone, except for the bed, which had gotten soaked when the window first broke. Now, it's sitting in the middle of the room, fully made, with mildew growing on the comforter. The contents of my drawers are scattered on the floor. I pick up my dictionary, hoping to save it, but the pages are warped and swollen. I turn to the *D* section, and there is a line of mold across the page like the beginning of an *X*. My walls are spotted with mildew, and the corners are dark with mold. The carpet has that same fuzzy look as the carpet at the church. All the food has been taken out of my closet, and my clothes are gone too, except for the suits. They are still hanging on the back wall. In the bathroom, everything is gone. All the tissue, soap, shampoo. Whatever we left has been cleared out. But the odor is still there. The toilet is crusted over inside with brown rings, and there is a layer of something like sand on the tile.

"About that album," Pastor Charles says, looking around the bedroom, "do you see it?"

"It's not here," I say, and my stomach gets real tight.

He shakes his head. "Ruth's not gonna be happy."

"I have it. I snuck it out of here. I was going to sneak it back in."

Pastor Charles looks at me like I just slapped him. "Why would you hide that?"

"I don't know." I shrug my shoulders. It's hard to explain. When I snuck the album out, it made sense to me, but now I don't know why. It seems stupid.

"I don't understand," Pastor Charles is talking with his hands. "First, you say I'm your father, and we let that lie ride. But this?" Pastor Charles raises his voice. It's not his preaching voice, though. He's mad at me. "Now you're lying about something as dumb as an album?"

"But Grandma—"

"Don't blame this on Ruth. You chose to lie. She had nothing to do with it." He kicks the dictionary across the room and lets out a big sigh. "Well, at least we can bring her album back to Houston. Let's get this stuff out of here, so we can pull up this carpet."

For the first time in my life, I feel uncomfortable with Pastor Charles, and it's my own fault. We bag what's left in my room and haul it out to the road without even talking to each other. When he finally gets a phone call, I'm relieved. He shoos me off and turns his back against the growing pile of debris at the road. I go back inside. The

only thing left to toss out are the suits on the back wall of the closet.
I don't care anything about those suits. What I care about is finding
out if there's actually a room behind the closet wall. I slide the suits
in both directions and start tapping the wall, looking for some kind
of weak spot. There's a soft spot from the top of the baseboard and up
about six inches. It's damp, which I can't figure out because the closet's
almost completely dry. There's barely even mold in here, just a little
mildew on the baseboards. I take all the suits down and toss them
to the floor. Maybe the opening is in one of the corners or along the
bottom. I'm sliding my hands up the wall from top to bottom when
Pastor Charles comes back in and says, "What exactly are you doing?"

Even though I know the whole reason we're not getting along is
because I lied twice, I say "I thought I heard something moving back
there, like a rat maybe."

"Likely, or a squirrel. Rodents usually find their own way to safety."

Pastor Charles looks at the suits. "We could have saved those, you
know?"

It's probably not a good idea to mention that Grandma only wanted
the album, so I just frown and say, "But they stink."

"I imagine so. Let's go ahead and bring them to the road."

Downstairs, Pastor Charles gets another call. It's Deacon Jackson,
and he wants to know if we need help at the house. Pastor says we're
almost done and just need to pull up the carpet and spray the bleach.
Deacon Jackson starts telling him about a Muslim family who needs
help not far from the church. I sneak off to my room while Pastor
Charles is explaining that we are the hands and feet of Jesus for anyone who needs it.

When I get back in my room, I go straight back to my closet and
keep feeling around because either it's real or I'm crazy, and I really
don't know which is true. I put my forehead on the wall and fold my
hands, and I ask God to show me the truth. But nothing happens.

"Great. I am crazy."

I hear Pastor Charles calling me from downstairs, but I don't want to go. He's mad and I'm tired, and now I have to face the fact that I'm losing my mind. I turn and rest my back against the wall, and I want more than anything to disappear, not to have to see Pastor Charles or hear how disappointed he is that I lied or go home to Grandma and give her the album that she won't even let me ask questions about or sit in that stupid writing club and talk about this dumb storm over and over again. I'm tired, and I don't want to face another day. I should have drowned in that storm. It should've been me and not Neil's mom, not even his dog, and definitely not Old Man Jake.

Pastor Charles calls again, and he sounds like he's almost at the top of the stairs, about to walk into my room. I can't deal with all of this. I just want to go back to the way everything was before the storm, before the water. I pull my knees to my chest and put my hands over my ears. My shoulders tighten. I don't want to hear whatever he has to say.

---

Suddenly, instead of sitting in the corner of my closet, I'm curled on my back like an egg, looking up at wooden ceiling beams. The room is brightly lit, the sun shining through the small window on the wall as if it's completely uncovered, only it's not, and the brightness in the room seems too much for the evening. I sit up, still holding my knees. This is different. I can't see into my room at all. The wall has resealed itself somehow, and I can't even hear Pastor Charles finish my name. In fact, I don't hear anything. I have never heard so much quiet in my life.

"Lord, am I going crazy?"

Again, I'm afraid to touch anything, but now I'm afraid not to. The first time I touched a chair, I ended up back in time with Half-face, a teenage Pastor Charles, and apparently Grandma too. But when I didn't touch nothing but the floor itself, I ended up in rising water. I don't know what to do. I stand to my feet and walk around the room, my hands up in the air like a criminal. Everything inside the room is the same, except the tools and cleaning stuff are gone. And that light, it's way too bright.

I study the map framed on the wall. It's a road map, and a green line is drawn from New Orleans, Louisiana, to Oxford, Mississippi. When I look real close, it kind of looks like someone cut two maps and taped them together to create one. New Orleans has a circle drawn around it in dark blue, so does Jackson, Mississippi, and Oxford. There are red X's on some places and others highlighted in yellow. I'm tempted to pull the map down and take it out of the frame, but I don't know if that's a good idea. What if I end up in the map or something crazy like that? So I just back up. I cross my arms because they hurt now, but I don't want to make a mistake and touch a thing. I back away from the map, just thinking, trying to figure out what to do. I almost fall when I bump into the table and grab hold of it to catch my balance, and that's it. That's all it takes.

Suddenly, I'm in a kitchen, leaning against something I can't see, my arms folded. There's a small air conditioner in the window, and it's rattling with a constant hum. The cold air blows against my wet skin, and I realize I'm sweaty from working all day. "Young man, turn around." Someone to my right nudges me, and I realize I'm still wearing my work boots, gloves, and mask. I remove my mask and gloves right away and shove them in my pocket. I turn and discover the same table I just stumbled on minutes before with Half-face at the head.

"The work we do opens the floodgate of equal opportunity for all. We're not just working for the advancement of Black people. We are working for the advancement of all people. That's what this is about." The man's voice is even deeper than I remember. He pulls out a large map and opens it wide so that it covers the full width of the table. "Even if you're not the one driving, all of you are accountable to one another. You understand? So, if the driver is doing something wrong, you have just as much right as anyone in that car to say something."

His voice drones on in the background: exit here, enter there, don't stop at this store, avoid that road. But I only half hear what he's saying. My mind is on other things, like where are Grandma and Pastor Charles?

"Shouldn't we wait for Charles Ray?" The voice is calm and soft but kind of sassy too. "He's our driver, I mean. So shouldn't we wait for him to arrive to go over all these details?"

This girl is beautiful. Her skin is the purest brown, and she has dark almond-shaped eyes. Her hair is in an Afro, like the kind I've seen in those old photos of Angela Davis, perfectly shaped. She taps her long fingers on the table softly. Half-face looks at her sternly, much like Pastor Charles looked at me when I confessed to having the album.

"Can't I just share an honest opinion?" she asks.

The other teens, who are standing around the table like me, look down. One is wringing her fingers and another inhales and makes a hissing sound. Now that I'm looking, these kids all seem younger than the girl who just spoke up. It's five of us standing, and we're all about the same age. But that one girl sitting at the table looks older than us, maybe even eighteen. Everyone else sitting down is an adult, forty years old at least. One of the ladies looks at the girl and opens her eyes wide.

"Ruth, watch yourself! How dare you disrespect Uncle Clarence that way!"

Half-face lets out a big sigh, and everyone shakes their heads. A kid next to me mumbles, "She's always the one who gets in trouble."

Grandma?

"And you're going to straighten that Afro before you go to Oxford too!"

"Mama, really?" Grandma frowns.

"Arrangements are already made. When you get to Jackson, Charles Ray will bring you to Ella Mae's house, and before you and her daughter Anne journey the rest of the way out to Oxford, Ella Mae is going to take care of that hair. Get it all respectable looking, like a college student that knows how to stay in her place."

Grandma crosses her arms tight and closes her eyes, and the vein in her temple is pulsing so hard, I think she's just going to explode. But when the door opens, and a tall teenager ducks his head down a little to clear the entrance, a huge smile spreads across her face. As soon as he crosses the threshold, he looks around the room slowly, smiles at Grandma, then turns to the adults and says, "Good morning. Mr. and Mrs. Calhoun. Mr. Clarence." He nods and extends his hand first to Mr. Calhoun, who I now think is my great-grandfather, and then to Mr. Clarence, who I can't help but call Half-face in my mind for obvious reasons.

Next the tall teen bends down and kisses Mrs. Calhoun, my great-grandmother, I assume, on the cheek. "Ma'am thank you for trusting me with Ruth. We'll be real careful." He says this with his mouth close to her ear like he's telling her a secret, but his voice is so deep I hear every word.

I look at Grandma and the smile on her eighteen-year-old face is unlike anything I've ever seen. So, this is Pastor Charles.

"Ruth ain't the only one you driving, Charles." This voice comes from a girl behind him, also about eighteen. She's carrying a hot pink purse on her arm. She rolls her eyes at Pastor Charles and pushes him a little to get to my great-grandmother. "Oh, Mrs. Calhoun," she says, "your cheekbones. So stunning. I have a blush you should try." She starts digging in her bag before she even notices my grandfather and great-uncle sitting at the table with the map.

"Charlese, take a seat, sweetheart. We are going to go over the plan again." Another woman taps the table lightly, and when I look closely, I recognize her as the same one who sat onstage that day Half-face, I mean Uncle Clarence, read the article about James Meredith. I squint to get a closer look. First Lady Ray?

"Yes, Auntie."

Charlese slips into the seat next to First Lady Ray and pushes her straightened bangs out of her eyes.

Another girl who walks in behind Pastor Charles is quiet. She says hello hardly above a whisper and then walks over to a nearby wall instead of sitting.

"Harriet Jo, you don't want to sit?"

Sister Harriet Jo? From church? The one who says she and Grandma used to be friends before college?

"No ma'am. I'm fine." Harriet Jo blows a large bubble with her pink gum.

The last guy comes in wearing a smile two sizes too big. He nearly shouts hello and greets everyone with a hug, even the men.

"Charlie." Uncle Clarence nods. "Let's get focused now."

"Yessir," Charlie says, still all smiles. "Oooh-weee! I can't wait to get to Mississippi." As soon as he says "Oooh-weee," I know this is Deacon Charlie Jackson, the frog leg connoisseur, and I almost laugh out loud. Deacon Jackson rubs his hands together fast, and that too-big smile gets even bigger.

Grandma rolls her eyes, then focuses her gaze on Pastor Charles.

Uncle Clarence moves two chairs close to him. "Charlie and Charles Ray, you two take a seat right here." He leans in closer to the map.

I start inching my way closer to him because I want to see if that's the same map from the wall, and right when I get close enough to see, he runs his finger along a highlighted green line. It's the same map alright.

"I know you think we've talked about this before, but you two will be driving. We want to make sure you understand. You do have your own copies of the map, correct?"

"Yessir," Charlie jumps in right away, but Pastor Charles only nods and swallows. His large Adam's apple moves up then down.

"Remember, avoid these spots marked with a red X. Also avoid small stores, private gas stations. Hell, small towns. Avoid small towns." Uncle Clarence massages the scar tissue on his lip as he speaks.

The kid next to me whispers in my ear. "It's a shame what they did to Mr. Clarence in Mississippi."

I want to ask what, but I'm guessing I should know. Plus, it's not a good time to talk.

"Take care of my niece," Uncle Clarence says. His eyes fall on Pastor Charles, and I turn my head to see Grandma squirming in her seat, her brown cheeks flushed.

Pastor Charles sits back and looks her way instead of at Uncle Clarence. "I will, sir. She's in good hands."

Time seems to stand still the next few seconds like someone pressed pause on a movie. I'm just looking at the two of them look at each other when I hear, "Eric!" I jump, startled, and turn in the direction of the voice. That's when I see Pastor Charles enter my closet doorway. I'm back in the closet again.

"What are you doing? I've been calling you."

I don't want to lie. I just want to tell the truth and get along with Pastor Charles again. So, I tell him. I tell him all about the room with the map on the wall that seems somehow connected to the closet and how I was just there again but can't figure out how I got there or back here.

He gives me that irritated look and shakes his head.

"Just tell me the truth! What are you so scared of?"

"I'm trying. I mean, I am. I'm telling you the truth. You and Grandma were at this table with Half-face and Ms. Harriet Jo and your cousin Charlese and my grandparents and some other kids were there too, kids my age. Half-face, I mean Uncle Clarence, had this map, and he was telling you and Deacon Jackson, I think, where to drive and what to avoid, and—"

Pastor Charles holds up his hand. "Eric, just stop. Obviously, you've gotten into your grandmother's files or something, and you found stuff. And now you're just trying to cover your tracks."

"I'm not! It really happened!"

I feel the sting of tears on my face, and my voice squeaks like a little kid's, and my throat sticks to itself so that it hurts to talk.

Pastor Charles turns and walks away. "Let's go," he says. "I should have never brought you down here. It's too much for a boy your age to handle. I'm taking you back to Houston."

# PART 3

# CROSSING THE LINE

# CHAPTER 13

"What's wrong with you lately?" Layla cuts me off in the hallway, keeping me from taking another step.

"What do you mean?" I can't bring myself to look at her. I know exactly what she means. I've been ignoring her for days, not even sitting with her, or anyone for that matter, at lunch. I spend every waking minute in the library trying to find out something about my grandmother or Uncle Clarence to prove I didn't just imagine the room with the map on the wall or the lamplit basement of the church or the kitchen table with Half-face at the head.

"You've missed two Refugee meetings." Her voice is soft and gentle. "Come on. I know you. Something has to be wrong."

"You don't know me." The words slip out of my mouth before I realize they're in my head. But I keep going even while I'm trying to stop. "What makes you think you know me? A little clothes shopping together? Lunch in a cafeteria with a bunch of other rejects? Oh, I forgot, not rejects, refugees." I feel anger rising, and it has nothing to do with her. I want to reach out and hug her, but instead I spit out stupid words I don't even mean.

Layla's lips tremble. Her eyes glaze over and fill with tears. "Forget it then. Forget me. I don't need you to be my friend."

She turns away and pushes past Paco like he's invisible. At first, he just grins and nods, like something funny happened. Then he turns around and calls out to Layla.

"Hey, Refugee! You blind or something?"

Layla turns around. The tears are still in her eyes, but now she looks angry, not sad.

"Don't mess with me, Paco!"

He repeats her words, imitating her high-pitched voice. Then, he drops down into a deep bass. "Or what?"

"You're such a jerk," Layla says. She turns to walk away.

"Oh no, you don't get away that easy, chica." Paco pulls her backpack, forcing her to take three steps backwards.

A crowd forms in the hallway.

"Paco, leave that girl alone. You gonna get in trouble."

"I'm not leaving her alone until she show me some respect."

Layla looks at me, and I feel the weight of her eyes, like she's asking me why I'm so quiet, begging me to say something. My heart is throbbing inside my chest. The last thing I want to do is cross Paco, but I can't just let him treat her like that.

He turns his head like he's following her eyes to mine. Then, he looks back at her. "'That your boyfriend, chica?" His laugh is loud and overexaggerated.

He's holding her backpack. Layla wiggles out of it and storms away. Paco throws the backpack and hits Layla in the calves, causing her to stumble and fall forward. Everything in my body tightens, especially my neck.

Paco laughs again. "Aw, look at what the storm washed up."

His laugh is taunting, reminding me of the days Neil and Raheem bullied me back home, and suddenly all that anger comes back.

I charge forward and punch him as hard as I can right in the neck, which is what I manage to reach, only the punch don't land hard. He moves, and my fist sort of grazes his skin.

"What the—" Paco tightens his eyes into slits thin as razor blades.

Layla scrambles up from the floor, grabs her backpack, and steps back into the crowd.

"Paco, no! Leave them alone!" Maria's high-pitched squeal is always the same.

He pulls back his fist and lands a full-force punch to the side of my head. I stumble against the lockers and a crowd of kids in the hall suddenly surround us on all sides. My vision's blurred, but I see Maria pulling at Paco, trying to keep him away from me. He pushes her back, and her cry comes out in slow motion. He lands another punch. This one to my chest, and I fall against the lockers again hitting my shoulder blade. The pain is awful. I charge back toward him, bringing my full body this time. I don't see Layla, and I can't hear her. But I'm replaying her last words, seeing the tears in her eyes. Paco puts his hand out, and I end up running into it only to have him push me back again. This time, I fall on the floor, and I see him coming at me when Neil and Jake walk up from behind.

"Hey, Paco!" Neil says. He's got this smirkish grin on his face that I remember too well.

Paco turns around. Neil punches him so hard, he stumbles back. I roll myself over and stand up.

Before Paco can get his balance, I land a punch to his shoulder. It's not much, but he stumbles a little before running toward me. Jake pulls him back, and Neil gets him in the face three times—whop, whop, whop. The next thing I know Bryson comes out of nowhere and jumps on Paco too. Then two of Paco's friends push their way through the crowd, and it's an all-out battle for about two minutes before the school's security officers walk up and break up the whole thing. They

handcuff me, Neil, Bryson, Paco, and his two friends. But Jake don't
get cuffed at all. The officers just point to him and say, "You too, come
on," like they're out of handcuffs or something.

They escort us right past Ms. Hornwell's room to the center staircase. Ms. Hornwell's standing in the door with Layla, whose eyes are
swollen even in the distance. I look back, and Ms. Hornwell is following us, but Layla shakes her head and goes the opposite direction.

---

"I don't understand what's gotten into you lately." Pastor Charles is the
first "parent" to arrive in the principal's office.

He's dressed in a suit with a shirt and tie, looking all polished and
perfect. He's been at the house now for about two weeks—ever since
we got back from New Orleans. The first night he stayed over, I heard
something about FEMA no longer covering his hotel bill and a single
man being last on the list for housing. There were no jokes about
Abraham or Sara or me lying and saying he's my dad. All of a sudden,
he was just sleeping on that velvet sofa, showering in my bathroom,
hanging his clothes in my closet. And now he's showing up at school
like he's my daddy, and ain't no one asking questions. Inside I'm all
conflicted, because on one hand I know Grandma would make a scene
if she came and he'll stay calm and all pastor-like, but somehow, I don't
want him here.

Ever since I tried to tell him the truth about the room behind my
closet, he don't even talk to me like he used to. It's just *hi* and *bye* and
*Can you pass me the crackers?* kind of talk. It's not anything like I imagined living with him would be. For one thing, Grandma is not nicer
with him around. She's tense, always telling me to pick up this, put
away that, speak up, look up, hush up because Pastor's on the phone
or Pastor's taking a nap. Besides that, there's Pastor himself—nothing
like I expected. Every time he looks at me, his eyes ask what's wrong.

But it's not the right kind of what's wrong. It's more like an accusation than a concern, not like what's wrong with your heart, more like what's wrong with your soul. If I say, "What's wrong is you don't believe me, and I need you to believe me. I need you to help me," he'll just think I'm making up something else. So again, the truth is not an option.

I just lean back in my seat and look at him. He folds his arms and looks mostly away, but every time our eyes lock, I feel like a sinner, and I didn't even lie—at least not about everything he thinks I lied about. The thing is . . . his not believing the truth is making me have to keep lying. I can't tell him or Grandma nothing about my research. I can't ask questions because they'll want to know where I got my information, and if Pastor Charles—the person I trusted more than anyone in the world—don't believe me, then I know I can't tell Layla, and I sure can't tell Neil.

And now this fight has just made everything worse.

I wonder what Ms. Hornwell and that principal are talking about. They've been behind the closed door of his office a long time. I'm sitting in a chair across from that door, and it has a window on it with open blinds, so I can see Ms. Hornwell's doing most of the talking, her hands moving more than her lips. He's just nodding and tapping his pen on his lip like he's in deep thought. Every now and then he writes something down in a notebook, and once I saw him shake his head and give Ms. Hornwell a brick wall. She stepped back and paused a long time after that. Then her hands and mouth were at it again.

A guy walks in, and I figure it's Jake's dad. Both him and Pastor Charles are wearing suits, like they got a memo on what to wear to the principal's office when your child gets in a fight. But it's not Jake's dad at all. When he signs in with the secretary, he says he's here to pick up his daughter Layla. Layla's never even mentioned her dad, and suddenly he's here. School let out over an hour ago, so I'm wondering what's with this man showing up late and out of the blue at that. Then again, I ain't been talking to Layla, so maybe he's in her life now. I don't know.

I'm looking back and forth from inside the principal's office to the receptionist's desk where Layla's dad explains that he came to surprise her. But I avoid looking at Pastor Charles who is literally sitting across from me, next to the principal's door, staring me down.

The receptionist looks up. She has a very small frown on her face, and she pulls her glasses down like that's the only way she can see. "Do you have an ID?"

A man comes in wearing boots, jeans, a hooded sweatshirt, and a neon orange vest. He rushes right to the counter and interrupts Layla's dad just as he's about to hand the receptionist his ID. The man's hair and clothes are dusty, and his hands look like he dropped them in plaster then tried to wipe it off with a paper towel. He cuts his eyes at Jake, and Jake looks away.

"I understand my son got in a fight and is being suspended from school."

He says this so loud everyone in the overcrowded office can hear. Not sure that matters though since all of us in the office are in trouble for fighting. Well, all of us except the receptionist, Pastor Charles, Layla's dad, Jake's dad, and some woman who just walked in with dreadlocks down her back. I'm thinking she's Bryson's mom. She's standing against the doorframe with her left hand on her hip and her right hand squeezing her temple, waiting for the two dads at the counter to get done.

"Sir, I'm going to have to ask you to take a seat. A principal will be with you soon."

The security officer steps forward when he says this like the receptionist needs to be rescued. He has handcuffs hanging off his belt loops, a warning that he'll put them back on us if he needs to.

Jake's dad grunts, looks around the room, then pushes himself between two empty seats to lean on the glass wall. He folds his arms across his chest and stares at Jake from his position across the room.

Layla's dad hands the secretary his ID. She types in something on the keyboard and says, "Sir, we don't have you on file. I am unable to call that student down for you."

"So she's still at school then? Stayed late for a club or something, right?"

"Sir, I'm going to have to ask you to leave. You are not on our list. Now, you can get the legal guardians to add you, but they'll have to come down in person to do that."

He slams his fist on the desk, and a small Snoopy figurine falls to the floor.

The man seems startled by his own actions. He jumps slightly then folds his hands over his face. "I'm sorry. I'll leave." He holds his hands up and turns around.

Pastor Charles suddenly looks like he's seen a ghost. "Jackson?"

The man don't respond to the name. He just glances around the room and says, "Y'all have a good afternoon."

Then he's out, and Pastor Charles is out too, following him. I turn and look out of the glass doors into the hallway. Pastor Charles does a fast trot to catch up with the man, cuts in front of him, and puts his hands on the man's shoulders. His lips move, but I can't read them. The man shakes his head, and again I can't make out the words coming from Pastor's lips, but his eyes look sad, like someone just took his last breath or something.

"Eric Calhoun." The associate principal steps out of his office with Ms. Hornwell by his side. "Is your parent here?"

"Well—"

Pastor Charles steps back in and waves his hand. "I'm here for Eric," he says.

"Come on in." The principal looks at Pastor Charles then back to me. "Both of you."

When we step into the office, the temperature drops right away. It's freezing cold. I rub my fingers over my bare arms.

"Take a seat," the principal says and gestures toward two chairs.

The seat is cushioned but hard and uncomfortable. The back is short and erect, so I have to sit up extra straight. There's no way to lean, no way to slouch. It's like the chair is already punishment.

"That was quite a fight," the principal says.

I drop my head, and Pastor Charles clears his throat, which I know is his way of saying make eye contact. So I look up, but I'm only pretending to look at the principal. Really, I'm staring out of the window behind him at the cars still in the parking lot.

"What started it?"

"Well," I take in a deep breath, "Layla got mad at me, and when she walked away, she bumped into Paco."

"Layla who?"

"Layla Everest. She's one of The Refugees." I twist my hand in my lap.

"Did you say Everest?" Pastor Charles turns sideways in his chair, his long legs somehow angled backwards. He leans in close to me. "Layla Everest?"

"Yes," I say. "Why?"

Pastor Charles holds up a finger and opens his mouth, but no words come out. He turns back to face the principal.

The principal looks back and forth from me to Pastor Charles to Ms. Hornwell.

He picks up his notebook and pen. "Is there something we should know about this Layla?"

# CHAPTER 14

"You know they could have expelled your little narrow behind from school, don't you?" Grandma leans forward on her recliner, knees bent, feet flat on the floor. "The only thing saved you is that pretty little teacher. Convinced the principal you all could work it out in that Refugee club."

The last time I saw her sitting like this, we had just found out the car wouldn't start, and we were stuck in New Orleans. Stuck. With the traffic all going one direction, and the storm on its way. But that day, her head was bent down, her face between her knees like she was going to vomit. Now, she's leaning forward with her elbows on her thighs, her head up, staring at me, her eyes squinting like she's trying to get them to focus.

"I just don't understand what's gotten into you lately," says Pastor Charles. "I mean, first lying. Now fighting." He is pacing the room, his hands moving with his words, up on lying, down on fighting.

"Lying?" Grandma turns toward Pastor Charles. "What has he been lying about?"

My stomach tightens. My eyes zoom in on Pastor Charles. He stops walking, stops dead in his tracks like a cat scared by headlights, and for a second he stares at me like he wants me to help him out. I bite my lip and think about what I'm gonna say when Grandma finds out I had the album all along or when she hears my story about the things I've been seeing.

"Charles Ray?"

He puts his hands on his face and pulls at his cheeks so they sag like an old man's. It's the first time I see him as old—old as Grandma. And I don't know why I expected an old man to understand anything about me anyway.

"It's nothing, Ruth." He avoids her eyes.

I look down at my hands, trying to think of something to say.

"One of you is going to tell me what's going on," Grandma says. Her eyes land on me. Even with my head down, I can feel her staring.

"Ruth, it's nothing. Just a little thing that happened on the trip home."

"What little thing? We're keeping secrets now? After all these years?"

"Ruth—" Pastor Charles starts pacing again. He taps his fingers on his cheek and looks at Grandma over the frame of his glasses.

"Well—"

"It's nothing. The boy just lied and said he had eaten raw oysters with you and liked them." He pauses and takes in a deep breath, and for a second when he closes his eyes, I think he must be looking at himself somehow. He shakes his head, and I realize I'm shaking mine too, only in slow motion. "I blew a Grant on the things. That's all."

"A Grant, hanh?" Grandma grunts. "Charles Ray, you know full well I don't eat oysters." On her way back to her room, she mumbles, "Who ever heard of spending fifty dollars on oysters for two people."

Pastor Charles looks at me real quiet a few seconds. Without saying a thing, he picks up his car keys and heads to the door. He don't say come on, but I follow anyway. I have no idea where he's going, but

I figure the best thing to do right now is give Grandma some space because if she comes out of her room and it's just me, I have a lot of explaining to do—which might include having to lie to cover Pastor Charles's lie that just covered my lie. And I want to avoid that as long as possible.

As soon as we get to the door, Grandma calls out, "I wasn't born yesterday, Charles Ray."

He stops a long time, just standing in front of the door like he's thinking of turning around to talk it all out. But then he just exhales long and hard, walks out, and closes the door softly behind him.

"What'd you do that for?" I ask in the car.

"What?"

"You lied."

Pastor Charles pulls into the parking lot of a gas station. "There's a lot of things you don't understand."

"So explain it then. You say you're mad at me for lying. Now you're lying. So why's that okay?"

Pastor Charles clicks his tongue. "It's not okay. But it is complicated."

"So you believe me? Is that why you lied?"

He looks straight ahead at nothing. There's nothing there but the brick wall of the building, not even a person walking by.

"Tell me again. About what you saw," he says.

So I tell him everything all over again—about the dark room with the kerosene lamps, the man reading the article, the map on the table, the teenage Grandma, teenage him, and even how somebody said Grandma was always the one getting in trouble. He chuckles a little at that.

"Yep," he says, "she was. But you couldn't know that no matter what you found."

"I'm telling you I was there."

"That's impossible." He glances at me a second before shifting the car to reverse. "What's in the room again? Before you end up somewhere else, I mean. What's there?"

I describe the table, even down to its thick curved legs and mismatched chairs. I describe the map with its red and blue ink, yellow and green highlights. The articles framed on the walls. The wedding photo behind the backless bookcase.

Pastor Charles bites his lip and checks the rearview mirror to make sure no one's behind him. "We're going back," he says.

———

The best thing about me getting suspended is that Pastor Charles is talking to me again. The worst thing is that Grandma's not talking to him, and Layla's speaking to Neil and Jake but not me, and Ms. Hornwell and the principal made Paco and his friends join The Refugees. I don't know which of those things is the worst thing. They're all pretty bad.

"What happened with you and Layla?" Jake walks up to me in the library.

I'm skipping out on The Refugees meeting again, trying to find information about Uncle Clarence. The librarian showed me how to search old articles using the school's newspaper archive, and I'm sliding a film onto the microfiche machine when he walks up.

"Homegirl said you're a jerk."

"Yeah, pretty much."

I turn the knob to focus the image.

He pulls a stool over and sits down. "I tried to tell her you've just been working on some big project, trying to find stuff for the story you're writing, you know?"

I lean in closer to the screen. "Thanks, man."

"But she said she don't give a care about what you're working on or about you either."

I wince and turn to face Jake. "There's got to be a way to make things right with her."

"So what happened?"

"I don't know," I say. "I was dealing with some stuff going on at home, and she came up on me asking questions." I pause and close my eyes. I'm trying to remember what actually did happen. "Nah, she just wanted to know how I was doing, why I wasn't hanging out with y'all, you know?"

Jake nods. "Yeah, we been missing you."

I look at him a long time because I'm taking his words in, and they feel new. I ain't never had nobody except Pastor Charles tell me they miss me. "I just kind of lost it. Said some things I didn't mean, like—"

"Whoa! What's with dude's face, yo?" Jake points to the screen.

I turn around, and the news article is zoomed in real close. "Oh my God. That's him." I lean in. It's a mugshot of Uncle Clarence, and his face is bloody, barely recognizable.

"That's who?"

"My grandmother's uncle."

"What happened to him?"

"I don't know."

I turn the knob to zoom out and read the headline out loud. "New Orleans NAACP Branch President, Clarence Calhoun, Arrested in Clarke County."

"Where's that?"

"Says here in Mississippi, 1955." I keep reading. "Shubuta strikes again but not quite. Many say Clarence Calhoun is lucky to be alive in the town most known for its lynchings. According to Calhoun, there was no 'Colored Only' sign, but when he stepped out of the outdoor restroom of a local gas station, two men attacked him with crowbars." The last word comes out like I'm asking a question.

"They beat him like that for going to the bathroom?" Jake shakes his head. "Man, that's sick."

We look at each other a few seconds in shock. I turn and read a little more.

"The county sheriff is reported to have said Calhoun is an educated nigger and should have known better than to relieve himself in a white man's toilet. 'He's lucky I arrested him before they strung him up on the Shubuta Bridge,' the sheriff said."

"For going to the restroom?"

I read more. "The NAACP has hired Attorney Thurgood Marshall to handle Calhoun's case."

"This kind of stuff really happened? To real people?"

I slouch on my stool. "It really did," I whisper, not to answer Jake but just to take it all in.

Jake looks like he's seen a ghost. I feel sick to my stomach. We sit for a while and stare at the screen. It's different from the pictures in the history books where everything looks like a staged photo or painting. And even if there was a picture like this, which I ain't never seen in my life, it still would feel different now because Uncle Clarence is someone I know. Well, sort of. I can hear his voice in my head saying, "Be willing to be defaced if you have to." Up until this moment, I figured he did something to cause that beating, but all he did was pee somewhere he wasn't supposed to. Ain't no way going to the bathroom is worth all that.

I lean forward and take in every detail. It's hard to look at this photo, harder than it was to look at him in person. It looks like it was taken right after the beating, when the blood was still seeping out. His lip is half detached, and the fleshy meat of his cheek is completely exposed. His eyes bulge out of sunken sockets, and even though the picture is black and white, it's easy to see that the tears flowing from his eyes are bloody.

When the bell rings, I jump. It's the bell that says if you don't have approved after-school activities, you have to leave the building.

"Come on," Jake says. "We gotta get to writing club."

He heads to the door, but I press print and walk real slow to the librarian's desk.

"Better hurry," Jake says before he walks out. "I'll save you a seat next to Layla."

When I get to the desk, Ms. Adler smiles. She's a short lady with a round head, buzz cut, and a heart-shaped tattoo right under her earlobe. Nothing about her says librarian except the eyeglasses with a beaded strap. She pulls the article from the printer and hands it to me.

"I remember that happening," she says. "I was in fourth grade, and this picture was blasted all over the place."

While she's talking, my eyes drift outside the glass doors. I see Layla and Neil walk past, holding hands.

"The NAACP won that case, you know?" She taps the page. "Seven years later."

My stomach's in knots, and I don't know if it's because I'm thinking of Uncle Clarence being in jail seven years for using a toilet or because I wish I was the one holding Layla's hand. Whatever it is, I decide I'm not going to writing club today.

"I think I'm gonna do more research, if that's okay."

"Oh, of course," Ms. Adler says. "I'll be here a while longer. You'll find more if you check the cards. I'm still working on getting everything in the computer database. It's a slow process." She steps back from behind the counter. "Here, let me show you."

I follow her back to the reading room, and she goes over to a cabinet about chest high with small drawers. "It's a card catalog, kind of like a dictionary," she says. "Just use the words on the front of the drawer like guide words. Calhoun—" She runs her fingers along a few drawers then stops. "Ah, here. You see? This drawer says Britain through Columbia. That's B-R through C-O, so Calhoun would be in here."

She opens the drawer then runs her fingers back past a few labels: Britain, Brown, Brussels, Calhoun. "Here you go," she says. "There's a lot here. See? All of this." She folds her index finger and thumb around a set of cards half an inch thick between the labels Calhoun and Caesar. "These little numbers down here, that's where the codes are for the microfiche films. You can find related search terms too, right there on the very bottom."

I nod, taking it all in. When she leaves, I realize I don't even know where to start. When I searched the computer, I found only one entry, and that one was about Uncle Clarence getting arrested. But all of this? I'm reading through the cards like I'm reading a novel or something. News about this man has been published in the *Crisis* magazine, the *New York Times, Jackson Free Press*, the *Times Picayune, Louisiana Weekly*. I'm scanning the related subjects too. There's *NAACP, desegregation, Thurgood Marshall, justice, KKK, Supreme Court, Martin Luther King Jr., SNCC*. And on the last card I look at, right next to *SNCC*, there's *Ruth Calhoun*.

"No way!" I take out a piece of paper and write down the microfiche number. The article title is "Calhoun, Leader of Ole Miss SNCC, Denied Degree."

I go back to Ms. Adler to sign out the film.

"You're a Calhoun too, right?" She holds the film up to the light and squints.

"Yes, ma'am."

"Such a rich legacy. Is Ruth your grandmother?"

She says Ruth like she's been knowing her all her life. I nod.

"My father helped get all those kids out of jail, but then when they found out about Ruth's pregnancy—" She pauses and shakes her head. "It's just a shame what those Eastmores tried to do." She hands me the film, careful not to touch it with her finger. "But I'm sure she's told you all that."

"Yeah," I say and fake a slight laugh, pretending to know exactly what she's talking about.

When I turn to walk away, she's still talking out loud.

"And that Joseph boy—well, he's an old man by now. To think he never even got a chance to meet his daughter."

# CHAPTER 15

"But why do you have to go back to New Orleans now? It's less than a week before Christmas." Grandma follows Pastor Charles out to the car, trying to work her arm into her jacket. "I already started prepping Christmas dinner. Baked the cornbread and grinded up gizzards for the dressing. I done boiled the turkey necks already, even peeled shrimp for the mirliton. And the ham's already thawing in the fridge."

He's carrying a large duffle bag and a small suitcase. "Go ahead and get the dinner ready. We'll be back in time."

"I just don't understand why you and Eric are going out there again so soon. If you wait until after Christmas, I can slice up the leftover ham and make sandwiches for the road."

"Oh?" He looks at her a long time. "That sounds good, but ham's got nothing on your chicken salad."

"Well, I can't make chicken salad around the holiday, Charles Ray. There's too much to do."

"I'm just teasing, Ruth." Pastor Charles sits his bags in the bed of the truck and pulls his long trench coat closed. "The truth is, I need to check on Zion. The contractor called trying to add another six thousand dollars for new piping, and the insurance adjuster says there's no need. Besides, I had Deacon Jackson drive past your house, and he said the work's no further than when we left, and your second check was cut almost a month ago. And—" He's talking with his hands again. "They're saying they need more money before putting the new cabinets up in my house. Something about unexpected mold." When he says more money, he stretches his arms wide like he's wrapping them around a big ball. "The insurance company's first payment was supposed to cover the mold treatment. These contractors are scamming people, Ruth."

"Well, I can't send you off with no food." Grandma zips her jacket and drops her head like she's tucking her chin in the collar.

It's one of the few cold days we've had all winter, and I'm bouncing back from one foot to the other trying to warm up.

"There are some nice restaurants on the way, and the hotel has food too."

"You're going to drop another Grant on some oysters?" Grandma smirks and tilts her head a little to the side.

"Please let's not go there again." Pastor wraps his arms around her and lets his chin rest on her head a second. When he lets her go, he holds on to her hands a second longer. "I did apologize."

"Yes, you did. But truth is I still don't know the truth. That's why I think I'll go too." She turns around and heads back to the front door, talking the whole way there. "Let me just turn off the sweet potatoes. I can go ahead and put those in the fridge and just finish when we get back. No sense in you and Eric going out there alone again."

Pastor Charles looks at me, his mouth slightly open. I shrug my shoulders. We both thought leaving after Grandma started meal prepping was a surefire way to make sure she didn't invite herself along, especially since she invited Wilbur, Charlotte, and Scarlet over for Christmas dinner. But I can hear in her voice that she's made up her mind, and there ain't no stopping Grandma once that happens. Exactly what we're gonna do when we get there is beyond me. I put my suitcase and backpack in the truck, right next to Pastor's, and go back inside.

I've been doing research for over two weeks, but I ain't share it with nobody, not even with Pastor Charles. I'm afraid if I do, he'll be back to thinking I'm just making up stuff based on what I found. I even found a picture of Grandma with that Angela Davis Afro and big hoop earrings. It was taken the night of her arrest, and it's all members of the SNCC—twelve Black kids with Afros of varying lengths and one white kid who looks terrified to be involved. His name's not even listed in the caption, just the Black kids, the twelve who got arrested. I don't bring none of that up though, because at least Pastor Charles is trying to believe me, and I don't want nothing to set him back to his unbelief.

"Now Eric," he'd said, "there are certain things I don't want no part in going back to. So, if what you're saying is true, we have to be careful what we touch in there." Pastor Charles and I never talk about our plans when we are at the house. It's always when we go out, because he's even more afraid than I am that Grandma will overhear something and get to acting crazy again. She's been seeming real sane with him around all the time. Even the few days she didn't talk to him, she wasn't on edge like usual. So the mysterious room and our plan to see what we can find is our little secret. I always thought having someone to share a secret with would feel good, but really, it just makes me feel all conflicted inside. For one thing, Grandma is nosier and more suspicious than ever, like she knows something is going on, and that suspicion keeps me feeling nervous, covering almost everything I do, even things that probably don't need covering. The other thing is, it's weird having a secret with Pastor Charles and seeing him nervous and jumpy all the time, like he's holding a loaded gun and thinks he might accidentally pull the trigger at any moment.

It's not helping that I ain't slept well since that conversation with Ms. Adler. I used to be so preoccupied with figuring out who my daddy is. Now, it's all about my grandfather, who I hardly ever wondered about before. But I'm so close to an answer I can feel it. Ms. Adler's words keep coming back to me: that Eastmore boy never met his daughter. I figure Grandma's protest got her arrested and then expelled, and that's how she and my grandfather split up. Only I don't see the name Eastmore showing up in none of the articles about Grandma. And then there's the one part I can't make sense of at all. Ms. Adler said it was a shame what that Eastmore family tried to do. But what did they try to do? That's what I want to know, and it don't look like there's an article to be found about that. Everything that mentions an Eastmore is about some old guy, a white racist senator. He didn't seem to be a bad man, just ignorant is all. He really believed in keeping everything separate between the races, and I know Grandma went to Ole Miss as part of a movement to keep the college integrated. That's what Uncle Clarence said that first night I saw him, the night the kerosene lamps flickered in his eyes. So I can't imagine being related to someone who thought like that Eastmore senator. No, there can't be no connection to him. But a young Eastmore? Someone who might be my mother's father? That's possible. Only I can't find a thing that proves it.

Maybe Ms. Adler got the name wrong. Even if she did, she sparked a curiosity in me. If I ever get back in that mysterious room, I plan to look for something that can take me to Ole Miss back in the late '60s, when Grandma got pregnant and arrested and went from a fun and sassy teenager to Crazy Ruth.

"Charles Ray, maybe on your way back, we can go visit Charlese and your mother in Baton Rouge."

"We'll see. That would be nice, actually."

"Do you remember the first time I went to your house for dinner?" Grandma laughs. "Your mama cooked up a storm—gumbo and potato salad, red beans and rice, cornbread and candied yams, ham and pork roast, and the pies. My, my, my—"

"She was quite the cook. For a long time. Until—" His voice trails off as though he walked away, but he's right behind the steering wheel.

"Yes, she was, and that's why I had her teach me. Every time I came home from school, I went to your mother's to learn to cook. Sure did! Oh, I remember the first time I brought one of those sweet potato pies to Mrs. Eastmore. She paid me double." Grandma laughs, then mumbles something under her breath I can't hear.

I lean forward. Grandma cranes her neck left like she's checking the side mirror on Pastor's side. "Be careful. Watch that car," she says. "I don't know why that's coming to me now. I guess it's because I been cooking up a storm myself, and I still smell the sweet potatoes, like they're stuck in my nose."

Pastor Charles is quiet. He turns the radio on, but it's all static.

"Grandma, who's Mrs. Eastmore?"

Grandma looks back at me like she just remembered I'm in the truck. "A filthy rich, God-awful—"

"Now Ruth," Pastor taps her hand.

She clears her throat, rubs her hands on her thighs like she's smoothing down a skirt. "She was a senator's wife. I used to work for the family."

"Did they have kids?" I'm thinking, *Did they have a son?* but I just say kids because that feels safe.

Grandma pauses a long time.

Pastor's eyes rise to the rearview mirror and back to the road again.

"You know, there's much better memories than that." Grandma presses the knob to stop the radio on an old gospel station. "Like the time we stayed up half the night playing Spades and found that pecan pie in your mother's freezer."

Pastor laughs. "Mama was so mad."

"Looking back, we should have known it was for something special, the way she had it wrapped all pretty."

"We ate the whole thing," Pastor's voice rumbles real deep, deeper than usual.

"No," Grandma taps her thighs twice. "We saved two pieces for your parents. That's how we got caught so fast."

They both laugh at that, and at the same time they say, "Young and dumb. Yes, Lord."

They're still laughing when we cross into Louisiana. Right away, we hear sirens behind us. Pastor Charles raises his head and looks in the rearview mirror. I turn all the way around in my seat and look behind me.

"Boy, are you crazy? Face forward. You don't want trouble with the cops." Grandma's voice shifts from silly to snappy in a split second.

I turn back around and lean forward. "Are they stopping you, Pastor Charles?"

"Sit back boy. Shoulders straight." Grandma straightens her own shoulders. "And put on your seatbelt. Lord, have mercy, we don't want no trouble with the cops."

Pastor Charles looks from his speedometer and back to the rearview mirror. "He can't be pulling me over. I'm five under the speed limit."

"Are you sure?"

"Ruth, I've been driving this highway a long time. Yes, I'm sure."

Grandma turns her head slightly away from him. She grips her shoulders and presses her fingers into the soft tissue.

"I'm sorry, Ruth." Pastor Charles shifts into the right lane. "I don't mean to snap at you. It's just—"

The police car moves behind him. There ain't many cars on the road at all. If the officer was heading after someone else, he would have kept going.

"I know, Charles Ray. I already know." Grandma's sigh is exaggerated.

"I'm pulling over," Pastor Charles says. "He's definitely stopping me."

Grandma sits up in her seat and leans forward, massaging her shoulders. "Peace be still," she says, just a little above a whisper.

Pastor Charles puts the car in park and reaches into the middle console for his wallet. He places it on the dashboard.

"Ruth, open the glove compartment and pull out that black document holder, please."

Grandma unfastens her seatbelt and leans forward. Just then, the officer taps on the window. Grandma freezes in place.

Pastor Charles lowers the window. "Good evening, officer." He puts his hands on the steering wheel.

The officer grunts something that sounds like an affirmation and peeks his head so far into the window Pastor Charles has to move his seat back a bit.

"Why don't you have your seatbelt on?" His eyes fall on Grandma.

"I just unhooked it after we stopped," Grandma says. "To reach for the registration."

"And where is it?"

"It's still in the glove compartment," Grandma says.

The officer stands up and smiles. He taps his fingers on his gun. "What are you hiding in here?"

"Sir, would you like my license and registration?" Pastor Charles taps his thumbs on the steering wheel.

"I'd like to see what you hidin' in this car."

"With all due respect, officer, I do not give my consent to a search."
Pastor Charles's fingers are trembling. Grandma sits back in her seat.
The officer laughs a little, smacks his gum. "License, registration,
proof of insurance."

Pastor Charles reaches for his wallet, which sits just a little above
the steering wheel. He takes out his license and passes it to the officer.
Grandma reaches forward to open the glove compartment, but before
she can open it, the officer draws his gun and points it inside.

"Watch what you're doing, pretty lady."

Grandma freezes again. Her hand is trembling.

"Officer, the registration is in the glove compartment." Pastor
Charles keeps his hands on the wheel but turns his head slightly toward the officer. From where I'm sitting, it looks like his eyes are staring right down that barrel. My heart's beating so fast my chest hurts.

"That's what I don't get. She says she was out of her seatbelt to get
the registration. But now, she still has to get the registration? That
don't compute."

I lean forward a little bit. I can see the officer's badge. Number 548.
I say the numbers to myself three times. Grandma snaps her head to
the side and looks at me with narrow eyes. She makes a kind of hissing
sound.

"Well, who do we have back here?" His head is in the vehicle again.
He points the gun toward me like it's a flashlight. Grandma lets out a
short scream and pushes her back firm against the seat.

Pastor Charles's words come out sounding forced, like his lips are
still closed. "Officer, do I have permission to secure my registration
and insurance papers for you?"

"Well, I never stopped you."

"Could you please put your gun back in your holster?"

"Now, that's something I don't think I can do until I know I'm safe."
Badge 548 stands tall again, still holding his gun. "See, I don't know
what you're about to try to do, but I suspect it's not the right thing."

"Ruth, open the glove compartment, please." Grandma pulls the handle, and the door opens downward.

"You see officer, there's just papers in there. My registration and insurance are in that black folder on top."

"Go ahead."

Pastor Charles leans right, lifts his hand from the steering wheel.

"Not you. Her." The officer nods toward Grandma.

Grandma clears her throat and pulls the folder out. She opens it and pulls out two papers. "That's registration and proof of insurance," she says.

548 takes both and walks back to his car. I exhale real deep and realize I have to pee so bad it hurts.

Pastor Charles rotates his shoulders, cracks his neck. But he don't say a word.

"Charles Ray?"

He's quiet.

"It's almost over, Charles Ray."

Grandma's hands are trembling, but she leans left and puts her trembling hand on his.

"I don't even know what he pulled me over for." He finally speaks. "All that talking, and I don't even know why he stopped me."

When 548 returns, he hands Pastor Charles a ticket. "You were going 70 in a 65."

"Sir, I started slowing down as soon as I crossed into Louisiana. I'm sure of it. When you pulled me over, I was all the way down to 60."

"Well, you can take it to court, if you want to." He pulls a pen from his pocket. "Sign here, and you're free to go."

Pastor Charles looks down at the ticket. "It says speeding and seat-belt violation."

"That's right."

Pastor Charles sighs.

"Signing is just indicating you received the ticket. If you disagree, like I said, just take it to court. I'll be ready for you." Badge 548 smiles again.

Pastor Charles signs the ticket and hands it back to 548. "Am I free to go?" The words come out slow, like he's forcing them one by one, having a conversation with each one in between.

548 nods. "Y'all have a nice evening. I'd be careful if I was you."

When the officer goes back to his vehicle, Pastor Charles just sits a while. His hands tremble on the wheel, and when he finally speaks, his voice cracks. "That wasn't called for, Ruth. You know that wasn't."

"You did well, Charles Ray."

"We shouldn't have to be scared like that." Pastor Charles is speaking through clenched teeth. "Why is this still happening?"

Grandma looks out her window. "It's been worse," she says.

I can hear Pastor Charles breathing. The officer's still sitting behind us. After a while, he flashes his lights but leaves the siren on silent.

"I don't think he's leaving before we do," I say.

Pastor pulls off slowly, and 548 follows him back onto the interstate. For a long time, he stays right behind us. Every time Pastor gets over, he does too.

"Just stay in the same lane," Grandma says, "before he makes up another excuse to pull us over." There's something about the way she says *us* that stays with me.

When 548 finally takes an exit, Pastor Charles takes the next one and pulls over to the side of the road.

"What's wrong, Charles Ray?"

He steps out, walks over to the shoulder, bends his tall body almost in half, and vomits into the grass.

548. 548. 548. I repeat the numbers in my head, but I don't say them out loud. Just making sure I remember.

# CHAPTER 16

Other than the weather being cold, the city don't feel like much has changed since our last time home. It's been four months since the storm, and it's just about a ghost town almost everywhere we go. Some neighborhoods look like no one's been back at all. The houses look lonely. That's the only way I can think to describe it. There's a look a house has when someone's been inside to check on it, and there's a look a house has when ain't nobody been around. On those houses, the waterline is solid from the front door to the frame and siding beside it. But when that door has been opened, when people have stepped inside, the waterline has just a tiny bit of space. For some reason, I notice this, and every time I see a house up close that no one has checked on, I feel sad.

Grandma keeps saying, "Oh, Lord. Look at that." She's pointing and gasping and repeating, "It looks like a war zone here. It's so much worse than on the news."

"I didn't really want you to see it like this, Ruth. Thought it might be too much." Pastor Charles puts his hand on her hand. I'm noticing they're doing this hand-holding thing a lot more often.

Grandma pinches her nose, "And that smell. It's so awful."

I want to say *It's better than it was,* but what's the point in that? I don't need Grandma getting all concerned about what I've seen or smelled for that matter.

When we turn on Carrollton Avenue to head to Zion, I look for the peach-and-yellow house. I'm wondering if that dog is still there. It turns out when we pass that house, it's the only one on the block that's being fixed up. All the windows are open, and I can see that the inside is completely without walls, just wooden beams like a naked skeleton. And yet, two men are on the porch scrubbing the outside of the house with yard brooms. I don't know what they're using, but whatever it is, it's not cutting through those spray-painted markings. One of the men pauses and wipes his forehead with the back of his hand. He steps back and takes a good look at his work, shakes his head, and gets right back to it.

It's different pulling in Zion this time because there's no one following behind us. Pastor Charles parks next to a truck in the parking lot with buckets in the back and ladders strapped to the top.

"Good. Contractor's here." He steps out and walks around to open Grandma's door, but she just sits a long time like she's glued to the seat or something. He holds his hand out to help her climb down.

We walk to the bottom step of the sanctuary and look up. "The elevator's not working right now. No electricity. I'm thinking you don't want to climb those steps." Pastor Charles looks at Grandma over his glasses.

Grandma shakes her head.

Pastor takes his keys out and walks to his office door. There's a new door up, but it's propped open, so we just walk in. The walls are nothing but studs. No sheetrock. No insulation. It's hard to tell where the office ends and the hall begins.

"Oh, Charles Ray," Grandma says, almost like a small child. She stands still and turns her body in a circle, looking around like one wall would show something different from another.

It's clean in here now. If Grandma had seen the desk falling apart or the photos crashing from the walls or the mold growing high and thick in the corners, I don't know if she could have taken it.

"Hello?" Pastor Charles calls out.

We hear voices coming from the kitchen area, so we follow them. The contractors are there, looking over a blueprint, and when they see Pastor, they look up and smile.

"Pastor!"

"Brothers." Pastor extends his hand.

One of the men wipes his dusty hand on his pants but then declines a handshake. "When we have running water, and I can clean my hands, then I can greet you the respectable way."

Pastor nods. "So, tell me about these pipes." He puts his hands on his hips and looks around.

The man who seems to be in charge walks him over to the exposed pipes behind where the kitchen sink used to be and explains that they are rusting out. "See these rust spots?" He points. "They are going to leak, one by one. And you can't fix pipes like these. All you can do is clog a leak. It'll just add pressure somewhere else, and whoosh! Another leak."

"Why won't the insurance company cover this?"

"It's not hurricane damage. It's just aging. When they built these buildings back in the '50s, they didn't know the steel would rust out like this. They were just trying to get away from lead piping."

Pastor sighs, ends it with a low whistle. "You know we barely have income coming in right now. I can't pay what the insurance company's not covering."

"It's less expensive to change them out now, while the walls are open. I'll tell you what—" The man pulls Pastor Charles to the side, and they turn their backs so the rest of the conversation is muffled.

Grandma walks back toward Pastor's office, and I follow her. It's like walking in a maze no one wants to play in. When she gets to his office, she leans her weight against a beam of the doorway.

"You know," she says. "I didn't know how I would feel when we got here, but truth is, it just feels so matter of fact. So what? The building's destroyed. We're here. We made it out alive. That's everything, Eric. That's absolutely everything."

Our hotel suite has two connected rooms with a sofa area and small kitchen in between. Grandma and I are in one room, and Pastor Charles is in the other. I wake up to the sound of Grandma singing in the kitchen. "I don't feel no ways tired." She bellows out the word *tired*, and Pastor and I show up in our bedroom doorways at the same time just to look at her. "I've come too far from where I started from." Grandma is standing in front of several plates: one with pancakes, another with bacon, a third with eggs, and a fourth with grits.

"Well, you're in a good mood." Pastor Charles's morning voice is deep and raspy.

"I went downstairs and got you sleepyheads some breakfast," Grandma says. She's dishing food from the plates like she's fixing it right out of a pot. When she has a plate with everything prepared, she holds it up. "This is for you, Charles Ray." Then, she turns to me. "You're next." And she goes right back to singing. "Nobody told me the road would be easy, and I don't believe he brought me this far to leave me."

Pastor Charles smiles and walks back into the bedroom. "I'll be out in a minute," he calls back.

But I have my eye on that bacon, and I go straight to the tiny little table and sit down. Grandma sits a plate in front of me, and she don't even ask if I washed my hands.

Grandma hums the whole drive to our neighborhood, but once we turn on our block, she stops. I hear a small whimper come out, and she cranes her head out of the window like she's trying to make sure she's seeing clearly.

Mostly everything looks the same as a few weeks ago, except Shelia's house is painted and the Nguyen's house is too. Every other house still has the spray-painted X's and waterlines. The debris outside's not piled as high as it was, but there's still a lot of carpet pulled to the road, and the refrigerators and freezers are at the curb up and down the block. Most of the furniture has been hauled off or broken down into smaller pieces though. There's a big dumpster on the side of Neil's house, and it's filled with stuff.

Pastor Charles pulls in front of our house and parks the truck. This time, when he walks around to help Grandma out, she's totally stiff. It's like she's trying to tell her body to move, but nothing's happening.

"Come on, Ruth. You said it was time for you to see it."

"Oh my God, Charles Ray. I didn't know it was this bad."

The house looks about the same as it did in November. No progress except that someone hauled off the porch steps, which is a strange thing to take away first. The refrigerator and freezer are still out front, and so is a bunch of wet carpet, and the velvet recliner, now covered in mildew. There's still a big gaping space where the oak tree had fallen. The wood beams are snapped in random places, and without the steps and porch in place, it's hard to see what the house used to be, impossible to imagine it ever coming back to what it once was. A blue tarp is spread out on the grass instead of covering the house. We can see men working inside, removing the broken beams. One of them is pointing at what should be the ceiling when we walk in.

"Gentlemen." Pastor Charles lowers his head out of habit as if the low doorframe is still there.

"Buenos dias!" A man in suspenders and a white t-shirt steps forward. "¿Su casa?" He smiles like he just offered us dessert.

"It's my house." Grandma steps forward. "I'm Ruth Calhoun."

"Ah, Señorita Ruth." Another man walks up. This one has on a yellow hard hat and a bright orange vest. "I'm Hector, the head on this project. We spoke on the phone."

Grandma walks slowly in the open space, looking up and around. "Ah ha," she says, like she can't find her usual "Nice to meet you."

Hector motions for her to come over to view the blueprints spread across a big worktable. He tells her she has the option to make the front different from how it was before, something about a loft and cathedral ceilings, maybe even a full second story instead of a camelback. I'm thinking this is a good time to wander upstairs. Maybe I can check out my closet and get back before she even finishes her conversation.

Pastor Charles sees me walking off and follows.

"What are you doing?" he says, his teeth clenched.

"I want to see if I can find anything in the closet," I whisper.

"You can't go up there now with her down here. What are you thinking?" He's doing that loud whisper-thing adults do when they want to fuss at you in public.

I feel a real lecture coming on, but Grandma calls out, "Charles Ray!" and that ends that.

He backs away from the staircase, the word *don't* unfolding on his lips. He don't turn around until he's all the way back to Grandma.

My room looks so empty now. The lower half of the sheetrock is gutted. The carpet is gone, and even the baseboards have been ripped out. The bathroom's not so bad. The ceramic held up well at least. It just smells like bleach has been dumped everywhere, but that beats the smell of mold. My eyes burn though. I close the bathroom door, which helps just a little because there's bleach sprayed on the walls and floors of my bedroom too.

I'm thinking about what Pastor Charles said, and I want to listen. But I'm also thinking I need to figure out why I only have these dreams or visions or whatever they are when I'm near my closet. Now that all my clothes are gone, when I step back and look in the closet, it's clear there's no button or trapdoor on that back wall. It's just a wall. There's not even a seam.

I get real close to the wall, down on my knees, and I'm so close I'm practically touching the wall with my nose. I'm moving real slow and pressing real soft because I want to notice exactly where the soft spot is—if that is what it is. In my mind, I'm dividing the wall into one-inch squares, and I'm checking each of them one by one. I'm about six inches up with more than eight feet to go when I hear, "Man, what are you doing?"

I freeze. My neck tightens. It's Neil. Of all people, it's Neil.

I get up real slow, and I'm wondering what I'm gonna tell him to explain this because I am not telling him the truth.

"What are you doing here?" I stand up and turn around.

He's all the way in the closet with me.

"We're at our house working. Been here all week. My grandpa and me, and we saw the truck." He pauses and walks to the window. "With Mama gone, he's thinking of selling the house."

He's quiet a few seconds, like he wants me to say something, but I can't think of words to follow "with Mama gone." So, I just look at him.

"Man, there ain't been nobody back here all week. Shelia's family came through two days ago and painted outside, but then they left." He points over to her house. "From here it looks like it's back to normal, but inside, it's just like all the other houses. Just a bunch of wood and pipes."

"You saw Shelia?"

"Yeah, she was here. Lost a lot of weight. Girl is fine now. Like, on fire, yo." He laughs. "Still Shelia though. Just funny like. She say some dumb stuff."

I narrow my eyes and frown a bit. "You talking about Shelia fine? I thought you were with Layla."

"I'm just saying homegirl fine. That's all I'm saying. She always liked you anyway. Everybody know that."

"Who?"

"Shelia, fool. Who else?"

I exhale because part of me was hoping he'd say Layla, even though I have sense enough to know she's his girl now. "Nah, I don't believe that. Not Shelia. What's up with you and Layla?"

"You know, we just do what we do. Hang out and talk a lot about missing my mama and hating her daddy." He nods and sucks his lip a little. "You the one brought us together. Man, you just went off the map all of a sudden. Layla missed you. Started hanging with me."

I roll my eyes and look at the back wall. I'm wishing I could just walk right through it.

"So thank you man. I really like her." He stands a while looking at the back wall with me like he's expecting something to happen. "Anyway, my grandpa saw the truck, and he wanted to stop by to say hello. Your grandma told me you were here." He gives this little half laugh. "Doing only God knows what is what she said."

ow he wants to crack some Crazy Ruth joke, but he don't.

ome up here, and you kneeling on the floor with your nose

g all over it." He walks deeper into the closet and

from me. "Weird, man."

"Why'd you pretend to be my friend?" I feel my heart beating fast. I just want him to leave.

"What?" Neil scrunches up his face. "What in the world are you talking about?"

"Did you just fake it to get Layla?"

"Man, what the—" He grunts and narrows his eyes. "I wasn't faking anything." He's pacing the closet. "After my mama died, and this city—our city—fell apart, the only thing I had to hold on to was you." He moves real close to me, pokes my shoulder with his index finger. "Then you just, you just left, like I was nothing."

I don't know what to say to that. I'm thinking it through when the words, "I guess that's your excuse for taking Layla," come out of my mouth.

I see Neil ball up his fist, a vein pulsing in his neck. The dimple in his chin hardly shows at all. "I got in a fight with Paco for you and everything. And that was after you started acting like you was too good for us or something. We all fought for you."

"Don't blame me for that. You wanted to fight him anyway."

"But I didn't. Not until he hit you. Then, it was on. And not a moment before that."

"Was it because he hit me? Or was it because he pushed your new girlfriend?"

"Forget you." Neil pushes me hard, like my last words were worse than any I could have said. I stumble into the back wall and hit my head just as Pastor Charles approaches the room and asks, "What's going on up here?"

# CHAPTER 17

There's noise all around—clamoring voices, moving feet, and sliding tables. I'm lying on my back, and all I can see are ceiling tiles and fluorescent lights. The floor is cold against my neck, and my head is throbbing. I try to get up, but someone pushes down my shoulders and puts a knee in my chest.

"You college niggers gettin' younger and younger," a voice says.

The man behind this voice leans over me so close my eyes can't focus. I blink twice and squint. A badge comes into view, number 548. The officer smiles, his lips thin and chapped.

"And dumber and dumber. Burning the Confederate flag." He shifts his weight and forces me to turn over and then stand up.

"I didn't—" I try to speak, but when he tightens handcuffs around my wrists, my throat closes. Inside my head, I'm screaming for Pastor Charles. I think I must be dreaming, but I can't wake myself up.

The officer kicks me behind the right knee and laughs when I stumble. As he pushes me toward a long line of students in cuffs, I see Grandma. She's on the floor, her face down, an officer's knee in the center of her back. He has one hand up her skirt, the other pressing her face to the floor.

I'm almost at the door when this man in a suit and shiny black shoes walks in. He's got a billy club in his hand, and he walks right over to Grandma. The officer pulls her to her feet then turns her to face this suited-up man, his hair slicked down and crossed over to the side like it's covering a bald spot. He gets real close to Grandma, leans in, and whispers something in her ear. I crane my neck trying to see better, trying to hear. Badge 548 pushes against my head. "Ain't nothing back there concerning you. You got enough trouble of your own."

But I look anyway, just long enough to see the man hit Grandma in the face, right along the left side of her mouth. The blood trickles out. All around us white students line up along the walls, just watching. Not one of them's in handcuffs. Everybody cuffed is Black. This one white boy jumps down from the stage, like he's been in shock the whole time and just realized something's going on. He tries to force himself between Grandma and the man. He's yelling something I can't hear, but I can tell he's yelling by the stretch of his mouth. The man slaps him in the face so hard there's a red handprint left on his cheek. Then, the man hands him some keys and points to the door. When the white kid walks away, the man turns around and hits Grandma in the face again. This time, it's the other side, and her eye swells.

I gasp and forget to take another step.

The officer presses hard in my back. "Keep moving."

The white boy turns around and storms toward the man with his fist balled at his side. I'm moving forward but looking back, the officer's fists pressing against my back. When that white man who hit Grandma looks at the boy running his way, the boy freezes. They both stand still a few seconds and stare at each other. The man smiles, and there must be something awful in that smile because the white boy unballs his fist, turns away, and runs straight for the exit.

I'm walking through the door when the white boy pushes past me and almost knocks me down. I follow him with my eyes the whole time Badge 548 is walking me toward the paddy wagon. Right when he's pushing me inside, the white boy gets in a black Maserati and speeds off.

So many of us are crammed in the back of the police vehicle, my shoulders are pressed into the chest of the guy on my right and the shoulder of the girl on my left. There's eleven of us in this one vehicle. Some are pretty beat up but no one as bad as Grandma.

"Where's Ruth?" The girl next to me is the first to speak.

"I don't know, Anne. But dear God I hope they didn't kill her." The girl saying this is the only one without an Afro. She has a short bob instead. No one seems alarmed or shocked at her words, like the possibility of being killed is an everyday thing. A whole bunch of them exhale at one time though, and someone clicks her tongue.

"Me too," Anne says.

"You know they have it in for her." The guy next to me, who has a split lip, is talking with his eyes closed. "I told that girl leave that Eastmore alone. You know he had to be the one to give the cops a heads-up about tonight's protest. Whoever heard of a white boy in the SNCC? And look around. He ain't back here handcuffed with us."

"Shhhhh." The girl with the bob snaps. "You betta act like we don't know nothin' about them."

An officer pushes Grandma into the wagon just then, and everyone gets real quiet and just looks at her. He closes the door, and we hear the lock click.

"I guess your Prince Charming couldn't save you." The words come through raspy but harsh.

Grandma cuts her eyes at the boy with the split lip, but she's quiet. Anne tears off a piece of her shirt and folds it. She hands it to Grandma. "Put this on your lip," she says. "It'll help stop the bleeding."

"Thanks." Grandma presses the cloth softly to her lip, and her eyes roll back like the pain is almost unbearable. Even so, she looks at me, like she's the first one to notice I'm there and don't belong. "Who are you? I ain't never seen you nowhere on campus."

I act like I think maybe she's talking to someone else at first, but then all eyes turn to me. I can say Eric, but I sure can't say Calhoun. That would raise too many questions. The next thing I know, the name coming out of my mouth is Neil Rose.

"Well, I don't know where you came from Neil Rose, but welcome to the SNCC. I'm Ruth Calhoun, the president of our Ole Miss chapter."

---

The jail cell has a cold steel bench that connects on three dark gray cinder block walls. The lights are dim. There's nothing else here. No phone. No toilet.

"If they don't move us out of here," Grandma says, "then they won't keep us long. It's only a holding cell."

"I'm tired of this, man. The white kids protested yesterday, and nothing happened to them. We hold up some Black power fists and ask them to get rid of those Confederate images, and we end up here?" He looks at Grandma a second. "And your face looks like crap Ruth. For what?"

"You didn't have to burn that flag, Titus."

"And you didn't have to sleep with that white boy, Ruth."

Grandma lowers her voice. "Whatever's happening between me and Joseph Eastmore has nothing to do with this." She sits back. "Besides, we're getting married. Right after I graduate in three months. You just wait and see."

There's a whole lot of head shaking then.

"Let me tell you something, Ruth. When we get back to campus, and this here moment is behind us, I'm putting together a petition to remove you as president. You're crossing lines that don't need to be crossed."

"Titus, that's enough," Anne stands to her feet. "We don't need to turn against each other at a time like this."

That night, most of us don't sleep. For one thing, the steel bench is too hard and cold. And then there's the noises—yelling, screaming, and crying and a constant tapping, almost like dripping water but something else.

Early in the morning, Half-face shows up at the cell door with an officer. "By the time y'all finish rescuing these bullheaded protestors, you're gonna be out of money, Clarence."

"We'll do what we have to do," Uncle Clarence says.

"You know we don't want no race mixing here in Mississippi." The officer unlocks the cell, but he don't open it right away. "You got some kids in Ole Miss. Enough is enough." He opens the cell, but none of us move. "You coloreds asking for too much, ought to appreciate the chance to go to one of the finest institutions in the South."

"Are the kids free to go?" Uncle Clarence narrows his eyes at the deputy, but he don't say nothing against his last words.

"Y'all come on out," the officer says. "And I don't want to see y'all back in here again. Next time, you might not get out so soon."

I don't know where I'm going, and I keep hoping I end up back in my closet at any moment, even if that does put me face-to-face with Neil again. But nothing happens. It's like this time, I'm stuck on the other side.

There's Black people in a few cars lined up outside the jail to take us back to campus, and the students split up and get into cars like they know the drill.

Grandma turns to me, "Neil Rose, why don't you ride with me and my uncle?"

We get in Uncle Clarence's town car. I sit in the back, and Grandma sits in the front.

"Ruth, there's something I have to tell you."

Grandma turns, the cut running from her left cheek to the corner of her mouth is still fleshy and wet looking.

"They're not gonna let you graduate."

"What?" Grandma almost jumps out of her seat. "That's not right, Uncle Clarence. I finished my program in the fall. I'm just taking extra courses right now." Her voice is elevated an octave, each syllable cut short with a gasp for air.

"The word is Senator Eastmore's out to get you. You know he's a big donor, and it's thought he's got something to do with the halt on your degree."

Grandma shakes her head.

"Is there something I should know about?"

"No sir," Grandma says. "Nothing at all."

They are quiet a long time.

"We can try to see the president in person," he finally says. "But I've spoken to him twice, and his mind seems made up." He parks the vehicle in a parking lot beside a red brick building with what looks like twenty windows on the side. "Neil, do you want me to drop you off closer to Baxter Hall? I assume that's where you're staying? Or do you want to get out here by the Lyceum?"

I don't know the difference between Baxter Hall and the Lyceum, so I just say it's fine to drop me off right where we are. We all get out, and I follow them to the front of the building. It has huge white columns and a white door that looks like something from a movie. Before Uncle Clarence and Grandma turn to go in, Uncle Clarence stops walking. He extends his hand to me. "I'm sorry for not doing a proper introduction. I was unraveled when I picked you all up. But look," he pauses and looks around, "keep up the good work. Our people need young people like you to keep fighting for equality." He says these last words in almost a whisper. Then he puts his arm around Grandma's waist and escorts her into the building.

I'm trying to stall, so I walk real slow to the other side of the building. I notice gashes and holes in the brick, and I remember something about this from my readings in Ms. Hornwell's class. I place my index finger in each gash one by one. There are so many.

"Amazing history," someone says.

I jump and turn around to find a lawn man standing nearby, holding a rake, shards of grass splattered all over his clothing.

"Name's Kevin," he says. "I never seen you around here, and ain't that many of us." He points to the back of his hand when he says "us" and I know what he means. "This ain't no kinda place for a runaway. That's what you is, ain't ya?"

I figure only two things can come from this conversation. One, I tell him I'm not a runaway and he leaves me alone, but I still have no place to stay. Two, I tell him I am a runaway, and he tries to figure out how to help me get back home and maybe he finds me a place to sleep until I get there.

"Yessir, but I—"

He puts up his hand. "Listen, son. I don't know what ya runnin' from, but you must don't have nowhere to go if you showed up here." He looks around. "I tell you what. Meet me right here after dark. I got somebody can take you in for a while."

---

"Well, Kevin. Good to see you."

She's no taller than me and thin with a small belly and slightly hunched shoulders. Her head is covered with a red scarf, and her skin is a deep brown. She smiles at me with evenly spaced, dark-stained teeth.

"Mama Evelyn, this here is Neil Rose. He's a runaway."

"Well, what'cha runnin' from?" She says this as she opens the door wide to let us in. The screen door slams behind us and rattles on its hinges.

I don't answer, and she don't really seem to care, like she's used to taking in stray kids or something.

"Come on to the kitchen. Let's get some food in that skinny body of yourn."

The kitchen is small and dingy, but the food smells like Grandma's cooking, and I realize I'm hungry.

Mama Evelyn piles greens and rice on a plate and adds a huge slice of cornbread. The food's so good I almost forget I'm stuck somewhere I don't want to be. There's a big pig tail in the greens. It sticks to my fingers when I pick it up, and when I bite into it a little bit of salty juice squirts into my mouth. I close my eyes and chew like my life depends on it.

"Well, you hungry, I see."

"Yes ma'am."

Mama Evelyn pours me a tall glass of iced tea, bigger than I ever get at home. It's sweeter too. She sits across from me at the table. Her eyes are shiny and cloudy, an almost unreal combination.

"I reckon you can help me around here for a while. I got some yard work needs doing." She turns to Kevin. He's standing up close to the stove finishing off a plate of greens. "Kevin's been too busy lately to get it done."

"Aw, Mama Evelyn, you know I'll get to it soon as I can." He takes a huge bite of cornbread and dusts his hands off inside the sink. He walks to the table, bends down, and gives Mama Evelyn a kiss on the forehead. Then, he's gone, just that fast. And I'm alone with the old lady.

I close my eyes and imagine myself back at home. I just wanna figure out how to get there, but I have no idea. Under the table, I'm clapping my heels together like that just might work, but it don't. When I open my eyes, I'm still sitting across from Mama Evelyn.

"Honey, I don't need you to tell me why you runnin', but whatever you runnin' from ain't goin' nowhere at all. The longer you stay away, the bigger it'll grow, and by the time you decide to face it, it'll be too big for you—bigger than you imagined it could be. I'll tell you what I tell all of 'em, you better off goin' back where you came from, facin' the problems head on."

She looks at me long and hard. I don't say a thing.

"Ah, well," she says. "Don't nobody listen to little, old me. I'm just here servin' the lost the best way I can."

A loud roar of thunder shakes the house; a flash of lightning brightens the room for a second, then the room seems darker than before. Mama Evelyn looks around and grunts. A pot in the corner of the kitchen pings with water dripping from the ceiling.

There's a sharp knock at the door. She slides her seat back and heads out of the kitchen. When she gets to the door, she flicks a light switch, but nothing happens. She seems unfazed, turns around, and says, "Seems to me dishes is as good a first job as any." Nothing about the sudden darkness or the lack of power.

I finish my food and stand up to gather the dishes. From the front door, I hear Mama Evelyn say, "Senator Eastmore, sir. What brings you here? You got another girl for me?"

I put the dishes down and move close to the kitchen door so I can hear better. The screen door slams, and Senator Eastmore's shoes clop against the hardwood.

"That son of mine got this one pregnant. Name's Ruth Calhoun. She's a student over at Ole Miss, a senior."

"How far along?"

"Six months they think, but she's flat as a board. Not showing at all."

"You wanna sit?"

There's a pause. "You know I don't sit in this rat's nest."

Mama Evelyn's quiet.

"I need you to birth this one. Here. I'll have her here tonight. Arrangements have already been made at the university, so they're not expecting her to return."

"Senator, I never kept none of the girls three whole months."

"The money's good, Evelyn. Might be able to get you a new place with this."

"Yessir."

"The thing is my son loves this girl." He pauses. "Imagine that. An Eastmore loving a nigger. Makes me wonder what I did wrong raising him." He takes several steps, like he's pacing the room. Outside the thunder booms, but no lightning follows, not that I can see. "I need her here because I need eyes on her at all times. Otherwise, those two are liable to run off to New York and get married."

"I see." Mama Evelyn's voice is soft.

"What I need you to understand, Evelyn, is we might adopt this one ourselves, depending on how it turns out. No need to get anyone else involved."

"But you say might, sir."

The senator coughs slightly. "My son Frank and his wife, Margaret, have no children. If this child is white enough, they will adopt it and raise it as their own."

"And if the child ain't white enough?"

"Then do what you always do, Evelyn. Find a buyer." He takes a few steps, and I hear the screen door creak as it opens.

The rain sounds fierce now, unrelenting. I shiver, remembering the manhole covers popping loose, the water rising from the ground up.

"But don't say a word to anyone about this child until we know for sure. Understand?"

"Yes, Senator."

"Good then. I'll have Ruth to you before morning."

# CHAPTER 18

"Neil!"

I wake up to the smell of Mama Evelyn cooking in the kitchen and the sound of a male voice calling my name—well, Neil's name. I sit up in the bed. The mattress is hard. I have no idea how I slept. There's a constant drip of water from the ceiling into an overflowing silver bucket. The rain outside hasn't slowed at all since the night before. It claps against the windows, which sound off like rusted tin instead of windowpane. The dark curtains are pulled closed, so tight I can barely see the occasional lightning. The only continuous light in the room is from a dim lamp beside the bed.

I sit up and stretch. I'm wearing the same clothes I've been in for the last two days. I'm starting to smell like I did when we were stuck without a shower. This room I'm in is musty too, kind of mildewy, maybe from the dripping ceiling. I get out of bed and follow the male voice, but it seems like it's taking me away from the kitchen. The floor is damp beneath my feet as if water's entering from beneath the house. I remember walking with Grandma, fast then slow, fast then slow, with Mr. Chris passing out ribs as neighbors ran indoors. But it's different being alone, harder to be brave in this house with an old woman I don't know. I pause and think of going back to the bed, but what would that do? Eventually, I'd have to get up, get back home. Somehow. I listen carefully, trying to make out the voice. Is it Kevin's? No, it's not. It's a familiar voice though—a man's voice. I run a list of names through my head and cancel them one by one. Whoever this is, I don't know him. Maybe the old lady has a husband or a son.

Mama Evelyn's singing some song while she's cooking, but the more I walk toward the male voice, the fainter her voice becomes and the less I smell bacon sizzling in what I imagine is a cast iron skillet. I pause and listen, hoping I'm getting it wrong. Surely the voice calling me is inviting me to breakfast.

"Neil!"

I walk down a hall toward another door I don't even remember from the night before.

I put my hand on the knob, and as I turn it, I hear, "Boys?"

*Boys?* Who else is here? I pause, listening for more voices, but I hear no more than a rustling, like a scratching on a wall. I open the door wide and step through. Beside me, Neil is kneeling, running his fingers along the wall. I turn around. The door I just walked through is gone.

Neil stands, and just as he is about to speak, his grandpa rounds the corner to my closet.

"What's taking you boys so long?"

Neil turns to his grandpa then back to me, his mouth and eyes wide open.

---

"If you look real close," the contractor says, "there's a waterline right here." He runs the crowbar in his hand along the back wall of my closet from left to right. "It's soft too. Definitely water damage. The only way to fix it is to cut through the wall."

"You sure that's the only way?" Pastor Charles says. "I mean, can't we just dry it out?"

"Pastor, look here." The contractor gets down on his knees and points to several spots on the baseboard. "That's mildew. This is only the beginning. What we can't see is the water damage on the other side." He stands on his feet and levels his hat on his head. "If we try to patch that up instead of replacing it, we'll be back here in a few months dealing with mold. You don't want that. Not after renovating everything else.

Grandma's quiet, just leaning against the doorframe with her arms folded.

"Sometimes," the contractor says, "tearing something down is the only way to build it up again."

Pastor walks to Grandma and puts his hands on her shoulders. He looks down. She looks up. "Ruth?"

Grandma closes her eyes a long time, like she's telling herself a story. "Go ahead," she says finally.

The contractor nods. "You'll be glad you did." He calls downstairs and asks another worker to bring up his rotary saw. "We'll keep it real clean for you." He kneels and pries the crowbar under the baseboard, popping it out of place.

"Let's go," Pastor says, and he walks away from the closet. "We can come back tomorrow. No need to see this."

But Grandma don't move. She stands in the doorway, staring into the closet with this look on her face like she's expecting a special guest.

"All right, then." Pastor takes a few more steps. "Eric, come on. Let's give your grandmother a moment."

We head into the hall and down the stairs just as the other worker comes up with the saw.

"What happened with you and Neil up here?" Pastor says. "He looked like he'd seen a ghost."

"I'm not sure you'll believe me," I say.

"Why don't you try me?"

I take in a deep breath, not because I don't know where to start, but because I don't know where to end.

"I went back again," I say.

"And?"

"And I ended up getting arrested with Grandma and a bunch of other college students. And she was pregnant, with my mother, I think."

Pastor nods. "Timing's right."

"And my great-grandfather is a bad, bad man, but my grandfather might not have been so bad. I don't think he was bad at all, just stuck."

"Oh?" Pastor stops walking at this. "What makes you say that?"

Before I can answer him, Neil and his grandpa walk through the kitchen door, and just as they do, we hear one of the workers upstairs yell, "What is all this?"

Pastor Charles and I both turn and run back up. Neil and his grandpa follow.

Grandma's still standing in the same place, just staring into space like she's in shock. We make our way past her, back into the closet. The workers have cut a perfect rectangle about four feet high and pulled the sheetrock down like it's on a hinge. I look at Pastor Charles, and he looks at me. Then it hits me. The workers have found a hidden room behind my closet.

One worker leans over and picks a frame off the floor. Glass is shattered all around it. I close my eyes, and my whole body gets tense like I'm in a car that's about to crash. Any second now, I'm expecting him or all of us to be swept to another place and time. I hear a voice say, "Calhoun, President of Ole Miss SNCC, Denied Degree."

Oh no. Here we go again. I open my eyes, expecting to be somewhere else, somewhere in the past. But I'm still in the same spot and so is everyone else. The head construction guy is holding that frame I knocked off the wall and reading the article out loud. He looks at Pastor Charles. "Is this about her? Ms. Ruth?" He points at Grandma.

"This place is amazing," Neil says. "Look at all of this stuff."

His grandfather stops in front of the article about black market adoptions and reads silently. His mouth opens wider and wider as he reads.

Pastor stands before the map, tracing his finger along the green line.

On the back wall, I see the backless bookcase, just below the window. I walk over and push it to the side. A few books crash to the floor.

Before I can even turn to look at the picture behind it, Neil gasps. "No way! Eric, that's Layla's dad."

---

Sometimes, when you finally get the thing you want, it's the last thing you want. That's how it is with finally meeting my daddy. For one thing, when Pastor Charles called him out that day I got suspended, he pretended to be someone else. And then there's the whole idea that he's Layla's dad too. So, when Pastor Charles convinces Grandma to add Layla's and Neil's families to the Christmas dinner list, I am not excited. It's even worse that they don't even tell Layla's family why. Pastor stays out of making contact because he already tried confronting my daddy, and it didn't work. Grandma don't make direct contact either because she's thinking if he hears her voice or full name, he won't show up, might even leave town, and then Layla's without him again. So, Grandma works it out with Neil's grandpa. She invites him to the house for dinner and tells him he can invite up to four more people. Of course, he invites Layla, her grandparents, and her dad. They all pretend it just accidentally worked out that way, but we know the truth.

Charlotte and Wilbur are the first to arrive. Charlotte comes in with a big peach cobbler. "Oh Ruth, I'm so glad to see you." She hands Pastor the cobbler and gives Grandma a hug so big it lifts her from the ground.

Wilbur hugs everyone in the kitchen and living room.

I keep peeking through the blinds because I'm so nervous. I feel sick to my stomach, and the smell of Christmas dinner is making it worse. I can't imagine sitting across from my dad or even being in the same room. I'm running through my mind what I'm gonna ask, what I'm gonna say. And I'm coming up with blanks. "So, what does it feel like to be a deadbeat?" don't seem like the right thing to say, but it's the only thing on my mind.

My mood lightens a little when Scarlet hops out of a silver car and gets Milaya from the back.

"Scarlet's here," I say.

Grandma rushes to the door, her arms already out and ready for Milaya. When Scarlet crosses the threshold, Wilbur signs "I love you," and Charlotte blows her a kiss. Grandma gives Scarlet a hug and pulls Milaya close to her.

"Ms. Ruth, it's so good to see you," Scarlet says. "Thank you so much for the invite."

Right then, a tall man, taller than Pastor Charles walks through the door. "Good afternoon, everyone." He holds his head down slightly like he's afraid he might bump the ceiling.

Scarlet smiles real big. "Ms. Ruth, this here is Marvin, Milaya's dad."

Grandma inhales and then lets out a squeal. "Marvin! It is so nice to meet you."

"Scarlet talks about you all the time," Marvin says. "I'm so glad she had you when we were separated after the storm."

Meeting Marvin ruins my mood. I'm feeling sad instead of happy that Milaya knows her dad. I leave the kitchen and go back to my room. I sit in the window a while and just stare out. As usual, that tabby cat is sitting by the tree, licking himself like he belongs to us. He turns to face me and yawns before getting up and scratching his side against the rough bark. You'd think that cat came with the house or something.

"Hey man, you okay?" I turn my head. Neil is standing in my bedroom doorway. "I figure this ain't an easy day for you."

"You think?" I say.

He laughs a little. "But yo, it's not every day you get to meet your dad."

I stand up and walk over to my rock collection. It's in a small cup on top of this chest Grandma got from the Salvation Army. I dig around for the smooth rock and rub it between my finger and thumb. "Or that you find out your friend's really your sister," I say.

Neil smirks and the dimple in his chin deepens. "But that does mean we can stop fighting over her."

I roll my eyes. "You really are a jerk."

"That's how most people feel about their brother-in-law. I'm just gettin' a head start, man."

He laughs, and I'm caught somewhere between mad and silly.

"Come on, Eric. Sometimes man, you just gotta be less serious. You can't change this stuff, you know? Look, I don't even know who my dad is. Just—" He lets out a big exhale.

We can hear the laughter and talking from the living room. It sounds like everyone's having a good time, like it's a normal holiday meal with no expected drama. But when the doorbell rings, everyone gets quiet on cue.

"Come on," Neil says.

I can't move. I sink down to the floor and sit with my knees up, my back resting underneath the window. Neil comes over and sits next to me.

"I wanna throw up, man."

Neil's quiet a while. After a few seconds, he says, "You know all that stuff we were reading about your grandma?"

"Yeah. Why?"

"Because man, no matter who your daddy is or what he do, or don't do, that's what's in you. Her. She's a real G, yo. I don't even know how she kept going, but she did. And even after your mama died, and your daddy disappeared, she was still a G. When everybody turned their backs on her, she just kept going. That's power, man. And you got that. It's in you."

I look at Neil a long time because it's the first time I really believe he's a real friend. I'm avoiding going to meet my daddy as long as possible. The voices have quieted, but there's definite conversation going on. We can hear a constant mumble, but we can't make out the words. I'm glad Neil's not forcing me to talk. We're just sitting, side by side, our backs to the wall. I'm rubbing my smooth rock, and he's tapping his knees with his hands.

Pastor Charles peeks his head in my door. "Can I come in?"

"Sure."

Neil stands up. "I'll be in the room with everybody else," he says.

Pastor pats Neil on the shoulder on his way in. Neil closes the door behind him.

"A lot's been going on lately. You okay in here?" Pastor takes a seat on the bed.

"Yeah. Just feeling sick."

"Well, let me warn you. This night might not get any easier."

I groan. I don't have the words to say what I feel. Pastor Charles reaches out for my hand and pulls me to my feet. I put my hands around Pastor Charles and hug him real tight, but I don't say a thing. He lets me hug him until Grandma calls our names.

"Ready?" he says. He's asking and answering himself at the same time, so I don't respond.

I ain't ready and he knows it, and we both know it don't matter.

Pastor leads the way to the living room. When I walk in, I'm confused, like I have to get my bearings or something. It's kind of crowded. There's Scarlet, Marvin, and Maliya sitting in two mismatched chairs pulled from the kitchen. Charlotte and Wilbur in the two wing chairs. Grandma in her recliner, and on the sofa, Layla, her grandparents, and two men who look exactly the same.

---

"What I don't understand," Grandma says, "is how you both have the same last name."

My daddy's name is Jackson; Layla's dad's name is Jason. They're twins, separated at birth, and sold on the black market. They were two of more than 150 interracial babies sold in illegal adoptions. Most of the time, the moms were Black women who worked for the white men they got pregnant by. They were given hush money and promised their babies would be raised in wealthy white homes with privileges they would never get if the women tried raising them themselves. Some of the women were just lied to and told their babies died in childbirth.

I'm wondering which is true about my daddy's mama, and what kind of woman is this grandma I never met, and who's my other grandpa, and how many family members is it possible not to know? I'm staring at a line on the hardwood because I can't imagine making eye contact with this daddy of mine, with either of them really.

Layla's dad is the one talking first. He's saying he was raised with abusive parents who beat him because his hair wouldn't stop curling, and when he played out in the sun, his tan got too dark. He ran away at sixteen and ended up meeting this attorney who was working on a big adoption scandal. Somehow, this guy connected him to his bio-logical mom. "It was just a God thing," he says. "This guy would find me every day and bring me food. We'd just talk, and he started putting pieces together. I don't know how he did it, but he brought me to my real mom. Her name is Ilesha Everest. When I first met her, I was shocked by her brown skin, but otherwise, she looked just like me. I mean, I guess I looked just like her."

There's an awkward silence in the room before he goes on. "And I didn't want to be found by the parents who raised me. They were so cruel. So, I legally changed my name to my birth mother's last name."

He tells us his birth mother ended up being a mess. She was strung out on pills and kept getting evicted. So when he turned eighteen, he ended up leaving her.

"Why'd you leave me?" Layla says the words without looking up.

"I didn't want to, but when that adoption ring crashed, it was like my life fell apart. You were just a baby, Layla, and I had never told your mom the truth about any of my stuff. I just said my parents were dead. Then there was this big blow up on the news, and she was following the story so close."

"So? What does that have to do with you leaving?"

Jason's quiet a long time. I'm wondering if I should call him Mr. Jason or Uncle Jason, but I can't get more than Jason to stick in my head.

"Well?" Layla holds the word a few seconds.

"Your mother was so vocal about the adoption ring and how sick it was that white men wanted to be with Black women at all. I just—"

"You're blaming mom? uh-uh . . . You don't get to do that." Layla storms out of the room. I think of running after her, but I'm wonder-ing what my own daddy has to say. I look at Neil, and he nods, then follows Layla.

Jason's just twisting his fingers in his lap. He don't even move, and I'm thinking there's a whole lot of coward in my bloodline.

"I didn't ask you this when you first showed up," Layla's grandfather says, "but why'd you come back? Why not just leave her alone."

"The storm. I knew Kyleigh moved to Biloxi after we split up, so when Katrina hit, I started searching for her. I really just wanted to make sure they were both okay. I wasn't going to come back, but then when I found Kyleigh, she was in rehab, and I know what that's like, having a mom with an addiction. I just had to try to be there for her."

Layla's grandfather shakes his head, but it's not clear what he's shaking his head about—Jason leaving, his return, Kyleigh's addiction, the whole crazy story, or just because he don't know what else to do. I find myself shaking my head too, and I don't know why that makes a bit of sense.

"And you, Jackson?" Grandma's voice is harsh. I look her way and see something new in her eyes. They're not wild, not calm either. It's something I ain't never seen. Maybe that's the look of every emotion combined, like anger and hurt and fear and relief all balled up into one. "You knew I would have even preferred a Black man for June. You knew that. I was vocal about just that." Grandma raises her voice and stands on her feet, and now I do see anger. "But you left right when I started trusting you, and right when I needed you." Her eyes narrow. I can see that she's losing her cool. I want to walk over to her and hold her, not really hug her but hold her back. Only I can't get my legs to move.

"It was more than that I was one of those babies, Ms. Ruth. My adopted parents were Frank and Margaret Eastmore, the same people who tried to take June from you."

I realize I'm not sitting down. I'm not even leaning on a wall, and all of sudden, I lose my balance. I don't know where Neil comes from, but he braces himself behind me, and I rest all my weight on him. My knees are trembling. Pastor Charles grabs a folding chair from the kitchen and puts it down next to me, but then Layla, who also seemed to return out of nowhere, has to actually make me sit, like my legs are too stiff to bend. She pulls up a chair and sits so we can see each other eye to eye, like she's letting me know we're in this together, and we are not the sum of our parents' failures.

Grandma gasps and sways a little to her left. Pastor Charles rushes away from me to her. He wraps his hand around hers, and Grandma lets out a deep breath. "Joseph's brother, Frank? That's who raised you?"

Jackson Everest keeps talking, and I realize I can't figure out what to call him either. It ain't gon' be daddy no time soon, maybe never. But I'm looking at him real close. His hands are slightly darker than my mother's. His hair is dark, almost black, and it's cut into a low taper on the sides, longer on top. Unlike Jason, he got a couple of curls in the front that hang over his eyes, but it's mostly straight. I'm feeling my curls and thinking about Whittaker's biology lesson.

"I found out about my adoption at sixteen. Overheard them talking about how scared they were that I was gonna get so dark people would know I couldn't be theirs. I didn't even know I was adopted. Then Mother—Margaret—said if I got too dark, they would just have to send me off to school and transition me out of the country." He takes a deep breath. "So I ran away at sixteen. I went to my Uncle Joseph first, and he sent me to Mama Evelyn. That woman would do anything for money. She gave me Ilesha Everest's name, and I went out and found her." He looks down. "I took on her name, just to break my ties from the Eastmores, but I just kept pretending to be white."

"Lord have mercy!" Grandma rocks back and forth in her seat.

Pastor rubs his face like he's trying to wake up from a nightmare.

And I'm still just shaking my head, but now I'm shaking it so fast it feels like it's going to just fall off. My eyes are welling with tears, and everything in the room is blurred. I'm ready for him to stop talking, for this to all be over. But he keeps going.

"Then the day before Eric was born, the adoption ring crashed, and I found out what they tried to do to you and June. I tried to get in touch with my uncle about it. He never was like the rest of them. You know? Uncle Joseph loved all people, and my grandfather hated him for that. But I never could reach him. The adoption ring crashed, and he disappeared." He shakes his head and stares off into space a few seconds. "All day long, I had been spinning it around in my head, trying to figure out whether or not to tell you or just pretend I didn't know. But when June died, I got scared I couldn't take care of a child without running back to them for help. And I didn't want to risk bringing my son into that world of evil. I just wanted to keep him from it."

The room's so quiet, every breath, every sigh, every sniffle is heard. I look at Layla, and Layla looks at me, and our faces don't say a thing. They're just blank, like we're both too numb to take it all in.

Pastor breaks the silence after a while. "Well, I guess at a time like this everyone wants a word from the Lord, and it's hard to think of the right one. The thing is I'm not sure I have the right one. Sometimes it's easier when your heart's not so close to the matter. But when it comes to Ruth, my heart's always all tangled up. And Jackson, Eric might be your biological son, but he's really mine."

I focus my eyes on Pastor Charles. I'm his? He sees me as his son? I'm not sure how I'm supposed to feel. What I always wanted is here, but it don't feel like I expected. It's like my happy and my angry have canceled each other out, and I'm numb. Confused. I look around, wondering if everyone heard what I heard. Layla's eyes are red and swollen. Neil reaches out and holds her hand. But this time, I don't mind. I'm glad he's there for her, and I guess I'm glad he's there for me too. Pastor Charles looks at me and our eyes lock, and I start thinking of all the times he's been there for me, all the things he's taught me. I'm thinking I don't need Jackson Everest at all, and I'm wishing he'd just leave and take his twin and his cowardly genes and let us get back to living our lives without him. I want to tell him that. I want to tell him to stop all the explaining because there ain't no good reason to walk out on your child. I want to tell him if he was any kind of man, he would have stayed no matter what. But won't nothing in my mouth work right, so I'm just quiet.

Pastor Charles keeps talking though. He turns to Grandma, and he gets real close to her, like there ain't nobody else in the room. "We been so busy over the years burying the past we never really allowed ourselves to build a future. So I guess what I want to say is, somehow, we got it all wrong." He looks around the room then, like he just remembered the rest of us. "I guess a lot of us in here got a lot of things wrong. And we might not be too pleased with ourselves or with each other—"

Wilbur signs something, and Charlotte pats him on the back. Pastor nods, not at Wilbur, not at anything really. "But we can still pick up the pieces—all that garbage from the past—and use it to press ahead. I know that's nothing grand or marvelous, no lightning bolt word from God, and it sure don't do nothing to take away all this pain. It's just a small piece of truth. I'm hoping it'll do."

# CHAPTER 19

We stay in Houston a full year, but in September 2006 instead of renewing the lease, we head back to New Orleans. Layla, her grandparents, and Jason Everest, they all stay in Houston. So does Bryson and his mom. My daddy, Jackson, finds out his Uncle Joseph is real sick, and he goes back to Mississippi to take care of him. Pastor asks Grandma if she wants to visit him because the doctors say he's getting close to his final days, but Grandma says some doors ain't meant to walk back through. When Pastor wasn't home one day though, I heard her on the phone with Joseph Eastmore, telling him she knew it wasn't his fault, and Jackson's presence was just one way God was letting them both know they weren't forgotten.

"Maybe," she'd said. "If I hadn't fallen in love with you and given birth to June, that adoption ring would have never come down. But I made it my life's work to bring it under. I would have preferred we be a family, but the timing wasn't right, Joseph. Timing can be everything."

I think about that a lot now. Timing is everything.

An hour after that phone call, when Pastor Charles came home, he pulled Grandma close to him, like he knew she had finally let Joseph Eastmore go.

"I've been thinking, Ruth. You and me, we been together nearly all our lives. Why don't we make it official?"

He opened a small box, and there was a diamond ring perfectly sized for Grandma's finger. I don't think they knew I was eavesdropping, but before I knew it, I had run out into the living room yelling, "Yes!" So when we moved back to New Orleans, we didn't move into two different houses. Pastor Charles rented out his and moved into ours.

The remodeled house has two rooms upstairs and an office with a loft that doubles as a library. All the articles from the hidden room are on the walls in the loft, out in the open. There are built-in bookcases across two walls. Between Grandma's books and Pastor's, the shelves are almost full.

It's Monday, September 11, 2006. Pastor's watching the morning news, and there's a moment of silence in recognition of the fifth anniversary of the attacks on the World Trade Center and Pentagon. I close my eyes, and I'm thinking it's also exactly one year after I met my cousin Layla shopping in the Salvation Army. There are some things we just don't forget.

I grab my backpack and step outside the house. The leaves on the trees have returned, and the grass is green again. Next door, Mr. Chris's house has been repainted, and a For Sale sign is out front. The young couple with two toddlers never returned at all. Their blue paint is peeling. The waterline is still visible above the doorknob. The big X and its spray-painted markings *9/22*, *MM*, *CAJNVY*, *0* are still dark and unfaded. Ms. Jackie's back home though, and she's outside on the porch repainting her iron bars. Next to her, the house that used to have a family of ten is surrounded with grass so high the house can hardly be seen. Across the street, Shelia's house looks like a storm never hit. It's not only painted, but her mother has planted a flower garden and placed large flowerpots on the porch. Ms. Carolyn's house is freshly painted too. Two men in overalls and boots are taking the boards off Old Man Jake's windows. I watch the spray-painted board fall to the ground, the words *Jake, where are you?* still clinging to the wood. Another man is replacing the siding, so the house looks striped, alternating the faded peach with the new cream-colored boards.

Down the street, I see Neil and Alejandro meet each other and dap off. They turn toward the bus stop and walk. I pause for a second to look at Old Man Jake's house, to remember the old man, and how he danced in the street, and I hear that second line music in my head. My feet start moving, and suddenly I'm dancing up the street like no one's around, like there's a whole group of Mardi Gras Indians egging me on. And somehow I think it's Old Man Jake telling me he's still here and reminding me that I am too, and I can't stop dancing. Even when Neil and Alejandro point my way and laugh, I keep going, headed straight for them, ready to get on that bus and head to the back to talk and laugh and get to class on time.

"Why we dancing?" Shelia asks.

Suddenly, she's next to me, and our feet are moving to the rhythm of the song in my head, so in sync I wonder if she hears it too.

"For Old Man Jake," I say.

Shelia nods and moves her right arm up like she's holding a boom box. With her left hand, she mimics holding a can. Neil and Alejandro make it to the bus stop then look our way. When they see Shelia's Old Man Jake impersonation, they start dancing toward us, like we're at a big party all hearing the same song. Before I know it, we're all together in the middle of the street—Alejandro and Neil on one side of the newly planted pothole flowers, Shelia and I on the other—stepping forward and backward but never far apart. Out of the corner of my eye, I see the Nguyen's house still boarded, still marked, still for sale. But next door, Ms. Joan is putting cat food on the porch, something she does every morning. Only, the cats never come. Then she starts shouting for her brother Jeffery, another thing she does every day, but he never comes either. The bus stops at the corner, and I wave my hands up like a lasso and start moving toward it, because if I've learned anything, I've learned to keep going. No matter what.

Shelia follows, then Alejandro and Neil, and we dance the rest of the way to the bus stop and then up the steps.

Mr. Lionel laughs, "Well, looka here," he says, and he begins to drive forward while we second line to the back.

An old man with cataract eyes like Old Man Jake turns up his radio to a Rebirth Brass Band tune and joins in. Mr. Lionel stops the bus, tells everyone to get their dance on then sit down because he can't keep driving like this.

He leans against the silver bar that runs from ceiling to floor behind his seat. He don't dance exactly, but he taps his foot to the rhythm of the music and moves his shoulders up and down. Every now and then he dips his hips a bit, like it's taking everything he has not to go all in. The rest of us dance in the narrow bus aisle, side by side. Cataract Eyes challenges me with a low dip, and a forward kick. I answer with a double low dip and a full turn.

When the song ends, we laugh and dap each other off like we're saying hello all over again. Cataract Eyes sits across two seats and leans his back against a window.

"Thanks for the music," I say.

"No problem, young blood. Had a good time. Yes, Lord, a mighty good time."

We make our way to the seats lining the back row of the nearly empty bus, and Mr. Lionel sits back behind the wheel.

"Man, Eric, I didn't know you had moves like that." Neil's mouth forms an *O* after *that*, but no sound comes out, like he's thinking *oooo-weee* but can't bring himself to say it.

"Me neither," I say and laugh.

"Where'd that come from?" Alejandro asks.

"Looking at Old Man Jake's house, I guess. Just came on me out of nowhere."

Neil nods. "That's righteous, man. I feel you. He was a legend. You know?"

"We are too," I say. "Everybody who lives and breathes and survives is a legend in some way. Just need to find it."

"Look at you, pulling up your inner Ms. Hornwell," Shelia says.

I take a close look at her and smile. Neil's right. That girl is fine, and we're even the same height now.

"Yeah, well, I did have her the rest of ninth grade."

"Lucky you." Shelia turns up her nose like whoever she had wasn't so good.

"You ever write that story? 'My Grandma Makes the Best Chicken Salad?'" Alejandro leans in to dap Neil off, and they laugh like crazy, heads bobbing up and down.

I'm not fazed though. "Nah, I wrote so much more." I hold my hands up like I'm writing in the air. "My grandma makes the best chicken salad, but before that she made history."

"Word?" Alejandro says.

"Tell us about it." Shelia leans forward on her backpack.

I sit up straight and tall, my back pressed firm against the seat. "Let me tell you the legend of Crazy Ruth," I say. "First of all, she wasn't crazy at all but strong."

"A real G," Neil says.

And so, the legend begins.